NON SANS DROICT.

William Shakespeare

The Tragedy of
JULIUS CAESAR

With New Dramatic Criticism
and an Updated Bibliography

Edited by William and Barbara Rosen

The Signet Classic Shakespeare
GENERAL EDITOR: SYLVAN BARNET

CC

A SIGNET CLASSIC

SIGNET CLASSIC
Published by the Penguin Group
Penguin Books USA Inc., 375 Hudson Street,
New York, New York 10014, U.S.A.
Penguin Books Ltd, 27 Wrights Lane,
London W8 5TZ, England
Penguin Books Australia Ltd, Ringwood,
Victoria, Australia
Penguin Books Canada Ltd, 2801 John Street,
Markham, Ontario, Canada L3R 1B4
Penguin Books (N.Z.) Ltd, 182-190 Wairau Road,
Auckland 10, New Zealand

Penguin Books Ltd, Registered Offices:
Harmondsworth, Middlesex, England

33   32   31   30   29   28   27   26   25

 REGISTERED TRADEMARK—MARCA REGISTRADA

Library of Congress Catalog Card Number: 86-62298

Printed in the United States of America

Contents

Shakespeare: Prefatory Remarks

Between the record of his baptism in Stratford on 26 April 1564 and the record of his burial in Stratford on 25 April 1616, some forty documents name Shakespeare, and many others name his parents, his children, and his grandchildren. More facts are known about William Shakespeare than about any other playwright of the period except Ben Jonson. The facts should, however, be distinguished from the legends. The latter, inevitably more engaging and better known, tell us that the Stratford boy killed a calf in high style, poached deer and rabbits, and was forced to flee to London, where he held horses outside a playhouse. These traditions are only traditions; they may be true, but no evidence supports them, and it is well to stick to the facts.

Mary Arden, the dramatist's mother, was the daughter of a substantial landowner; about 1557 she married John Shakespeare, who was a glove-maker and trader in various farm commodities. In 1557 John Shakespeare was a member of the Council (the governing body of Stratford), in 1558 a constable of the borough, in 1561 one of the two town chamberlains, in 1565 an alderman (entitling him to the appellation "Mr."), in 1568 high bailiff—the town's highest political office, equivalent to mayor. After 1577, for an unknown reason he drops out of local politics. The birthday of William Shakespeare, the eldest son of this locally prominent man, is unrecorded; but the Stratford parish register records that the infant was baptized on 26 April 1564. (It is quite possible that he was born on 23 April, but this date has probably been assigned by tradition because it is the date on which, fifty-two years later, he died.) The attendance records of the Stratford grammar school of the period are not extant, but it is reasonable to assume that the son of a local official attended the school and received substantial training in Latin. The masters of the school from Shakespeare's seventh to fifteenth years held Oxford degrees; the Elizabethan curriculum excluded mathematics and the natural sciences but taught a good deal of Latin rhetoric, logic, and literature. On 27 November 1582 a marriage license was issued to Shakespeare and Anne Hathaway, eight years his senior. The couple had a child in May, 1583. Perhaps the marriage was necessary, but perhaps the couple had earlier engaged in a formal "troth plight" which would render their children legitimate even if no further ceremony were performed. In 1585 Anne Hathaway bore Shakespeare twins.

That Shakespeare was born is excellent; that he married and had children is pleasant; but that we know nothing about his departure from Stratford to London, or about the beginning of his theatrical career, is lamentable and must be admitted. We would gladly sacrifice details about his children's baptism for details about his earliest days on the stage. Perhaps the poaching episode is true (but it is first reported almost a century after Shakespeare's death), or perhaps he first left Stratford to be a schoolteacher, as another tradition holds; perhaps he was moved by

> Such wind as scatters young men through the world,
> To seek their fortunes further than at home
> Where small experience grows.

In 1592, thanks to the cantankerousness of Robert Greene, a rival playwright and a pamphleteer, we have our first reference, a snarling one, to Shakespeare as an actor and playwright. Greene warns those of his own educated friends who wrote for the theater against an actor who has presumed to turn playwright:

> There is an upstart crow, beautified with our feathers, that with his *tiger's heart wrapped in a player's hide* supposes he

is as well able to bombast out a blank verse as the best of you, and being an absolute Johannes-factotum is in his own conceit the only Shake-scene in a country.

The reference to the player, as well as the allusion to Aesop's crow (who strutted in borrowed plumage, as an actor struts in fine words not his own), makes it clear that by this date Shakespeare had both acted and written. That Shakespeare is meant is indicated not only by "Shake-scene" but by the parody of a line from one of Shakespeare's plays, *3 Henry VI*: "O, tiger's heart wrapped in a woman's hide." If Shakespeare in 1592 was prominent enough to be attacked by an envious dramatist, he probably had served an apprenticeship in the theater for at least a few years.

In any case, by 1592 Shakespeare had acted and written, and there are a number of subsequent references to him as an actor: documents indicate that in 1598 he is a "principal comedian," in 1603 a "principal tragedian," in 1608 he is one of the "men players." The profession of actor was not for a gentleman, and it occasionally drew the scorn of university men who resented writing speeches for persons less educated than themselves, but it was respectable enough: players, if prosperous, were in effect members of the bourgeoisie, and there is nothing to suggest that Stratford considered William Shakespeare less than a solid citizen. When, in 1596, the Shakespeares were granted a coat of arms, the grant was made to Shakespeare's father, but probably William Shakespeare (who the next year bought the second-largest house in town) had arranged the matter on his own behalf. In subsequent transactions he is occasionally styled a gentleman.

Although in 1593 and 1594 Shakespeare published two narrative poems dedicated to the Earl of Southampton, *Venus and Adonis* and *The Rape of Lucrece*, and may well have written most or all of his sonnets in the middle nineties, Shakespeare's literary activity seems to have been almost entirely devoted to the theater. (It may be significant that the two narrative poems were written in years when the plague closed the theaters for several months.) In 1594 he was a charter member of a theatrical company called the

Chamberlain's Men (which in 1603 changed its name to the King's Men); until he retired to Stratford (about 1611, apparently), he was with this remarkably stable company. From 1599 the company acted primarily at the Globe Theatre, in which Shakespeare held a one-tenth interest. Other Elizabethan dramatists are known to have acted, but no other is known also to have been entitled to a share in the profits of the playhouse.

Shakespeare's first eight published plays did not have his name on them, but this is not remarkable; the most popular play of the sixteenth century, Thomas Kyd's *The Spanish Tragedy*, went through many editions without naming Kyd, and Kyd's authorship is known only because a book on the profession of acting happens to quote (and attribute to Kyd) some lines on the interest of Roman emperors in the drama. What is remarkable is that after 1598 Shakespeare's name commonly appears on printed plays—some of which are not his. Another indication of his popularity comes from Francis Meres, author of *Palladis Tamia: Wit's Treasury* (1598): in this anthology of snippets accompanied by an essay on literature, many playwrights are mentioned, but Shakespeare's name occurs more often than any other, and Shakespeare is the only playwright whose plays are listed.

From his acting, playwriting, and share in a theater, Shakespeare seems to have made considerable money. He put it to work, making substantial investments in Stratford real estate. When he made his will (less than a month before he died), he sought to leave his property intact to his descendants. Of small bequests to relatives and to friends (including three actors, Richard Burbage, John Heminges, and Henry Condell), that to his wife of the second-best bed has provoked the most comment; perhaps it was the bed the couple had slept in, the best being reserved for visitors. In any case, had Shakespeare not excepted it, the bed would have gone (with the rest of his household possessions) to his daughter and her husband. On 25 April 1616 he was buried within the chancel of the church at Stratford. An unattractive monument to his memory, placed on a wall near the grave, says he died on 23 April. Over the grave itself are the lines, perhaps by Shakespeare, that (more than his literary fame) have kept his bones undisturbed in the crowded burial ground where old bones were often dislodged to make way for new:

> Good friend, for Jesus' sake forbear
> To dig the dust enclosed here.
> Blessed be the man that spares these stones
> And cursed be he that moves my bones.

Thirty-seven plays, as well as some nondramatic poems, are held to constitute the Shakespeare canon. The dates of composition of most of the works are highly uncertain, but there is often evidence of a *terminus a quo* (starting point) and/or a *terminus ad quem* (terminal point) that provides a framework for intelligent guessing. For example, *Richard II* cannot be earlier than 1595, the publication date of some material to which it is indebted; *The Merchant of Venice* cannot be later than 1598, the year Francis Meres mentioned it. Sometimes arguments for a date hang on an alleged topical allusion, such as the lines about the unseasonable weather in *A Midsummer Night's Dream,* II.i.81–117, but such an allusion (if indeed it is an allusion) can be variously interpreted, and in any case there is always the possibility that a topical allusion was inserted during a revision, years after the composition of a play. Dates are often attributed on the basis of style, and although conjectures about style usually rest on other conjectures, sooner or later one must rely on one's literary sense. There is no real proof, for example, that *Othello* is not as early as *Romeo and Juliet,* but one feels *Othello* is later, and because the first record of its performance is 1604, one is glad enough to set its composition at that date and not push it back into Shakespeare's early years. The following chronology, then, is as much indebted to informed guesswork and sensitivity as it is to fact. The dates, necessarily imprecise, indicate something like a scholarly consensus.

PLAYS

1588–93	*The Comedy of Errors*
1588–94	*Love's Labor's Lost*

1590–91	*2 Henry VI*
1590–91	*3 Henry VI*
1591–92	*1 Henry VI*
1592–93	*Richard III*
1592–94	*Titus Andronicus*
1593–94	*The Taming of the Shrew*
1593–95	*The Two Gentlemen of Verona*
1594–96	*Romeo and Juliet*
1595	*Richard II*
1594–96	*A Midsummer Night's Dream*
1596–97	*King John*
1596–97	*The Merchant of Venice*
1597	*1 Henry IV*
1597–98	*2 Henry IV*
1598–1600	*Much Ado About Nothing*
1598–99	*Henry V*
1599	*Julius Caesar*
1599–1600	*As You Like It*
1599–1600	*Twelfth Night*
1600–01	*Hamlet*
1597–1601	*The Merry Wives of Windsor*
1601–02	*Troilus and Cressida*
1602–04	*All's Well That Ends Well*
1603–04	*Othello*
1604	*Measure for Measure*
1605–06	*King Lear*
1605–06	*Macbeth*
1606–07	*Antony and Cleopatra*
1605–08	*Timon of Athens*
1607–09	*Coriolanus*
1608–09	*Pericles*
1609–10	*Cymbeline*
1610–11	*The Winter's Tale*
1611–12	*The Tempest*
1612–13	*Henry VIII*

POEMS

1592	*Venus and Adonis*
1593–94	*The Rape of Lucrece*

Shakespeare's Theater

In Shakespeare's infancy, Elizabethan actors performed wherever they could—in great halls, at court, in the courtyards of inns. The innyards must have made rather unsatisfactory theaters: on some days they were unavailable because carters bringing goods to London used them as depots; when available, they had to be rented from the innkeeper; perhaps most important, London inns were subject to the Common Council of London, which was not well disposed toward theatricals. In 1574 the Common Council required that plays and playing places in London be licensed. It asserted that

> sundry great disorders and inconveniences have been found to ensue to this city by the inordinate haunting of great multitudes of people, specially youth, to plays, interludes, and shows, namely occasion of frays and quarrels, evil practices of incontinency in great inns having chambers and secret places adjoining to their open stages and galleries,

and ordered that innkeepers who wished licenses to hold performances put up a bond and make contributions to the poor.

The requirement that plays and innyard theaters be licensed, along with the other drawbacks of playing at inns, probably drove James Burbage (a carpenter-turned-actor) to rent in 1576 a plot of land northeast of the city walls and to build here—on property outside the jurisdiction of the city—England's first permanent construction designed for plays. He called it simply the Theatre. About all that is known of its construction is that it was wood. It soon had imitators, the most famous being the Globe (1599), built across the Thames (again outside the city's jurisdiction), out of timbers of the Theatre, which had been dismantled when Burbage's lease ran out.

There are three important sources of information about the structure of Elizabethan playhouses—drawings, a contract, and stage directions in plays. Of drawings, only the so-called De Witt drawing (c. 1596) of the Swan—really a friend's copy of De Witt's drawing—is of much significance. It shows a building of three tiers, with a stage jutting from a wall into the yard or center of the building. The tiers are roofed, and part of the stage is covered by a roof that projects from the rear and is supported at its front on two posts, but the groundlings, who paid a penny to stand in front of the stage, were exposed to the sky. (Performances in such a playhouse were held only in the daytime; artificial illumination was not used.) At the rear of the stage are two doors; above the stage is a gallery. The second major source of information, the contract for the Fortune, specifies that although the Globe is to be the model, the Fortune is to be square, eighty feet outside and fifty-five inside. The stage is to be forty-three feet broad, and is to extend into the middle of the yard (i.e., it is twenty-seven and a half feet deep). For patrons willing to pay more than the general admission charged of the groundlings, there were to be three galleries provided with seats. From the third chief source, stage directions, one learns that entrance to the stage was by doors, presumably spaced widely apart at the rear ("Enter one citizen at one door, and another at the other"), and that in addition to the platform stage there was occasionally some sort of curtained booth or alcove allowing for "discovery" scenes, and some sort of playing space "aloft" or "above" to represent (for example) the top of a city's walls or a room above the street. Doubtless each theater had its own peculiarities, but perhaps we can talk about a "typical" Elizabethan theater if we realize that no theater need exactly have fit the description, just as no father is the typical father with 3.7 children. This hypothetical theater is wooden, round or polygonal (in *Henry V* Shakespeare calls it a "wooden *O*"), capable of holding some eight hundred spectators standing in the yard around the projecting elevated stage and some fifteen hundred additional spectators seated in the three roofed galleries. The stage, protected by a "shadow" or "heavens" or roof, is entered by two doors; behind the doors is the "tiring house" (attiring house, i.e., dressing room), and above the doors is some sort of gallery that may sometimes hold spectators but that can be used (for example) as the bedroom from which Romeo—according to a stage direction in one text—"goeth down." Some evidence suggests that a throne can be lowered onto the platform stage, perhaps from the "shadow"; certainly characters can descend from the stage through a trap or traps into the cellar or "hell." Sometimes this space beneath the platform accommodates a sound-effects man or musician (in *Antony and Cleopatra* "music of the hautboys is under the stage") or an actor (in *Hamlet* the "Ghost cries under the stage"). Most characters simply walk on and off, but because there is no curtain in front of the platform, corpses will have to be carried off (Hamlet must lug Polonius' guts into the neighbor room), or will have to fall at the rear, where the curtain on the alcove or booth can be drawn to conceal them.

Such may have been the so-called "public theater." Another kind of theater, called the "private theater" because its much greater admission charge limited its audience to the wealthy or the prodigal, must be briefly mentioned. The private theater was basically a large room, entirely roofed and therefore artificially illuminated, with a stage at one end. In 1576 one such theater was established in Blackfriars, a Dominican priory in London that had been suppressed in 1538 and confiscated by the Crown and thus was not under the city's jurisdiction. All the actors in the Blackfriars theater were boys about eight to thirteen years old (in the public theaters similar boys played female parts; a boy Lady Macbeth played to a man Macbeth). This private theater had a precarious existence, and ceased operations in 1584. In 1596 James Burbage, who had already made theatrical history by building the Theatre, began to construct a second Blackfriars theater. He died in 1597, and for several years this second Blackfriars theater was used by a troupe of boys, but in 1608 two of Burbage's sons and five other actors (including Shakespeare) became joint operators of the theater, using it in the winter when the open-air Globe was unsuitable. Perhaps such a smaller theater, roofed, artificially illuminated, and with a tradition of a courtly audience, exerted an influence on Shakespeare's late plays.

Performances in the private theaters may well have had intermissions during which music was played, but in the public theaters the action was probably uninterrupted, flowing from scene to scene almost without a break. Actors would enter, speak, exit, and others would immediately enter and establish (if necessary) the new locale by a few properties and by words and gestures. Here are some samples of Shakespeare's scene painting:

> This is Illyria, lady.
>
> Well, this is the Forest of Arden.
>
> This castle hath a pleasant seat; the air
> Nimbly and sweetly recommends itself
> Unto our gentle senses.

On the other hand, it is a mistake to conceive of the Elizabethan stage as bare. Although Shakespeare's Chorus in *Henry V* calls the stage an "unworthy scaffold" and urges the spectators to "eke out our performance with your mind," there was considerable spectacle. The last act of *Macbeth*, for example, has five stage directions calling for "drum and colors," and another sort of appeal to the eye is indicated by the stage direction "Enter Macduff, with Macbeth's head." Some scenery and properties may have been substantial; doubtless a throne was used, and in one play of the period we encounter this direction: "Hector takes up a great piece of rock and casts at Ajax, who tears up a young tree by the roots and assails Hector." The matter is of some importance, and will be glanced at again in the next section.

The Texts of Shakespeare

Though eighteen of his plays were published during his lifetime, Shakespeare seems never to have supervised their publication. There is nothing unusual here; when a playwright sold a play to a theatrical company he surrendered his ownership of it. Normally a company would not publish the play, because to publish it meant to allow competitors to acquire the piece. Some plays, however, did get published: apparently treacherous actors sometimes pieced together a play for a publisher, sometimes a company in need of money sold a play, and sometimes a company allowed a play to be published that no longer drew audiences. That Shakespeare did not concern himself with publication, then, is scarcely remarkable; of his contemporaries only Ben Jonson carefully supervised the publication of his own plays. In 1623, seven years after Shakespeare's death, John Heminges and Henry Condell (two senior members of Shakespeare's company, who had performed with him for about twenty years) collected his plays—published and unpublished—into a large volume, commonly called the First Folio. (A folio is a volume consisting of sheets that have been folded once, each sheet thus making two leaves, or four pages. The eighteen plays published during Shakespeare's lifetime had been issued one play per volume in small books called quartos. Each sheet in a quarto has been folded twice, making four leaves, or eight pages.) The First Folio contains thirty-six plays; a thirty-seventh, *Pericles*, though not in the Folio, is regarded as canonical. Heminges and Condell suggest in an address "To the great variety of readers" that the republished plays are presented in better form than in the quartos: "Before you were abused with diverse stolen and surreptitious copies, maimed and deformed by the frauds and stealths of injurious impostors that exposed them; even those, are now offered to your view cured and perfect of their limbs, and all the rest absolute in their numbers, as he [i.e., Shakespeare] conceived them."

Whoever was assigned to prepare the texts for publication in the First Folio seems to have taken his job seriously and yet not to have performed it with uniform care. The sources of the texts seem to have been, in general, good unpublished copies or the best published copies. The first play in the collection, *The Tempest*, is divided into acts and scenes, has unusually full stage directions and descriptions of spectacle, and concludes with a list of the characters, but the editor was not able (or willing) to present all of the succeeding texts so fully dressed. Later texts occasionally show signs of carelessness: in one scene of *Much Ado About Nothing* the names of actors, instead of characters, appear as speech prefixes, as they had in the quarto, which the Folio reprints; proofreading throughout the Folio is spotty and apparently was done without reference to the printer's copy; the pagination of *Hamlet* jumps from 156 to 257.

A modern editor of Shakespeare must first select his copy; no problem if the play exists only in the Folio, but a considerable problem if the relationship between a quarto and the Folio—or an early quarto and a later one—is unclear. When an editor has chosen what seems to him to be the most authoritative text or texts for his copy, he has not done with making decisions. First of all, he must reckon with Elizabethan spelling. If he is not producing a facsimile, he probably modernizes it, but ought he to preserve the old form of words that apparently were pronounced quite unlike their modern forms—"lanthorn" "alablaster"? If he preserves these forms, is he really preserving Shakespeare's forms or perhaps those of a compositor in the printing house? What is one to do when one finds "lanthorn" and "lantern" in adjacent lines? (The editors of this series in general, but not invariably, assume that words should be spelled in their modern form.) Elizabethan punctuation, too, presents problems. For example in the First Folio, the only text for the play, Macbeth rejects his wife's idea that he can wash the blood from his hand:

> no: this my Hand will rather
> The multitudinous Seas incarnardine,
> Making the Greene one, Red.

Obviously an editor will remove the superfluous capitals, and he will probably alter the spelling to "incarnadine," but will he leave the comma before "red," letting Macbeth speak of the sea as "the green one," or will he (like most modern editors) remove the comma and thus have Macbeth say that his hand will make the ocean *uniformly* red?

An editor will sometimes have to change more than spelling or punctuation. Macbeth says to his wife:

> I dare do all that may become a man,
> Who dares no more, is none.

For two centuries editors have agreed that the second line is unsatisfactory, and have emended "no" to "do": "Who dares do more is none." But when in the same play Ross says that fearful persons

> floate vpon a wilde and violent Sea
> Each way, and moue,

need "move" be emended to "none," as it often is, on the hunch that the compositor misread the manuscript? The editors of the Signet Classic Shakespeare have restrained themselves from making abundant emendations. In their minds they hear Dr. Johnson on the dangers of emending: "I have adopted the Roman sentiment, that it is more honorable to save a citizen than to kill an enemy." Some departures (in addition to spelling, punctuation, and lineation) from the copy text have of course been made, but the original readings are listed in a note following the play, so that the reader can evaluate them for himself.

The editors of the Signet Classic Shakespeare, following tradition, have added line numbers and in many cases act and scene divisions as well as indications of locale at the beginning of scenes. The Folio divided most of the plays into acts and some into scenes. Early eighteenth-century editors increased the divisions. These divisions, which provide a convenient way of referring to passages in the plays, have been retained, but when not in the text chosen as the basis for the Signet Classic text they are enclosed in square brackets [ ] to indicate that they are editorial additions. Similarly, although no play of Shakespeare's published during his lifetime was equipped with indications of locale at the heads of scene divisions, locales have here been added in square brackets for the convenience of the reader, who lacks the information afforded to spectators by costumes, properties, and gestures. The spectator can tell at a glance he is in the throne room, but without an editorial indication the reader may be puzzled for a while. It should be mentioned, incidentally, that there are a few authentic stage directions—perhaps Shakespeare's, perhaps a prompter's— that suggest locales: for example, "Enter Brutus in his orchard," and "They go up into the Senate house." It is hoped that the bracketed additions provide the reader with the sort of help provided in these two authentic directions, but it is equally hoped that the reader will remember that the stage was not loaded with scenery.

No editor during the course of his work can fail to recollect some words Heminges and Condell prefixed to the Folio:

> It had been a thing, we confess, worthy to have been wished, that the author himself had lived to have set forth and overseen his own writings. But since it hath been ordained otherwise, and he by death departed from that right, we pray you do not envy his friends the office of their care and pain to have collected and published them.

Nor can an editor, after he has done his best, forget Heminges and Condell's final words: "And so we leave you to other of his friends, whom if you need can be your guides. If you need them not, you can lead yourselves, and others. And such readers we wish him."

SYLVAN BARNET
Tufts University

Introduction

Thomas Platter, a Swiss traveler to England, recorded his visit of September 21, 1599, to a London theater: at about two o'clock, after lunch, he and his party crossed the river, and in a house with a thatched roof saw an excellent performance of the tragedy of the first Emperor Julius Caesar. (Platter was mistaken in giving to Caesar the title of "Emperor," either because he was weak in history or because he was impressed by the imperious portrayal of the title role.) He went on to note that there was a cast of about fifteen, and that after the play, according to custom, there was a most elegant and curious dance, two participants being dressed in men's clothes, and two in women's.

The dance that Platter saw was the jig, and the play was undoubtedly Shakespeare's *The Tragedy of Julius Caesar*, performed at the newly constructed Globe Theatre. It is quite probable that Shakespeare wrote the play early in 1599, and it marks an important stage in his development. His previous work, *Henry V* (1599), was the last of a long series of English history plays; and while attention shifts to Roman times in *Julius Caesar*, Shakespeare incorporates those ideas of history that grew through the English plays. Starting as a chronicle of wars and bloody events, the histories progressively move toward a recognition of tragedy through historical process. As the histories unfold, Shakespeare's horror of civil war becomes increasingly apparent; and as the focus narrows to individual rulers, we see the development of his intense belief in the divine quality of kingship as the only possible safeguard against civil dissension.

In *Julius Caesar* Shakespeare continues to explore the drama of power politics and personal conscience; only now, as if to gain perspective on the great issues of the histories, he moves the setting to a more distant time. The shift to ancient history would have sharpened rather than blunted the play's contemporary relevance because of the acknowledged Elizabethan habit of viewing history as a series of object lessons for present conduct.

We must not forget how widespread was the longing for unshakable rule and how overwhelming was the dread of civil war at the time *Julius Caesar* was first performed. Elizabeth I had come to the throne in 1558 when the country was in such a state of rebellion and confusion that it seemed likely to slip back into the horrors of the Wars of the Roses. Elizabeth had given her subjects peace, and the nation had prospered; for many years she had been a strong ruler, despite the repeated Catholic claims that she was illegitimate and therefore not a true successor. Attempts at assassination had been many. By 1599 she was old and visibly failing. She had no direct heir; there was no one whose claim to the throne after her was beyond dispute. Childless like Caesar, she could pass on the office only by naming an heir, and this she refused to do, perhaps in order to prevent the growth of factions. The shadow of war and dissension grew ominous. In such circumstances, we see first among the issues of *Julius Caesar* the very topical and concrete problem of a disputed succession, and the more abstract problem of killing—and replacing—the ruler.

Even without Machiavelli many Elizabethans knew that the moral problems of government are not necessarily the same as the moral problems of men. It was precisely because Elizabeth had compromised her personal beliefs whenever the public interest demanded it that she had been so successful a ruler; indeed, in many cases it is still impossible to know what she as a private person believed. Mary Tudor, who had tried to rule in accordance with religious principles, had brought about years of bloodshed. The theory of divine grace accorded to the public actions of a duly appointed ruler was not childish authoritarianism but a philosophical way of resolving the well-perceived gap between what the man might believe and what the ruler must do.

When we view *Julius Caesar* in the light of the political considerations of its own time, many of the difficulties of the play, which are discussed in critical articles in this volume, can be seen in perspective. Caesar *is* proud, and destined for the punishment of *hubris;* he is, nonetheless, "the ruler" by ability as well as power, as Plutarch himself suggests in *The Life of Julius Caesar*, a primary source for Shakespeare's work:

> . . . the Romans, inclining to Caesar's prosperity and taking the bit in the mouth, supposing that to be ruled by one man alone, it would be a good mean for them to take breath a little, after so many troubles and miseries as they had abidden in these civil wars, they chose him perpetual Dictator. . . . And now for himself, after he had ended his civil wars, he did so honorably behave himself, that there was no fault to be found in him. . . .

Plutarch goes on to list Caesar's achievements and enterprises, and suggests that his only failing is a desire to be *called* king. However, Caesar's personal faults have no bearing upon his public abilities.

Brutus is high-minded and disinterested, even though his love of political liberty leads him to transgress the rules of allegiance to a ruler and gratitude to a benefactor. His personal virtues, however, have no bearing upon his public abilities. He is naive enough to believe that a republic needs no power structure, that the removal of Caesar will simply allow power to flow back to the officers of the republic. But of course events prove otherwise, and he and Cassius are forced in their turn to assume power against those who would "destroy the revolution." Neither Brutus nor Cassius has the ability—or the right—to rule, and both are defeated. Yet the man who ultimately replaces them is not the man who roused the public against them, but the one whose impersonal manner from the beginning marks him as the next possessor of the power to rule—Octavius Caesar.

private vs. public

Brutus, Octavius, and Antony all become guilty as men. Brutus kills his friend; Octavius joins the others of the Triumvirate in condemning innocent men to death; Antony deliberately rouses a mob and turns it loose to do what mischief it will. What they do, however, does not matter in considering the fitness of each to rule. Personal innocence or guilt is not in question, and we are not asked to feel that one man or another is "right." We are asked to see that while a just man in private life is to be praised, a just man in public life may very well bring about catastrophe. The wicked—or, like Caesar, the conceited and superstitious— may be the genius as a ruler. Man's worth as a private individual does not necessarily ensure his value as a public ruler. Less sentimental than many of his critics, Shakespeare sees that a morally repulsive act may at times be a politically desirable one; that a man who acts from the highest of motives may be too busy keeping his conscience clean to lead well; that a man who once does evil in the expectation that good will be the final result may be forced more deeply into self-deception and impotence than a man who acts simply from expediency. But he also sees that the pursuit of expediency and lack of scruple do not in themselves guarantee ability to govern—else why not, ultimately, an Antony in command?

There is a natural inclination to desire unequivocal answers and absolute judgments, to simplify events until they can be seen as black or white; and we are naturally bewildered when forced into a position that requires us to judge but forbids us the use of simple terms of reference. It is not surprising, therefore, that we may be confounded by *Julius Caesar*, for often we confront situations in which personalities and actions are neither wholly right nor wholly wrong. We cannot feel unreserved hate or love for any character; each seems to call for a different response as he reacts to the seemingly irreconcilable demands of public and private life. Caesar is deaf, aging, subject to epileptic fits, inclined to superstition, warmhearted to his friends in private yet inflexible in public. But if we can believe Antony at all, Caesar has a genuine love of his country. His fault is a kind of ecstasy that the exercise of his office brings upon

him. As a private individual he shows many weaknesses;
as a public institution he sees himself superior to all ordinary
dangers, and believes that his office is a power that must
not be opposed. Indeed, Caesar constantly uses his name to
speak of his alter ego, the Dictator, and in an early speech
to Antony, in which he reveals his distrust of Cassius, he
sums up the two views of himself as he unwittingly contrasts
two attitudes: the public office that is perfect, and the
private individual who is defective. It is as though his public
self is quite dissociated from his personal weaknesses:

> I rather tell thee what is to be feared
> Than what I fear; for always I am Caesar.
> Come on my right hand, for this ear is deaf,
> And tell me truly what thou think'st of him.
>
> (I.ii.211–14)

Caesar may have a number of weaknesses, but none of the
personal defects impair the spirit of Caesar—the capacity
to rule. The play vividly demonstrates that there is more
stability, freedom, and justice in Rome with Caesar alive
than with Caesar dead.

We may be far more sympathetic to the personality of
Brutus; yet we must admit that neither he nor Cassius has
any specific charges that would warrant the killing of
Caesar. Cassius derides Caesar's weaknesses. His attacks
are the result of personal envy—why should the fact that
Caesar failed in a swimming contest, or suffered from fever,
make him contemptible as a ruler? And Brutus admits that
he has no immediate cause for indicting his friend. His
soliloquy at the beginning of Act II is an agonized attempt
to reconcile the idea of tyranny with the personal Caesar he
knows. He begins his analysis of the situation with the
conclusion—"It must be by his death"—and then, unable
to find anything concrete for which Caesar deserves death,
he has to resort to possibilities and probabilities: "He would
be crowned./How that might change his nature, there's the
question." In the end he convinces himself of the necessity
of murder by thinking not of what is but what might be, by
imagining the future abuse of power, and finally, by em-
ploying false analogy:

> And therefore think him as a serpent's egg
> Which hatched, would as his kind grow mischievous,
> And kill him in the shell.
>
> (II.i.32–34)

But Caesar is a man, not a serpent's egg; and Brutus is no less mistaken when he tries to kill the spirit of Caesar by doing away with the man. He only succeeds in killing the man, not his spirit—and this is forcefully dramatized when, after the assassination, the people are eager to transfer their allegiance to Brutus, just as they had abandoned Pompey for Caesar:

Third Plebeian. Let him be Caesar.
Fourth Plebeian.   Caesar's better parts
  Shall be crowned in Brutus.

> (III.ii.52–53)

It is not only Brutus' misfortune but his fault that his achievements turn out, ironically, to be the reverse of his best intentions. He brings to Rome anarchy and the horrors of civil war, not "Peace, freedom, and liberty."

In dramatizing the complex issues of power politics, *Julius Caesar* offers no easy solution to problems that are no less baffling to our own age. Many will find that this work is one of Shakespeare's most perplexing, for it is disconcerting when a play—or history itself—appeals to man's earnest desire to judge actions in terms of simple, personal standards of right and wrong and then betrays and mocks his deepest convictions by suggesting that Power is better than Virtue,—that efficiency may be preferable to goodness, or that conscience may be dangerously inadequate in determining political action.

An individual's scrupulous concern for morality may, indeed, be disastrously impolitic. Cassius leads Brutus to an abhorrent deed, but when the consequences involve Brutus in the exercise of power, Brutus continues to think and act in accordance with private morality. His scruples about killing Antony or about unjustly raising money hinder the success of the conspiracy. His wish to fight a pitched battle, to decide the matter once and for all, instead of following stratagems and winning by attrition, is also the decision of a man who refuses to take on the role of politician. It is noteworthy that Cassius, after his initial victory, consistently defers to Brutus' moral scruples; knowing him to be wrong in his strategy, he is still swayed by the very image of nobility for which Brutus was chosen as the figurehead of the conspiracy. The irony is unmistakable: the politic man sets up an image of virtue, dissociated from politics, to serve his own purposes, to endear him to the populace; but once that image is established, his freedom to act without it is curbed, and he is hampered in the achievement of his political ends by the very image he has fostered.

The spirit of Caesar that dominates the play is to be associated, finally, with the exercise of supreme power. When Caesar dies, power is without a master, and as such, indiscriminately destructive. Each man in his turn tries to grasp the lightning that has been set free, and is fearfully transformed, until finally it comes to rest upon the man who alone, by gift of personality and legitimate succession, may wield it unscathed.

Shakespeare fully delineates the intriguing pattern of shifting power as an old Caesar is succeeded by a young one. The politic Cassius gives in to an impolitic Brutus and both fail as a result. Antony, Octavius, and Lepidus begin with complete ruthlessness; however, this does not guarantee them power or even win the battle for them—their opponents defeat themselves through mistakes. Lepidus, the "straw man," is first burdened with responsibility, then eliminated; and afterward, effortlessly, Antony, the ruthless and emotional partner, is displaced by the man without a temperament, the personification of impersonal rule.

The transfer of power from Antony to Octavius is subtly and swiftly dramatized in Act V, Scene i, when Octavius suddenly opposes Antony's command and leads his troops in his own way—"I do not cross you," he tells Antony, "but I will do so." From this point Antony refers to his partner as "Caesar," whereas until that moment he had called him only "Octavius." Even when Octavius asks for advice immediately after he has asserted his independence (V.i.23), Antony calls him "Caesar" before bidding him "Make forth." And soon afterward Octavius is seen as the one who is beginning to prevail; it is he who gives directions: "Come, Antony; away!" In the last scene of the play Octavius is in total charge of the action, while Antony is returned to his first prominent role, that of funeral orator. Antony may deliver the wonderful eulogy for Brutus, but Octavius, in businesslike fashion, gives the orders for burial, and without consulting or mentioning Antony, says to his former adversaries: "All that served Brutus, I will entertain them," as if he were in sole command. Finally, Octavius renders the play's concluding speech, which is conventionally given by the person of highest rank, whose task is to restore order to the state.

In portraying Octavius and describing his rise to power, Shakespeare departs from his primary source, Plutarch's *Lives*, and his changes are important for our understanding of the play. Plutarch's Octavius is not an exceptional soldier but an outwardly pleasant person of charm and wit, the very opposite of Shakespeare's characterization. And whereas Shakespeare's Octavius gains stature at the battle of Philippi, in Plutarch's *The Life of Marcus Antonius* he is sick at this time, and Antony "had the chiefest glory of all this victory." In Plutarch's *Life of Marcus Brutus* it is further reported that Octavius was absent from the battle; he had himself carried from his camp because of a friend's ominous dream, "and no man could tell what became of Octavius Caesar after he was carried out of his camp."

Shakespeare's independent treatment of Octavius reveals his conception of the kind of man who can wield power in the spirit of Caesar. Brutus, Cassius, and Antony grasp at power and are unable to retain it, perhaps because in exercising it they are more swayed by personal passions than Caesar. Octavius had no part in the murder; he is the only person in the play as free of the passions of love or hate as Caesar claimed to be. In his speech at the beginning of Act V he identifies himself with the spirit of Caesar, makes himself spiritually his heir, and assumes the duty of revenge:

Look,
I draw a sword against conspirators.
When think you that the sword goes up again?
Never, till Caesar's three and thirty wounds
Be well avenged; or till another Caesar
Have added slaughter to the sword of traitors.

(V.i.50–55)

At the close of the play we are meant to feel that the exercise of power necessary for these times has once more been placed in adequate hands. The spirit of Caesar, for good or ill, has not been put to rest.

WILLIAM ROSEN
BARBARA ROSEN
University of Connecticut

The Tragedy of
JULIUS CAESAR

Julius Caesar
Octavius Caesar ⎫
Marcus Antonius ⎬ triumvirs after
M. Aemilius Lepidus ⎭ the death of Julius Caesar

Cicero ⎫
Publius ⎬ senators
Popilius Lena ⎭

Marcus Brutus
Cassius
Casca
Trebonius ⎫
Ligarius ⎬ conspirators against Julius Caesar
Decius Brutus
Metellus Cimber ⎭
Cinna

Flavius ⎫
Marullus ⎬ tribunes

Artemidorus of Cnidos, a teacher of rhetoric
A Soothsayer
Cinna, a poet
Another Poet

Lucilius ⎫
Titinius ⎪
Messala ⎬ friends to Brutus and Cassius
Young Cato ⎪
Volumnius ⎭

Varro ⎫
Clitus ⎪
Claudius ⎬ servants to Brutus
Strato ⎪
Lucius ⎪
Dardanius ⎭
Pindarus, servant to Cassius
Calphurnia, wife to Caesar
Portia, wife to Brutus
Senators, Citizens, Guards, Attendants, &c.

Scene: During most of the play, at Rome;
afterward near Sardis, and near Philippi]

The Tragedy of Julius Caesar

ACT I

Scene I. [*Rome. A street.*]

Enter Flavius, Marullus, and certain Commoners over the stage.

Flavius. Hence! Home, you idle creatures, get you home!
　Is this a holiday? What, know you not,
　Being mechanical,°1 you ought not walk
　Upon a laboring day without the sign
　Of your profession?° Speak, what trade art thou?　　5

Carpenter. Why, sir, a carpenter.

Marullus. Where is thy leather apron and thy rule?
　What dost thou with thy best apparel on?
　You, sir, what trade are you?

Cobbler. Truly, sir, in respect of a fine° workman, I am　10
　but, as you would say, a cobbler.°

Marullus. But what trade art thou? Answer me directly.°

Cobbler. A trade, sir, that, I hope, I may use with a

---

1 The degree sign (°) indicates a footnote, which is keyed to the text by
line number. Text references are printed in *italic* type; the annotation
follows in roman type.
I.i. 3 *mechanical* of the working class　4–5 *sign/Of your profession*
mark of your trade, i.e., working clothes　10 *in respect of a fine* in
comparison with a skilled　11 *cobbler* (1) shoemaker (2) bungler
12 *directly* straightforwardly

33

15   safe conscience, which is indeed, sir, a mender of bad
      soles.°

Flavius. What trade, thou knave? Thou naughty° knave,
      what trade?

Cobbler. Nay, I beseech you, sir, be not out° with me:
      yet, if you be out,° sir, I can mend you.°

20 *Marullus.* What mean'st thou by that? Mend me, thou
      saucy fellow?

Cobbler. Why, sir, cobble you.

Flavius. Thou art a cobbler, art thou?

Cobbler. Truly, sir, all that I live by is with the awl: I
25   meddle with no tradesman's matters, nor women's
      matters; but withal,° I am indeed, sir, a surgeon to
      old shoes: when they are in great danger, I recover°
      them. As proper men as ever trod upon neat's
      leather° have gone upon my handiwork.

30 *Flavius.* But wherefore art not in thy shop today?
      Why dost thou lead these men about the streets?

Cobbler. Truly, sir, to wear out their shoes, to get
      myself into more work. But indeed, sir, we make
      holiday to see Caesar and to rejoice in his triumph.°

Marullus. Wherefore rejoice? What conquest brings he
35   home?
      What tributaries° follow him to Rome,
      To grace in captive bonds his chariot wheels?
      You blocks, you stones, you worse than senseless
      things!
      O you hard hearts, you cruel men of Rome,
40   Knew you not Pompey?° Many a time and oft
      Have you climbed up to walls and battlements,
      To tow'rs and windows, yea, to chimney tops,

15 *soles* (pun on "souls") 16 *naughty* worthless 18 *out* angry
19 *be out* i.e., have worn-out shoes 19 *mend you* (1) mend your
shoes (2) improve your character 26 *withal* (1) nevertheless (2) with
awl (3) with all 27 *recover* (1) resole (2) cure 28–29 *neat's leather*
cattle's hide 34 *triumph* triumphal celebration 36 *tributaries* captives 40 *Pompey* (defeated by Caesar in 48 B.C., later murdered)

Citizens are fickle

Your infants in your arms, and there have sat
The livelong day, with patient expectation,
To see great Pompey pass the streets of Rome.   45
And when you saw his chariot but appear,
Have you not made an universal shout,
That Tiber trembled underneath her banks
To hear the replication° of your sounds
Made in her concave shores?°   50
And do you now put on your best attire?
And do you now cull out a holiday?
And do you now strew flowers in his way
That comes in triumph over Pompey's blood?°
Be gone!   55
Run to your houses, fall upon your knees,
Pray to the gods to intermit° the plague
That needs must light on this ingratitude.

Flavius. Go, go, good countrymen, and, for this fault,
Assemble all the poor men of your sort;   60
Draw them to Tiber banks and weep your tears
Into the channel, till the lowest stream
Do kiss the most exalted shores of all.°
                    Exeunt all the Commoners.
See, whe'r° their basest mettle° be not moved;
They vanish tongue-tied in their guiltiness.   65
Go you down that way towards the Capitol;
This way will I. Disrobe the images,
If you do find them decked with ceremonies.°

Marullus. May we do so?
You know it is the feast of Lupercal.°   70

Flavius. It is no matter; let no images
Be hung with Caesar's trophies. I'll about

---

49 *replication* echo   50 *concave shores* hollowed-out banks   54 *in
triumph over Pompey's blood* as the conqueror of Pompey's sons
57 *intermit* hold back   63 *most exalted shores of all* highest water
mark   64 *whe'r* whether   64 *mettle* (1) substance (2) disposition
68 *ceremonies* robes (or ornaments)   70 *Lupercal* (fertility festival
held on February 15; Caesar's triumph really took place in the preceding October, but Shakespeare combines events and shortens time
spans for dramatic effect)

And drive away the vulgar° from the streets;
So do you too, where you perceive them thick.
75 These growing feathers plucked from Caesar's wing
Will make him fly an ordinary pitch,°
Who else would soar above the view of men
And keep us all in servile fearfulness.   *Exeunt.*

[handwritten: falcony]

[handwritten: try to take his power]

[Scene II. *A public place.*]

*Enter Caesar, Antony (for the course), Calphurnia, Portia,
Decius, Cicero, Brutus, Cassius, Casca, a Soothsayer;
after them, Marullus and Flavius.*

Caesar. Calphurnia!

Casca.   Peace, ho! Caesar speaks.

Caesar.   Calphurnia!

Calphurnia. Here, my lord.

Caesar. Stand you directly in Antonius' way
When he doth run his course. Antonius!

5 *Antony.* Caesar, my lord?

Caesar. Forget not in your speed, Antonius,
To touch Calphurnia; for our elders say
The barren, touchèd in this holy chase,
Shake off their sterile curse.

Antony.   I shall remember:
10 When Caesar says "Do this," it is performed.

Caesar. Set on, and leave no ceremony out.

Soothsayer. Caesar!

Caesar. Ha! Who calls?

73 *vulgar* common people   76 *pitch* height

puts blame on her (barren)

Casca. Bid every noise be still; peace yet again!

Caesar. Who is it in the press° that calls on me?　　15
I hear a tongue, shriller than all the music,
Cry "Caesar." Speak; Caesar is turned to hear.

Soothsayer. Beware the ides of March.°

Caesar.　　　　　　　　　What man is that?

Brutus. A soothsayer bids you beware the ides of March.

Caesar. Set him before me; let me see his face.　　20

Cassius. Fellow, come from the throng; look upon
Caesar.

Caesar. What say'st thou to me now? Speak once again.

Soothsayer. Beware the ides of March.

Caesar. He is a dreamer, let us leave him. Pass.
Sennet.° Exeunt. Mane[n]t° Brutus and Cassius.

Cassius. Will you go see the order of the course?°　　25

Brutus. Not I.

Cassius. I pray you do.

Brutus. I am not gamesome:° I do lack some part
Of that quick spirit° that is in Antony.　　*obedience*
Let me not hinder, Cassius, your desires;　　30
I'll leave you.

Cassius. Brutus, I do observe you now of late;
I have not from your eyes that gentleness
And show of love as I was wont° to have;
You bear too stubborn and too strange a hand°　　35
Over your friend that loves you.

I.ii.15 *press* crowd　18 *ides of March* March 15　24 s.d. *Sennet* flourish of trumpets marking ceremonial entrance or exit　24 s.d. *Mane[n]t*
(they) remain　25 *order of the course* progress of the race　28 *gamesome* (1) fond of sport (2) merry　29 *quick spirit* (1) lively nature
(2) prompt obedience　34 *wont* accustomed　35 *bear . . . hand* treat
too haughtily and distantly, keep at arm's length (the metaphor is from
horsemanship)

Brutus.   Cassius,
    Be not deceived: if I have veiled my look,
    I turn the trouble of my countenance
    Merely upon myself.° Vexèd I am
40   Of late with passions of some difference,°
    Conceptions only proper to myself,°
    Which give some soil,° perhaps, to my behaviors;
    But let not therefore my good friends be grieved
    (Among which number, Cassius, be you one)
45   Nor construe° any further my neglect
    Than that poor Brutus, with himself at war,
    Forgets the shows° of love to other men.

Cassius. Then, Brutus, I have much mistook your
      passion;°
    By means whereof° this breast of mine hath buried
50   Thoughts of great value, worthy cogitations.
    Tell me, good Brutus, can you see your face?

Brutus. No, Cassius; for the eye sees not itself
    But by reflection, by some other things.

Cassius. 'Tis just:°
55   And it is very much lamented, Brutus,
    That you have no such mirrors as will turn
    Your hidden worthiness into your eye,
    That you might see your shadow.° I have heard
    Where many of the best respect° in Rome
60   (Except immortal Caesar), speaking of Brutus,
    And groaning underneath this age's yoke,
    Have wished that noble Brutus had his eyes.

Brutus. Into what dangers would you lead me, Cassius,
    That you would have me seek into myself
65   For that which is not in me?

37–39 *if I have . . . upon myself* i.e., if I have seemed withdrawn, it is because I am displeased with myself and no one else (*Merely* = wholly)
40 *passions of some difference* conflicting emotions   **41** *Conceptions
. . . myself* ideas concerning me only   **42** *soil* blemish   **45** *construe* in-
terpret   **47** *shows* manifestations   **48** *passion* feelings   **49** *By means
whereof* as a consequence of which   **54** *just* true   **58** *shadow* reflection, i.e., yourself as others see you   **59** *best respect* highest reputation

Cassius. Therefore, good Brutus, be prepared to hear;
  And since you know you cannot see yourself
  So well as by reflection, I, your glass°
  Will modestly discover to yourself
  That of yourself which you yet know not of.   70
  And be not jealous on° me, gentle Brutus:
  Were I a common laughter,° or did use
  To stale with ordinary oaths my love
  To every new protester;° if you know
  That I do fawn on men and hug them hard,   75
  And after scandal° them; or if you know
  That I profess myself° in banqueting
  To all the rout,° then hold me dangerous.

                                Flourish° *and shout.*

Brutus. What means this shouting? I do fear the people
  Choose Caesar for their king.

Cassius.   Ay, do you fear it?   80
  Then must I think you would not have it so.

Brutus. I would not, Cassius, yet I love him well.
  But wherefore do you hold me here so long?
  What is it that you would impart to me?
  If it be aught toward the general good,°   85
  Set honor in one eye and death i' th' other,
  And I will look on both indifferently;°
  For let the gods so speed me,° as I love
  The name of honor more than I fear death.

Cassius. I know that virtue to be in you, Brutus,   90
  As well as I do know your outward favor.°
  Well, honor is the subject of my story.
  I cannot tell what you and other men
  Think of this life, but for my single self,

---

68 *glass* mirror   71 *jealous on* suspicious of   72 *laughter* object of
mockery   72–74 *did use . . . protester* were accustomed to make cheap
with glib and frequent avowals to every new promiser of friendship
(*ordinary* = [1] tavern [2] everyday)   76 *scandal* slander   77 *profess
myself* declare my friendship   78 *rout* vulgar crowd   78 s.d. *Flourish*
ceremonial sounding of trumpets   85 *general good* public welfare
87 *indifferently* impartially   88 *speed me* make me prosper   91 *favor*
appearance

95   I had as lief not be,° as live to be
      In awe of such a thing as I myself.°
      I was born free as Caesar; so were you;
      We both have fed as well, and we can both
      Endure the winter's cold as well as he:
100   For once, upon a raw and gusty day,
      The troubled Tiber chafing with° her shores,
      Caesar said to me "Dar'st thou, Cassius, now
      Leap in with me into this angry flood,
      And swim to yonder point?" Upon the word,
105   Accout'red° as I was, I plunged in
      And bade him follow; so indeed he did.
      The torrent roared, and we did buffet it
      With lusty sinews, throwing it aside
      And stemming it with hearts of controversy.°
110   But ere we could arrive the point proposed,
      Caesar cried "Help me, Cassius, or I sink!"
      I, as Aeneas,° our great ancestor,
      Did from the flames of Troy upon his shoulder
      The old Anchises bear, so from the waves of Tiber
115   Did I the tired Caesar. And this man
      Is now become a god, and Cassius is
      A wretched creature, and must bend his body
      If Caesar carelessly but nod on him.
      He had a fever when he was in Spain,
120   And when the fit was on him, I did mark
      How he did shake: 'tis true, this god did shake.
      His coward lips did from their color fly,°
      And that same eye whose bend° doth awe the world
      Did lose his° luster; I did hear him groan;
125   Ay, and that tongue of his, that bade the Romans
      Mark him and write his speeches in their books,
      Alas, it cried, "Give me some drink, Titinius,"

95 *as lief not be* just as soon not exist   96 *such a thing as I myself* i.e.,
another human being (Caesar)   101 *chafing with* raging against
105 *Accout'red* fully armed   109 *stemming . . . controversy* moving
forward against it (1) aggressively (2) in rivalry   112 *Aeneas* (legendary founder of the Roman state, and hero of Vergil's *Aeneid* Anchises
was his feeble father)   122 *His coward . . . fly* the color fled from his
lips like a deserter fleeing from his banner in battle (*color* = [1] hue
[2] banner)   123 *bend* glance   124 *his* its

As a sick girl. Ye gods! It doth amaze me,
A man of such a feeble temper° should
So get the start of° the majestic world,   130
And bear the palm° alone.   *Shout. Flourish.*

Brutus. Another general shout?
I do believe that these applauses are
For some new honors that are heaped on Caesar.

Cassius. Why, man, he doth bestride the narrow world   135
Like a Colossus,° and we petty men
Walk under his huge legs and peep about
To find ourselves dishonorable° graves.
Men at some time are masters of their fates:
The fault, dear Brutus, is not in our stars,°   140
But in ourselves, that we are underlings.
Brutus and Caesar: what should be in that "Caesar"?
Why should that name be sounded° more than yours?
Write them together, yours is as fair a name;
Sound them, it doth become the mouth as well;   145
Weigh them, it is as heavy; conjure with 'em,
"Brutus" will start° a spirit as soon as "Caesar."
Now, in the names of all the gods at once,
Upon what meat doth this our Caesar feed,
That he is grown so great? Age, thou art shamed!   150
Rome, thou hast lost the breed of noble bloods!
When went there by an age, since the great flood,°
But it was famed with° more than with one man?
When could they say (till now) that talked of Rome,
That her wide walks encompassed but one man?   155
Now is it Rome indeed, and room° enough,

129 *feeble temper* weak constitution   130 *get the start of* outdistance
131 *bear the palm* carry off the victor's prize   136 *Colossus* (an immense statue of Apollo, said to straddle the entrance to the harbor of Rhodes so that ships sailed under its legs)   138 *dishonorable* (because we are dominated by Caesar)   140 *stars* destinies (in Shakespeare's day one's temperament, and therefore one's actions and course of life, were thought to be largely determined by the position of the planets at one's birth)   143 *sounded* (1) spoken (2) proclaimed by trumpet   147 *start* raise   152 *great flood* (classical story told of the drowning of all mankind except Deucalion and his wife Pyrrha, spared by Zeus because of their virtue)   153 *But it was famed with* without the age being made famous by   156 *Rome . . . room* (homonyms, hence a pun)

When there is in it but one only man.
O, you and I have heard our fathers say,
There was a Brutus° once that would have brooked°
160 Th' eternal devil to keep his state in Rome
As easily as a king.

Brutus. That you do love me, I am nothing jealous;°
What you would work me to,° I have some aim;°
How I have thought of this, and of these times,
165 I shall recount hereafter. For this present,
I would not so (with love I might entreat you)
Be any further moved. What you have said
I will consider; what you have to say
I will with patience hear, and find a time
170 Both meet° to hear and answer such high things.
Till then, my noble friend, chew° upon this:
Brutus had rather be a villager
Than to repute himself a son of Rome
Under these hard conditions as this time
Is like to lay upon us.

175 *Cassius.*   I am glad
That my weak words have struck but thus much show
Of fire from Brutus.

Enter Caesar and his Train.°

Brutus. The games are done, and Caesar is returning.

Cassius. As they pass by, pluck Casca by the sleeve,
180 And he will (after his sour fashion) tell you
What hath proceeded worthy note today.

Brutus. I will do so. But look you, Cassius,
The angry spot doth glow on Caesar's brow,
And all the rest look like a chidden train:
185 Calphurnia's cheek is pale, and Cicero

---

159 *a Brutus* (Lucius Junius Brutus helped expel the Tarquins and
found the Republic in 509 B.C.)   159 *brooked* tolerated   162 *nothing
jealous* not at all doubtful   163 *work me to* persuade me of   163 *aim*
idea   170 *meet* suitable   171 *chew* reflect   177 s.d. *Train* retinue

Looks with such ferret° and such fiery eyes
As we have seen him in the Capitol,
Being crossed in conference° by some senators.

Cassius. Casca will tell us what the matter is.

Caesar. Antonius.   190

Antony. Caesar?

Caesar. Let me have men about me that are fat, >lazy
Sleek-headed men, and such as sleep a-nights.
Yond Cassius has a lean and hungry look;
He thinks too much: such men are dangerous.   195

Antony. Fear him not, Caesar, he's not dangerous;
He is a noble Roman, and well given.°

Caesar. Would he were fatter! But I fear him not.
Yet if my name were liable to fear,°
I do not know the man I should avoid   200
So soon as that spare Cassius. He reads much,
He is a great observer, and he looks
Quite through the deeds° of men. He loves no plays,
As thou dost, Antony; he hears no music;°
Seldom he smiles, and smiles in such a sort°   205
As if he mocked himself, and scorned his spirit
That could be moved to smile at anything.
Such men as he be never at heart's ease
Whiles they behold a greater than themselves,
And therefore are they very dangerous.   210
I rather tell thee what is to be feared
Than what I fear; for always I am Caesar.
Come on my right hand, for this ear is deaf,

COCKY

186 *ferret* ferretlike (a ferret is a vicious, weasel-like animal with red eyes)   188 *conference* debate   197 *given* disposed   199 *if my name . . . to fear* i.e., if the idea of fear could ever be associated with me   203 *through the deeds* i.e., to the hidden motives of actions   204 *hears no music* (cf. *Merchant of Venice*, V.i.83ff: "The man that hath no music in himself,/Nor is not moved with concord of sweet sounds,/Is fit for treasons. . . . Let no such man be trusted")   205 *sort* manner

And tell me truly what thou think'st of him.
                         Sennet. Exeunt Caesar and his Train.

Casca. You pulled me by the cloak; would you speak
215 with me?

Brutus. Ay, Casca; tell us what hath chanced today,
That Caesar looks so sad.°

Casca. Why, you were with him, were you not?

Brutus. I should not then ask Casca what had chanced.

220 *Casca.* Why, there was a crown offered him; and being
offered him, he put it by° with the back of his hand,
thus; and then the people fell a-shouting.

Brutus. What was the second noise for?

Casca. Why, for that too.

225 *Cassius.* They shouted thrice; what was the last cry for?

Casca. Why, for that too.

Brutus. Was the crown offered him thrice?

Casca. Ay, marry,° was't, and he put it by thrice, every
time gentler than other; and at every putting-by mine
230 honest neighbors shouted.

Cassius. Who offered him the crown?

Casca. Why, Antony.

Brutus. Tell us the manner of it, gentle Casca.

Casca. I can as well be hanged as tell the manner of it:
235 it was mere foolery; I did not mark it. I saw Mark
Antony offer him a crown—yet 'twas not a crown
neither, 'twas one of these coronets°—and, as I told
you, he put it by once; but for all that, to my thinking, he would fain° have had it. Then he offered it to
240 him again; then he put it by again; but to my thinking, he was very loath to lay his fingers off it. And

217 *sad* serious 221 *put it by* pushed it aside 228 *marry* truly (originally an oath, "By the Virgin Mary") 237 *coronets* small crowns
239 *fain* gladly

then he offered it the third time. He put it the third
time by; and still° as he refused it, the rabblement
hooted, and clapped their chopt° hands, and threw
up their sweaty nightcaps,° and uttered such a deal   245
of stinking breath because Caesar refused the crown,
that it had, almost, choked Caesar; for he swounded°
and fell down at it. And for mine own part, I durst
not laugh, for fear of opening my lips and receiving
the bad air.   250

Cassius. But, soft,° I pray you; what, did Caesar
swound?

Casca. He fell down in the market place, and foamed
at mouth, and was speechless. *Ceasar's weakness*

Brutus. 'Tis very like he hath the falling-sickness.°

Cassius. No, Caesar hath it not; but you, and I,   255
And honest Casca, we have the falling-sickness.° *We are bowing to Ceesar*

Casca. I know not what you mean by that, but I am
sure Caesar fell down. If the tag-rag people° did not
clap him and hiss him, according as he pleased and
displeased them, as they use° to do the players in the   260
theater, I am no true man.

Brutus. What said he when he came unto himself?

Casca. Marry, before he fell down, when he perceived
the common herd was glad he refused the crown, he
plucked me ope his doublet° and offered them his   265
throat to cut. An I had been a man of any occupation,°
if I would not have taken him at a word, I would I
might go to hell among the rogues. And so he fell.
When he came to himself again, he said, if he had

---

243 *still* every time   244 *chopt* rough, chapped   245 *nightcaps* (contemptuous term for workingmen's caps)   247 *swounded* fainted   251
soft slowly, "wait a minute"   254 *falling-sickness* epilepsy   256 *we
have the falling-sickness* i.e., we are becoming powerless and are
declining under Caesar's rule   258 *tag-rag people* ragged mob
260 *use* are accustomed   265 *ope his doublet* open his jacket   266 *man
of any occupation* (1) workingman, i.e., one of those to whom Caesar's
speech was addressed (2) "man of action"

270 done or said anything amiss, he desired their worships to think it was his infirmity. Three or four wenches, where I stood, cried "Alas, good soul!" and forgave him with all their hearts; but there's no heed to be taken of them; if Caesar had stabbed their
275 mothers, they would have done no less.

Brutus. And after that, he came thus sad away?

Casca. Ay.

Cassius. Did Cicero say anything?

Casca. Ay, he spoke Greek.

280 *Cassius.* To what effect?

Casca. Nay, an I tell you that, I'll ne'er look you i' th' face again. But those that understood him smiled at one another and shook their heads; but for mine own part, it was Greek to me. I could tell you more news
285 too: Marullus and Flavius, for pulling scarfs off Caesar's images, are put to silence.° Fare you well. There was more foolery yet, if I could remember it.

Cassius. Will you sup with me tonight, Casca?

Casca. No, I am promised forth.°

290 *Cassius.* Will you dine with me tomorrow?

Casca. Ay, if I be alive, and your mind hold,° and your dinner worth the eating.

Cassius. Good; I will expect you.

Casca. Do so. Farewell, both.   *Exit.*

295 *Brutus.* What a blunt fellow is this grown to be! He was quick mettle° when he went to school.

Cassius. So is he now in execution Of any bold or noble enterprise,

---

286 *put to silence* silenced (by being stripped of their tribuneships, and perhaps exiled or executed)   289 *am promised forth* have a previous engagement   291 *hold* does not change   296 *quick mettle* of a lively disposition

However he puts on this tardy form.°
This rudeness is a sauce to his good wit,° 300
Which gives men stomach° to disgest° his words
With better appetite.

Brutus. And so it is. For this time I will leave you.
Tomorrow, if you please to speak with me,
I will come home to you; or if you will, 305
Come home to me, and I will wait for you.

Cassius. I will do so. Till then, think of the world.°

Exit Brutus.

Well, Brutus, thou art noble; yet I see
Thy honorable mettle° may be wrought
From that it is disposed;° therefore it is meet° 310
That noble minds keep ever with their likes;
For who so firm that cannot be seduced?
Caesar doth bear me hard,° but he loves Brutus.
If I were Brutus now, and he were Cassius,
He should not humor° me. I will this night, 315
In several hands,° in at his windows throw,
As if they came from several citizens,
Writings, all tending to° the great opinion
That Rome holds of his name; wherein obscurely
Caesar's ambition shall be glancèd at.° 320
And after this, let Caesar seat him sure;°
For we will shake him, or worse days endure. *Exit.*

---

299 *tardy form* sluggish appearance   300 *wit* intelligence   301 *stomach* appetite   301 *disgest* digest   307 *the world* i.e., the current state of affairs   309 *mettle* (1) disposition (2) metal   309–10 *wrought . . . disposed* shaped (like iron) contrary to its natural form   310 *meet* fitting   313 *bear me hard* hold a grudge against me   315 *humor* cajole, influence by flattery   316 *several hands* different handwritings   318 *tending to* bearing on   320 *glancèd at* indirectly touched upon   321 *seat him sure* make his position secure

[Scene III. *A street.*]

Thunder and lightning. Enter [from opposite sides,]
Casca and Cicero.

Cicero. Good even, Casca; brought you Caesar home?
Why are you breathless? And why stare you so?

Casca. Are not you moved, when all the sway of earth°
    Shakes like a thing unfirm? O Cicero,
5   I have seen tempests, when the scolding winds
    Have rived° the knotty oaks, and I have seen
    Th' ambitious ocean swell and rage and foam,
    To be exalted with° the threat'ning clouds;
    But never till tonight, never till now,
10   Did I go through a tempest dropping fire.
    Either there is a civil strife in heaven,
    Or else the world, too saucy° with the gods,
    Incenses them to send destruction.

Cicero. Why, saw you anything more wonderful?

15 *Casca.* A common slave—you know him well by sight—
    Held up his left hand, which did flame and burn
    Like twenty torches joined, and yet his hand,
    Not sensible of° fire, remained unscorched.
    Besides—I ha' not since put up my sword—
20   Against° the Capitol I met a lion,
    Who glazed° upon me and went surly by
    Without annoying me. And there were drawn
    Upon a heap° a hundred ghastly° women,

I.iii.3 *all the sway of earth* i.e., the whole scheme of things (*sway:* ruling
principle) 6 *rived* split 8 *exalted with* elevated to 12 *saucy* pre-
sumptuous 18 *sensible of* sensitive to 20 *Against* directly opposite
(?) near (?) 21 *glazed* stared 22–23 *drawn/Upon a heap* huddled together 23 *ghastly* white as ghosts

Transformèd with their fear, who swore they saw
Men, all in fire, walk up and down the streets.   25
And yesterday the bird of night° did sit
Even at noonday upon the market place,
Hooting and shrieking. When these prodigies°
Do so conjointly meet,° let not men say,
"These are their reasons, they are natural,"   30
For I believe they are portentous things
Unto the climate° that they point upon.

Cicero. Indeed, it is a strange-disposèd° time:
But men may construe things after their fashion,°
Clean from the purpose° of the things themselves.   35
Comes Caesar to the Capitol tomorrow?

Casca. He doth; for he did bid Antonius
Send word to you he would be there tomorrow.

Cicero. Good night then, Casca; this disturbèd sky
Is not to walk in.

Casca.   Farewell, Cicero.   *Exit Cicero.*   40

Enter Cassius.

Cassius. Who's there?

Casca.   A Roman.

Cassius.   Casca, by your voice.

Casca. Your ear is good. Cassius, what night is this?

Cassius. A very pleasing night to honest men.

Casca. Who ever knew the heavens menace so?

Cassius. Those that have known the earth so full of
     faults.   45
For my part, I have walked about the streets,
Submitting me unto the perilous night,

---

26 *bird of night* owl (a bird of ill omen)   28 *prodigies* unnatural events
29 *conjointly meet* coincide   32 *climate* region   33 *strange-disposèd*
abnormal   34 *after their fashion* in their own way   35 *Clean from
the purpose* quite contrary to the real meaning

LION

And thus unbracèd,° Casca, as you see,
Have bared my bosom to the thunder-stone;°
50 And when the cross° blue lightning seemed to open
The breast of heaven, I did present myself
Even in the aim and very flash of it.

Casca. But wherefore did you so much tempt the
heavens?
It is the part° of men to fear and tremble
55 When the most mighty gods by tokens° send
Such dreadful heralds to astonish° us.

Cassius. You are dull, Casca, and those sparks of life
That should be in a Roman you do want,°
Or else you use not. You look pale, and gaze,
60 And put on° fear, and cast yourself in wonder,°
To see the strange impatience of the heavens;
But if you would consider the true cause
Why all these fires, why all these gliding ghosts,
Why birds and beasts from quality and kind,°
65 Why old men,° fools, and children calculate,°
Why all these things change from their ordinance,°
Their natures and preformèd faculties,°
To monstrous quality,° why, you shall find
That heaven hath infused them with these spirits°
70 To make them instruments of fear and warning
Unto some monstrous state.°
Now could I, Casca, name to thee a man
Most like this dreadful night,
That thunders, lightens, opens graves, and roars
75 As doth the lion in the Capitol;
A man no mightier than thyself, or me,

---

48 *unbracèd* with doublet unfastened   49 *thunder-stone* lightning bolt
50 *cross* jagged   54 *part* role   55 *tokens* prophetic signs   56 *astonish*
stun   58 *want* lack   60 *put on* display   60 *cast yourself in wonder* are
amazed   64 *from quality and kind* (act) against their natures   65 *old
men* i.e., the senile, in second childhood   65 *calculate* make predictions (cf. proverb, "Fools and children often do prophesy")   66 *ordinance* natural order of behavior   67 *preformèd faculties* innate qualities   68 *monstrous quality* unnatural condition   69 *spirits* supernatural powers   71 *monstrous state* abnormal state of affairs

Caesar wouldn't be great if Romans weren't so bad

In personal action, yet prodigious° grown
And fearful,° as these strange eruptions° are.

Casca. 'Tis Caesar that you mean, is it not, Cassius?

Cassius. Let it be who it is; for Romans now   80
Have thews° and limbs like to their ancestors;
But, woe the while!° Our fathers' minds are dead,
And we are governed with our mothers' spirits;
Our yoke and sufferance° show us womanish.

Casca. Indeed, they say the senators tomorrow
Mean to establish Caesar as a king;   85
And he shall wear his crown by sea and land,
In every place save here in Italy.

Cassius. I know where I will wear this dagger then;
Cassius from bondage will deliver Cassius.   90
Therein,° ye gods, you make the weak most strong;
Therein, ye gods, you tyrants do defeat.
Nor stony tower, nor walls of beaten brass,
Nor airless dungeon, nor strong links of iron,
Can be retentive to° the strength of spirit;   95
But life, being weary of these worldly bars,
Never lacks power to dismiss itself.
If I know this, know all the world besides,
That part of tyranny that I do bear
I can shake off at pleasure.   *Thunder still.*

Casca.   So can I;   100
So every bondman in his own hand bears
The power to cancel his captivity.

Cassius. And why should Caesar be a tyrant then?
Poor man, I know he would not be a wolf
But that he sees the Romans are but sheep;   105
He were no lion, were not Romans hinds.°

suicide

servants

77 *prodigious* ominous   78 *fearful* causing fear   78 *eruptions* disturbances of nature   81 *thews* sinews   82 *woe the while* alas for the times   84 *yoke and sufferance* servitude and the meek endurance of it   91 *Therein* i.e., in suicide   95 *be retentive to* hold in   106 *hinds* (1) female deer (2) peasants (3) servants

Those that with haste will make a mighty fire
Begin it with weak straws. What trash is Rome,
What rubbish and what offal, when it serves
110   For the base matter to illuminate
So vile a thing as Caesar! But, O grief,
Where hast thou led me? I, perhaps, speak this
Before a willing bondman; then I know
My answer must be made.° But I am armed,
115   And dangers are to me indifferent.°

Casca. You speak to Casca, and to such a man
That is no fleering° tell-tale. Hold, my hand.
Be factious° for redress of all these griefs,
And I will set this foot of mine as far
As who goes farthest.   [*They clasp hands.*]

120   *Cassius.*   There's a bargain made.
Now know you, Casca, I have moved already
Some certain of the noblest-minded Romans
To undergo° with me an enterprise
Of honorable dangerous consequence;
125   And I do know, by this° they stay for me
In Pompey's porch;° for now, this fearful night,
There is no stir or walking in the streets,
And the complexion of the element°
In favor's like° the work we have in hand,
130   Most bloody, fiery, and most terrible.

Enter Cinna.

Casca. Stand close° awhile, for here comes one in haste.

Cassius. 'Tis Cinna; I do know him by his gait;
He is a friend. Cinna, where haste you so?

114 *My answer must be made* I shall have to answer for my words
115 *indifferent* unimportant   117 *fleering* flattering   118 *factious* ac-
tive in forming a political party   123 *undergo* undertake   125 *by this*
by this time   126 *Pompey's porch* portico of Pompey's Theater
128 *complexion of the element* condition of the sky   129 *In favor's
like* in appearance is like   131 *close* hidden

Cinna. To find out you. Who's that? Metellus Cimber?

Cassius. No, it is Casca, one incorporate   135
To° our attempts. Am I not stayed° for, Cinna?

Cinna. I am glad on't.° What a fearful night is this!
There's two or three of us have seen strange sights.

Cassius. Am I not stayed for? Tell me.

Cinna.   Yes, you are.
O Cassius, if you could   140
But win the noble Brutus to our party—

Cassius. Be you content. Good Cinna, take this paper,
And look you lay it in the praetor's chair,°
Where Brutus may but find it;° and throw this
In at his window; set this up with wax   145
Upon old Brutus'° statue. All this done,
Repair° to Pompey's porch, where you shall find us.
Is Decius° Brutus and Trebonius there?

Cinna. All but Metellus Cimber, and he's gone
To seek you at your house. Well, I will hie,°   150
And so bestow these papers as you bade me.

Cassius. That done, repair to Pompey's Theater.
                                        Exit Cinna.
Come, Casca, you and I will yet ere day
See Brutus at his house; three parts of him
Is ours already, and the man entire   155
Upon the next encounter yields him ours.

135–36 *incorporate/To* intimately bound up with   136 *stayed* waited
137 *on't* of it (i.e., that Casca has joined the conspiracy)   143 *praetor's
chair* official chair in which Brutus would sit as chief magistrate, an
office next in rank to consul   144 *Where Brutus may but find it* where
only Brutus may find it   146 *old Brutus* (Lucius Junius Brutus, founder
of the Roman Republic)   147 *Repair* go   148 *Decius* (actually
Decimus, a kinsman of Marcus Brutus; the error is found in North's
Plutarch)   150 *hie* hurry

Casca. O, he sits high in all the people's hearts;
And that which would appear offense in us,
His countenance,° like richest alchemy,° *Brutus*
160   Will change to virtue and to worthiness.

Cassius. Him, and his worth, and our great need of him,
You have right well conceited.° Let us go,
For it is after midnight, and ere day
We will awake him and be sure of him.   *Exeunt.*

---

159 *countenance* support   159 *alchemy* (the "science" by which many experimenters tried to turn base metals into gold)   162 *conceited* (1) understood (2) described in an elaborate simile

ACT II

[Scene I. *Rome*.]

Enter Brutus in his orchard.°

Brutus. What, Lucius, ho!
  I cannot, by the progress of the stars,
  Give guess how near to day. Lucius, I say!
  I would it were my fault to sleep so soundly.
  When, Lucius, when? Awake, I say! What, Lucius!   5

Enter Lucius.

Lucius. Called you, my lord?

Brutus. Get me a taper° in my study, Lucius.
  When it is lighted, come and call me here.

Lucius. I will, my lord.   *Exit.*

Brutus. It must be by his death; and for my part,   10
  I know no personal cause to spurn at° him,
  But for the general.° He would be crowned.
  How that might change his nature, there's the ques-
    tion.
  It is the bright day that brings forth the adder,
  And that craves° wary walking. Crown him that,   15
  And then I grant we put a sting in him

II.i.s.d. *orchard* garden   7 *taper* candle   11 *spurn at*   rebel (literally
"kick") against   12 *general* public welfare   15 *craves* demands

55

That at his will he may do danger° with.
Th' abuse of greatness is when it disjoins
Remorse° from power; and, to speak truth of Caesar,
20   I have not known when his affections swayed°
More than his reason. But 'tis a common proof°
That lowliness° is young ambition's ladder,
Whereto the climber upward turns his face;
But when he once attains the upmost round,°
25   He then unto the ladder turns his back,
Looks in the clouds, scorning the base degrees°
By which he did ascend. So Caesar may;
Then lest he may, prevent.° And, since the quarrel°
Will bear no color° for the thing he is,
30   Fashion it° thus: that what he is, augmented,
Would run to these and these extremities;°
And therefore think him as a serpent's egg
Which hatched, would as his kind° grow mischievous,
And kill him in the shell.

Enter Lucius.

35   *Lucius.* The taper burneth in your closet,° sir.
Searching the window for a flint, I found
This paper thus sealed up, and I am sure
It did not lie there when I went to bed.
                                        Gives him the letter.

Brutus. Get you to bed again; it is not day.
40   Is not tomorrow, boy, the ides of March?

Lucius. I know not, sir.

Brutus. Look in the calendar and bring me word.

Lucius. I will, sir.   *Exit.*

---

17 *danger* harm   18–19 *disjoins/Remorse* separates mercy   20 *affections swayed* emotions ruled   21 *common proof* matter of common experience   22 *lowliness* humility   24 *round* rung   26 *base degrees* (1) low steps of the ladder (2) less important grades of office (3) common people   28 *prevent* take action to forestall   28 *quarrel* cause of complaint   29 *bear no color* have no excuse   30 *Fashion it* construct the case   31 *these and these extremities* such and such extremes (of tyranny)   33 *as his kind* according to its nature   35 *closet* study

Brutus. The exhalations° whizzing in the air
    Give so much light that I may read by them.   45
                Opens the letter and reads.

    "Brutus, thou sleep'st; awake, and see thyself.
    Shall Rome, &c.° Speak, strike, redress.
    Brutus, thou sleep'st; awake."

    Such instigations have been often dropped
    Where I have took them up.
    "Shall Rome, &c." Thus must I piece it out:°   50
    Shall Rome stand under one man's awe?° What,
       Rome?
    My ancestors did from the streets of Rome
    The Tarquin drive, when he was called a king.
    "Speak, strike, redress." Am I entreated   55
    To speak and strike? O Rome, I make thee promise,
    If the redress will follow, thou receivest
    Thy full petition at the hand of° Brutus!

              Enter Lucius.

Lucius. Sir, March is wasted fifteen days. *Knock within.*

Brutus. 'Tis good. Go to the gate; somebody knocks.   60
                [Exit Lucius.]
    Since Cassius first did whet° me against Caesar,
    I have not slept.
    Between the acting of a dreadful thing
    And the first motion,° all the interim is
    Like a phantasma,° or a hideous dream.   65
    The genius° and the mortal instruments°
    Are then in council, and the state of a man,
    Like to a little kingdom, suffers then
    The nature of an insurrection.°

44 *exhalations* meteors   **47, 51** *&c.* (read "et cetera")   **51** *piece it out*
develop the meaning   **52** *under one man's awe* in awe of one man
58 *Thy full . . . hand of* all you ask from   **61** *whet* incite   **64** *motion*
prompting   **65** *phantasma* hallucination   **66** *genius* guardian spirit
(?) reasoning spirit (?)   **66** *mortal instruments* the emotions and physical powers (which should be ruled and guided by reason)   **69** *nature of
an insurrection* a kind of insurrection

Enter Lucius.

70 *Lucius.* Sir, 'tis your brother° Cassius at the door,
　　Who doth desire to see you.

Brutus.   Is he alone?

Lucius. No, sir, there are moe° with him.

Brutus.   Do you know them?

Lucius. No, sir; their hats are plucked about their ears,
　　And half their faces buried in their cloaks,
75 　That by no means I may discover° them
　　By any mark of favor.°

Brutus.   Let 'em enter. [*Exit Lucius.*]
　　They are the faction. O conspiracy,
　　Sham'st thou to show thy dang'rous brow by night,
　　When evils are most free?° O, then by day
80 　Where wilt thou find a cavern dark enough
　　To mask thy monstrous visage? Seek none, con-
　　　　spiracy;
　　Hide it in smiles and affability:
　　For if thou path,° thy native semblance° on,
　　Not Erebus° itself were dim enough
85 　To hide thee from prevention.°

*Enter the conspirators, Cassius, Casca, Decius, Cinna,
　　Metellus [Cimber], and Trebonius.*

Cassius. I think we are too bold upon° your rest.
　　Good morrow, Brutus; do we trouble you?

Brutus. I have been up this hour, awake all night.
　　Know I these men that come along with you?

90 *Cassius.* Yes, every man of them; and no man here
　　But honors you; and every one doth wish

---

70 *brother* i.e., brother-in-law (Cassius was married to Brutus' sister)
72 *moe* more   75 *discover* recognize   76 *favor* appearance   79 *evils
are most free* evil things roam most freely   83 *path* walk (verb)
83 *native semblance* true appearance   84 *Erebus* dark region between
earth and Hades   85 *from prevention* from being forestalled and hindered   86 *upon* in intruding on

You had but that opinion of yourself
Which every noble Roman bears of you.
This is Trebonius.

Brutus.　　　　　　He is welcome hither.

Cassius. This, Decius Brutus.

Brutus.　　　　　　　He is welcome too.　　95

Cassius. This, Casca; this, Cinna; and this, Metellus
　　Cimber.

Brutus. They are all welcome.
　What watchful cares° do interpose themselves
　Betwixt your eyes and night?

Cassius. Shall I entreat a word?　　　*They whisper.*　100

Decius. Here lies the east; doth not the day break here?

Casca. No.

Cinna. O, pardon, sir, it doth; and yon gray lines
　That fret° the clouds are messengers of day.

Casca. You shall confess that you are both deceived.　105
　Here, as I point my sword, the sun arises,
　Which is a great way growing on° the south,
　Weighing° the youthful season of the year.
　Some two months hence, up higher toward the north
　He first presents his fire; and the high° east　110
　Stands as the Capitol, directly here.

Brutus. Give me your hands all over, one by one.

Cassius. And let us swear our resolution.

Brutus. No, not an oath. If not the face of men,°
　The sufferance° of our souls, the time's abuse°—　115

98 *watchful cares* cares that keep you awake　104 *fret* pattern, interlace　107 *growing on* tending toward　108 *Weighing* considering　110 *high* due　114 *the face of men* i.e., the sincere and resolute appearance of the conspirators, which should not be distrusted　115 *sufferance* patient endurance　115 *time's abuse* corruption of the age (i.e., Caesar's assumption of unconstitutional powers)

If these be motives weak, break off betimes,°
And every man hence to his idle bed.
So let high-sighted° tyranny range° on
Till each man drop by lottery.° But if these
120 (As I am sure they do) bear fire enough
To kindle cowards and to steel with valor
The melting spirits of women, then, countrymen,
What need we any spur but our own cause
To prick° us to redress? What other bond
125 Than secret Romans° that have spoke the word,
And will not palter?° And what other oath
Than honesty° to honesty engaged°
That this shall be, or we will fall for it?
Swear° priests and cowards and men cautelous,°
130 Old feeble carrions° and such suffering souls
That welcome wrongs; unto bad causes swear
Such creatures as men doubt; but do not stain
The even° virtue of our enterprise,
Nor th' insuppressive mettle° of our spirits,
135 To think that or our cause or° our performance
Did need an oath; when every drop of blood
That every Roman bears, and nobly bears,
Is guilty of a several bastardy°
If he do break the smallest particle
140 Of any promise that hath passed from him.

Cassius. But what of Cicero? Shall we sound him?
I think he will stand very strong with us.

Casca. Let us not leave him out.

Cinna.   No, by no means.

Metellus. O, let us have him, for his silver hairs

---

116 *betimes* immediately   118 *high-sighted* arrogant (viewing widely
from on high, like a falcon ready to swoop on prey)   118 *range* rove
or fly in search of prey   119 *by lottery* by chance, i.e., at the tyrant's
whim   124 *prick* urge   125 *secret Romans* the fact that we are
Romans capable of maintaining secrecy   126 *palter* equivocate
127 *honesty* personal honor   127 *engaged* pledged   129 *Swear* bind
by oath   129 *cautelous* deceitful   130 *carrions* wretches almost dead
and rotting   133 *even* unblemished, perfect   134 *insuppressive mettle*
indomitable temper   135 *or . . . or* either . . . or   138 *guilty . . .
bastardy* i.e., guilty of an act not truly Roman

Will purchase us a good opinion,°   145
And buy men's voices to commend our deeds.
It shall be said his judgment ruled our hands;
Our youths and wildness shall no whit° appear,
But all be buried in his gravity.°

Brutus. O, name him not! Let us not break with him;°   150
For he will never follow anything
That other men begin.

Cassius.   Then leave him out.

Casca. Indeed, he is not fit.

Decius. Shall no man else be touched but only Caesar?

Cassius. Decius, well urged.° I think it is not meet   155
Mark Antony, so well beloved of Caesar,
Should outlive Caesar; we shall find of° him
A shrewd contriver;° and you know, his means;
If he improve° them, may well stretch so far
As to annoy° us all; which to prevent,°   160
Let Antony and Caesar fall together.

Brutus. Our course will seem too bloody, Caius Cassius,
To cut the head off and then hack the limbs,
Like wrath in death and envy° afterwards;
For Antony is but a limb of Caesar.   165
Let's be sacrificers, but not butchers, Caius.
We all stand up against the spirit of Caesar,°
And in the spirit of men there is no blood.
O, that we then could come by° Caesar's spirit,
And not dismember Caesar! But, alas,   170
Caesar must bleed for it. And, gentle° friends,
Let's kill him boldly, but not wrathfully;

---

145 *opinion* reputation   **148** *no whit* not in the slightest   **149** *gravity*
sobriety and stability (Latin *gravitas*)   **150** *break with him* divulge
our plan to him   **155** *urged* suggested   **157** *of* in   **158** *shrewd con-*
triver cunning and malicious plotter   **159** *improve* make good use
of   **160** *annoy* harm   **160** *prevent* forestall   **164** *envy* malice, i.e.,
as though we were killing Caesar for personal spite and hatred
167 *the spirit of Caesar* the principles (of tyranny) for which
Caesar stands   **169** *come by* get possession of   **171** *gentle* noble

Let's carve him as a dish fit for the gods,
Not hew him as a carcass fit for hounds.
175 And let our hearts, as subtle masters do,
Stir up their servants° to an act of rage,
And after seem to chide 'em. This shall make
Our purpose necessary, and not envious;°
Which so appearing to the common eyes,
180 We shall be called purgers,° not murderers.
And for Mark Antony, think not of him;
For he can do no more than Caesar's arm
When Caesar's head is off.

Cassius.   Yet I fear him;
For in the ingrafted° love he bears to Caesar——

185 *Brutus.* Alas, good Cassius, do not think of him.
If he love Caesar, all that he can do
Is to himself—take thought° and die for Caesar.
And that were much he should,° for he is given
To sports, to wildness, and much company.

190 *Trebonius.* There is no fear° in him; let him not die,
For he will live and laugh at this hereafter.
                         Clock strikes.

Brutus. Peace! Count the clock.

Cassius.   The clock hath stricken three.

Trebonius. 'Tis time to part.

Cassius.   But it is doubtful yet
Whether Caesar will come forth today or no;
195 For he is superstitious grown of late,
Quite from the main° opinion he held once
Of fantasy, of dreams, and ceremonies.°
It may be these apparent prodigies,°
The unaccustomed terror of this night,

176 *servants* (1) the hands (2) the passions   178 *envious* malicious
180 *purgers* healers   184 *ingrafted* firmly rooted   187 *take thought*
grow melancholy with brooding   188 *that were much he should* that
would be too much to expect of him   190 *no fear* nothing to fear
196 *Quite from the main* at variance with the strong   197 *ceremonies*
omens   198 *apparent prodigies* obvious signs of disaster

And the persuasion of his augurers° 200
May hold him from the Capitol today.

Decius. Never fear that. If he be so resolved,
I can o'ersway him;° for he loves to hear
That unicorns may be betrayed with trees,°
And bears with glasses,° elephants with holes,° 205
Lions with toils,° and men with flatterers;
But when I tell him he hates flatterers,
He says he does, being then most flattered.
Let me work;
For I can give his humor° the true bent,° 210
And I will bring him to the Capitol.

Cassius. Nay, we will all of us be there to fetch him.

Brutus. By the eighth hour; is that the uttermost?°

Cinna. Be that the uttermost, and fail not then.

Metellus. Caius Ligarius doth bear Caesar hard,° 215
Who rated° him for speaking well of Pompey.
I wonder none of you have thought of him.

Brutus. Now, good Metellus, go along by him.°
He loves me well, and I have given him reasons;
Send him but hither, and I'll fashion° him. 220

Cassius. The morning comes upon 's; we'll leave you,
    Brutus.
And, friends, disperse yourselves; but all remember
What you have said, and show yourselves true
    Romans.

Brutus. Good gentlemen, look fresh and merrily.
Let not our looks put on° our purposes, 225

---

200 *augurers* augurs (priests who foretold, from omens, the future)
203 *o'ersway him* persuade him to change his mind   204 *betrayed with
trees* i.e., tricked into running at a tree (at the last moment its prey
steps aside so that the horn is deeply embedded and the unicorn is
helpless)   205 *glasses* mirrors   205 *holes* pitfalls   206 *toils* nets,
snares   210 *humor* temperament   210 *bent* direction   213 *uttermost*
latest   215 *bear Caesar hard* has a grudge against Caesar   216 *rated*
berated   218 *him* his house   220 *fashion* shape (to our designs)
225 *put on* display

But bear it° as our Roman actors do,
With untired spirits and formal constancy.°
And so good morrow to you every one.

Exeunt. Manet° Brutus.

Boy! Lucius! Fast asleep? It is no matter;
230   Enjoy the honey-heavy dew° of slumber.
Thou hast no figures nor no fantasies°
Which busy care draws in the brains of men;
Therefore thou sleep'st so sound.

Enter Portia.

Portia   Brutus, my lord.

Brutus. Portia, what mean you? Wherefore rise you now?
235   It is not for your health thus to commit
Your weak condition to the raw cold morning.

Portia. Nor for yours neither. Y'have ungently,° Brutus,
Stole from my bed; and yesternight at supper
You suddenly arose and walked about,
240   Musing and sighing, with your arms across;°
And when I asked you what the matter was,
You stared upon me with ungentle looks.
I urged you further; then you scratched your head,
And too impatiently stamped with your foot.
245   Yet I insisted, yet you answered not,
But with an angry wafter° of your hand
Gave sign for me to leave you. So I did,
Fearing to strengthen that impatience
Which seemed too much enkindled, and withal°
250   Hoping it was but an effect of humor,°
Which sometime hath his° hour with every man.
It will not let you eat, nor talk, nor sleep,
And could it work so much upon your shape

---

226 *bear it* play our parts   227 *formal constancy* consistent decorum
228s.d. *Manet* remains   230 *dew* i.e., refreshment   231 *figures . . .
fantasies* (both words specify figments of the imagination)   237 *ungently* discourteously   240 *across* folded (a sign of melancholy)
246 *wafter* waving   249 *withal* also   250 *effect of humor* i.e., sign of a
temporary mood   251 *his* its

As it hath much prevailed on your condition,°
I should not know you° Brutus. Dear my lord,   255
Make me acquainted with your cause of grief.

Brutus. I am not well in health, and that is all.

Portia. Brutus is wise and, were he not in health,
He would embrace the means to come by it.

Brutus. Why, so I do. Good Portia, go to bed.   260

Portia. Is Brutus sick, and is it physical°
To walk unbracèd° and suck up the humors°
Of the dank morning? What, is Brutus sick,
And will he steal out of his wholesome bed,
To dare the vile contagion of the night,°   265
And tempt the rheumy and unpurgèd air°
To add unto his sickness? No, my Brutus;
You have some sick offense° within your mind,
Which by the right and virtue of my place°
I ought to know of; and upon my knees   270
I charm° you, by my once commended beauty,
By all your vows of love, and that great vow
Which did incorporate° and make us one,
That you unfold to me, your self, your half,
Why you are heavy,° and what men tonight   275
Have had resort to you; for here have been
Some six or seven, who did hide their faces
Even from darkness.

Brutus.   Kneel not, gentle Portia.

Portia. I should not need, if you were gentle Brutus.
Within the bond of marriage, tell me, Brutus,   280
Is it excepted° I should know no secrets
That appertain to you? Am I your self

254 *condition* disposition   255 *know you* recognize you as   261 *physical* healthy   262 *unbracèd* with doublet unfastened   262 *humors* dampness, mist   265 *night* (night air was thought to be harmful, even poisonous)   266 *tempt . . . air* risk the damp and unpurified (by the sun) air   268 *sick offense* sickness that harms   269 *place* situation (as wife)   271 *charm* entreat   273 *incorporate* make us one flesh (cf. Matthew 19:5, "they twain shall be one flesh")   275 *heavy* dejected   281 *excepted* made an exception that

But, as it were, in sort or limitation,°
To keep with you at meals, comfort your bed,
And talk to you sometimes? Dwell I but in the
285   suburbs°
Of your good pleasure? If it be no more,
Portia is Brutus' harlot, not his wife.

Brutus. You are my true and honorable wife,
As dear to me as are the ruddy drops
290   That visit my sad heart. ·

Portia. If this were true, then should I know this secret.
I grant I am a woman; but withal°
A woman that Lord Brutus took to wife.
I grant I am a woman; but withal
295   A woman well reputed, Cato's daughter.°
Think you I am no stronger than my sex,
Being so fathered and so husbanded?
Tell me your counsels,° I will not disclose 'em.
I have made strong proof of my constancy,°
300   Giving myself a voluntary wound
Here in the thigh; can I bear that with patience,
And not my husband's secrets?

Brutus.   O ye gods,
Render me worthy of this noble wife!   *Knock.*
Hark, hark! One knocks. Portia, go in a while,
305   And by and by thy bosom shall partake
The secrets of my heart.
All my engagements° I will construe° to thee,
All the charactery of° my sad brows.
Leave me with haste.   *Exit Portia.*

---

283 *in sort or limitation* after a fashion or within a certain restriction
(legal terms)   285 *suburbs* outlying districts (where the brothels and
least respectable taverns were found)   292 *withal* at the same time
295 *Cato's daughter* (Marcus Porcius Cato was famous for his integrity; he joined Pompey against Caesar and killed himself at Utica
in 46 B.C. to avoid capture; he was Brutus' uncle as well as father-in-
law)   298 *counsels* secrets   299 *proof of my constancy* trial of my
resolution   307 *engagements* commitments   307 *construe* explain
308 *charactery of* writing upon, i.e., wrinkles of grief and worry

Enter Lucius and [Caius] Ligarius.

            Lucius, who's that knocks?

Lucius. Here is a sick man that would speak with you. 310

Brutus. Caius Ligarius, that Metellus spake of.
  Boy, stand aside. Caius Ligarius! How?°

Caius. Vouchsafe° good morrow from a feeble tongue.

Brutus. O, what a time have you chose out, brave° Caius,
  To wear a kerchief!° Would you were not sick! 315

Caius. I am not sick, if Brutus have in hand
  Any exploit worthy the name of honor.

Brutus. Such an exploit have I in hand, Ligarius,
  Had you a healthful ear to hear of it.

Caius. By all the gods that Romans bow before, 320
  I here discard my sickness! Soul of Rome,
  Brave son, derived from honorable loins,°
  Thou, like an exorcist,° hast conjured up
  My mortifièd° spirit. Now bid me run,
  And I will strive with things impossible, 325
  Yea, get the better of them. What's to do?

Brutus. A piece of work that will make sick men whole.°

Caius. But are not some whole that we must make sick?

Brutus. That must we also. What it is, my Caius,
  I shall unfold to thee, as we are going 330
  To whom° it must be done.

Caius.   Set on° your foot,
  And with a heart new-fired I follow you,

---

312 *How* how are you   313 *Vouchsafe* please accept   314 *brave* noble
315 *To wear a kerchief* (as a protection against drafts), i.e., to be sick
322 *from honorable loins* i.e., descent from Lucius Junius Brutus,
founder of the Roman Republic   323 *exorcist* conjurer   324 *morti-
fièd* deadened   327 *whole* healthy   331 *To whom* to the house of him
to whom   331 *Set on* advance

To do I know not what; but it sufficeth
That Brutus leads me on.   *Thunder.*

Brutus.   Follow me, then.   *Exeunt.*

[Scene II. *Caesar's house.*]

*Thunder and lightning. Enter Julius Caesar in his
nightgown.°*

Caesar. Nor heaven nor earth have been at peace
    tonight:
Thrice hath Calphurnia in her sleep cried out,
"Help, ho! They murder Caesar!" Who's within?

Enter a Servant.

Servant. My lord?

5 *Caesar.* Go bid the priests do present° sacrifice,
And bring me their opinions of success.°

Servant. I will, my lord.   *Exit.*

Enter Calphurnia.

Calphurnia. What mean you, Caesar? Think you to walk
    forth?
You shall not stir out of your house today.

Caesar. Caesar shall forth. The things that threatened
10 me
Ne'er looked but on my back; when they shall see
The face of Caesar, they are vanishèd.

Calphurnia. Caesar, I never stood on ceremonies,°
Yet now they fright me. There is one within,
15 Besides the things that we have heard and seen,
Recounts most horrid sights seen by the watch.°

II.ii.s.d. *nightgown* dressing gown   5 *present* immediate   6 *opinions
of success* judgment as to the future course of events   13 *stood on
ceremonies* paid attention to omens   16 *watch* nightwatchmen

A lioness hath whelpèd in the streets,
And graves have yawned, and yielded up their dead;
Fierce fiery warriors fought upon the clouds
In ranks and squadrons and right form° of war,   20
Which drizzled blood upon the Capitol;
The noise of battle hurtled° in the air,
Horses did neigh and dying men did groan,
And ghosts did shriek and squeal about the streets.
O Caesar, these things are beyond all use,°   25
And I do fear them.

Caesar.   What can be avoided
   Whose end is purposed by the mighty gods?
   Yet Caesar shall go forth; for these predictions
   Are to° the world in general as to Caesar.

Calphurnia. When beggars die, there are no comets seen;   30
   The heavens themselves blaze forth° the death of
      princes.

Caesar. Cowards die many times before their deaths;
   The valiant never taste of death but once.
   Of all the wonders that I yet have heard,
   It seems to me most strange that men should fear,   35
   Seeing that death, a necessary end,
   Will come when it will come.

Enter a Servant.

                    What say the augurers?

Servant. They would not have you to stir forth today.
   Plucking the entrails of an offering forth,
   They could not find a heart within the beast.   40

Caesar. The gods do this in shame of cowardice:
   Caesar should° be a beast without a heart°
   If he should stay at home today for fear.
   No, Caesar shall not; Danger knows full well
   That Caesar is more dangerous than he.   45

---

20 *right form* proper military formation   **22** *hurtled* clashed   **25** *use* normal experience   **29** *Are to* apply to   **31** *blaze forth* i.e., proclaim (by comets and meteors)   **42** *should* would   **42** *heart* (the organ of courage)

We are two lions littered in one day,
And I the elder and more terrible,
And Caesar shall go forth.

Calphurnia.   Alas, my lord,
Your wisdom is consumed in confidence.°
50   Do not go forth today. Call it my fear
That keeps you in the house and not your own.
We'll send Mark Antony to the Senate House,
And he shall say you are not well today.
Let me, upon my knee, prevail in this.

55   *Caesar.* Mark Antony shall say I am not well,
And for thy humor,° I will stay at home.

Enter Decius.

Here's Decius Brutus, he shall tell them so.

Decius. Caesar, all hail! Good morrow, worthy Caesar;
I come to fetch° you to the Senate House.

60   *Caesar.* And you are come in very happy time°
To bear my greeting to the senators,
And tell them that I will not come today.
Cannot, is false; and that I dare not, falser:
I will not come today. Tell them so, Decius.

Calphurnia. Say he is sick.

65   *Caesar.*   Shall Caesar send a lie?
Have I in conquest stretched mine arm so far
To be afeard to tell graybeards the truth?
Decius, go tell them Caesar will not come.

Decius. Most mighty Caesar, let me know some cause,
70   Lest I be laughed at when I tell them so.

Caesar. The cause is in my will: I will not come.
That is enough to satisfy the Senate.
But for your private satisfaction,
Because I love you, I will let you know.

49 *consumed in confidence* destroyed by too much confidence   56 *humor* whim   59 *fetch* escort   60 *happy time* favorable time (i.e., just at the right moment)

Handwritten annotation at top: *Ceasar Superstitious + arrogant*

Calphurnia here, my wife, stays° me at home.   75
She dreamt tonight° she saw my statue,°
Which, like a fountain with an hundred spouts,
Did run pure blood, and many lusty Romans
Came smiling and did bathe their hands in it.
And these does she apply for° warnings and portents°   80
And evils imminent, and on her knee
Hath begged that I will stay at home today.

Decius. This dream is all amiss interpreted;
   It was a vision fair and fortunate:
   Your statue spouting blood in many pipes,   85
   In which so many smiling Romans bathed,
   Signifies that from you great Rome shall suck
   Reviving blood, and that great men shall press
   For tinctures, stains, relics, and cognizance.°
   This by Calphurnia's dream is signified.   90

Caesar. And this way have you well expounded it.

Decius. I have, when you have heard what I can say;
   And know it now, the Senate have concluded
   To give this day a crown to mighty Caesar.
   If you shall send them word you will not come,   95
   Their minds may change. Besides, it were a mock
   Apt to be rendered,° for someone to say
   "Break up the Senate till another time,
   When Caesar's wife shall meet with better dreams."
   If Caesar hide himself, shall they not whisper   100
   "Lo, Caesar is afraid"?
   Pardon me, Caesar, for my dear dear love
   To your proceeding° bids me tell you this,
   And reason to my love is liable.°

Handwritten annotations in right margin: *appeals to his greed + ego*

75 *stays* keeps   76 *tonight* i.e., last night   76 *statue* (trisyllabic; pronounced "stat-u-a")   80 *apply for* explain as   80 *portents* (accent on
last syllable)   89 *tinctures . . . cognizance* (Samuel Johnson para-
phrases the line: "The Romans, says Decius, all come so you, as to a
saint, for relics; as to a prince, for honors")   *tinctures* (1) alchemical
elixirs (2) colors, metals, etc. used in heraldry   *stains* colors in a coat
of arms   *relics* venerated property of a martyr   *cognizance* mark of
identification worn by a nobleman's followers   96–97 *mock . . . rendered* jeering remark likely to be made   103 *proceeding* advancement
104 *reason . . . liable* i.e., my affection proves stronger than my judgment (of impropriety) in telling you this (*liable* = subordinate)

Caesar. How foolish do your fears seem now,
105   Calphurnia!
I am ashamèd I did yield to them.
Give me my robe,° for I will go.

*Enter Brutus, Ligarius, Metellus [Cimber], Casca,
Trebonius, Cinna, and Publius.*

And look where Publius is come to fetch me.

Publius. Good morrow, Caesar.

Caesar.   Welcome, Publius.
110   What, Brutus, are you stirred so early too?
Good morrow, Casca. Caius Ligarius,
Caesar was ne'er so much your enemy°
As that same ague which hath made you lean.
What is't o'clock?

Brutus.   Caesar, 'tis strucken eight.

115 *Caesar.* I thank you for your pains and courtesy.
              Enter Antony.

See! Antony, that revels long a-nights,
Is notwithstanding up. Good morrow, Antony.

Antony. So to most noble Caesar.

Caesar.   Bid them prepare° within.
I am to blame to be thus waited for.
120 Now, Cinna; now, Metellus; what, Trebonius,
I have an hour's talk in store for you;
Remember that you call on me today;
Be near me, that I may remember you.

Trebonius. Caesar, I will [*aside*] and so near will I be,
125   That your best friends shall wish I had been further.

Caesar. Good friends, go in and taste some wine with
     me,

---

107 *robe* toga 112 *enemy* (Ligarius had supported Pompey against
Caesar in the Civil War and had recently been pardoned by Caesar)
118 *prepare* i.e., set out the wine mentioned in line 126

And we (like friends) will straightway go together.

Brutus. [*Aside*] That every like is not the same,° O Caesar,
The heart of Brutus earns° to think upon.   *Exeunt.*

[Scene III. *A street near the Capitol, close to
Brutus' house.*]

Enter Artemidorus [*reading a paper*].

[*Artemidorus.*] "Caesar, beware of Brutus; take heed of
Cassius; come not near Casca; have an eye to Cinna;
trust not Trebonius; mark well Metellus Cimber;
Decius Brutus loves thee not; thou hast wronged
Caius Ligarius. There is but one mind in all these   5
men, and it is bent° against Caesar. If thou beest not
immortal, look about you: security gives way to
conspiracy.° The mighty gods defend thee!
      Thy lover,° ARTEMIDORUS."
Here will I stand till Caesar pass along,   10
And as a suitor° will I give him this.
My heart laments that virtue cannot live
Out of the teeth of emulation.°
If thou read this, O Caesar, thou mayest live;
If not, the Fates with traitors do contrive.°   *Exit.*   15

128 *That every like is not the same* i.e., what a pity that those who
appear like friends may actually be enemies   129 *earns* grieves
II.iii.6 *bent* directed   7–8 *security gives way to conspiracy* overcon-
fidence gives conspiracy its opportunity   9 *lover* devoted friend
11 *as a suitor* like a petitioner   13 *Out of the teeth of emulation*
beyond the reach of envious rivalry   15 *contrive* conspire

[Scene IV. *Another part of the street.*]

Enter Portia and Lucius.

Portia. I prithee, boy, run to the Senate House;
     Stay not to answer me, but get thee gone.
     Why dost thou stay?

Lucius.   To know my errand, madam.

Portia. I would have had thee there and here again
5   Ere I can tell thee what thou shouldst do there.
     O constancy,° be strong upon my side;
     Set a huge mountain 'tween my heart and tongue!
     I have a man's mind, but a woman's might.°
     How hard it is for women to keep counsel!°
     Art thou here yet?

10   *Lucius.*   Madam, what should I do?
     Run to the Capitol, and nothing else?
     And so return to you, and nothing else?

Portia. Yes, bring me word, boy, if thy lord look well,
     For he went sickly forth; and take good note
15   What Caesar doth, what suitors press to him.
     Hark, boy, what noise is that?

Lucius. I hear none, madam.

Portia.   Prithee, listen well.
     I heard a bustling rumor like a fray,°
     And the wind brings it from the Capitol.

20   *Lucius.* Sooth,° madam, I hear nothing.

II.iv.6 *constancy* resolution   8 *might* physical strength   9 *counsel* secret (Brutus has obviously told her of the conspiracy, though "stage time" has allowed no opportunity for this; the inconsistency is not noticeable during a performance)   18 *bustling rumor like a fray* confused noise as of battle   20 *Sooth* truly

Enter the Soothsayer.

Portia. Come hither, fellow. Which way hast thou been?

Soothsayer. At mine own house, good lady.

Portia. What is't o'clock?

Soothsayer.   About the ninth hour, lady.

Portia. Is Caesar yet gone to the Capitol?

Soothsayer. Madam, not yet; I go to take my stand,   25
  To see him pass on to the Capitol.

Portia. Thou hast some suit to Caesar, hast thou not?

Soothsayer. That I have, lady; if it will please Caesar
  To be so good to Caesar as to hear me,
  I shall beseech him to befriend himself.   30

Portia. Why, know'st thou any harm's intended towards
    him?

Soothsayer. None that I know will be, much that I fear
    may chance.°
  Good morrow to you. Here the street is narrow;
  The throng that follows Caesar at the heels,
  Of senators, of praetors, common suitors,   35
  Will crowd a feeble man almost to death.
  I'll get me to a place more void,° and there
  Speak to great Caesar as he comes along.   *Exit.*

Portia. I must go in. Ay me, how weak a thing
  The heart of woman is! O Brutus,   40
  The heavens speed° thee in thine enterprise!
  Sure, the boy heard me—Brutus hath a suit
  That Caesar will not grant—O, I grow faint.
  Run, Lucius, and commend me° to my lord;
  Say I am merry;° come to me again,   45
  And bring me word what he doth say to thee.
                    Exeunt [severally].

---

32 *chance* happen   37 *more void* more empty (less crowded)   41
speed prosper   44 *commend me* give my love   45 *merry* cheerful

ACT III

Flourish. Enter Caesar, Brutus, Cassius, Casca,
Decius, Metellus [Cimber], Trebonius, Cinna,
Antony, Lepidus, Artemidorus, Publius, [Popilius,]
and the Soothsayer.

Caesar. The ides of March are come.

Soothsayer. Ay, Caesar, but not gone.

Artemidorus. Hail, Caesar! Read this schedule.°

Decius. Trebonius doth desire you to o'er-read,
5   At your best leisure, this his humble suit.

Artemidorus. O Caesar, read mine first; for mine's a suit
That touches° Caesar nearer. Read it, great Caesar.

Caesar. What touches us ourself shall be last served.

Artemidorus. Delay not, Caesar; read it instantly.

Caesar. What, is the fellow mad?

10 *Publius.*   Sirrah, give place.°

Cassius. What, urge you your petitions in the street?
Come to the Capitol.

III.i.3 *schedule* scroll   7 *touches* concerns   10 *Sirrah, give place*
fellow, get out of the way

76

[Caesar goes to the Capitol, the rest following.]

Popilius. I wish your enterprise today may thrive.

Cassius. What enterprise, Popilius?

Popilius.   Fare you well.
                              [Advances to Caesar.]

Brutus. What said Popilius Lena?   15

Cassius. He wished today our enterprise might thrive.
   I fear our purpose is discoverèd.

Brutus. Look how he makes to° Caesar; mark him.

Cassius. Casca, be sudden,° for we fear prevention.°
   Brutus, what shall be done? If this be known,   20
   Cassius or Caesar never shall turn back,°
   For I will slay myself.

Brutus.   Cassius, be constant.°
   Popilius Lena speaks not of our purposes;
   For look, he smiles, and Caesar doth not change.°

Cassius. Trebonius knows his time; for look you, Brutus,   25
   He draws Mark Antony out of the way.
                              [Exeunt Antony and Trebonius.]

Decius. Where is Metellus Cimber? Let him go
   And presently prefer° his suit to Caesar.

Brutus. He is addressed.° Press near and second him.

Cinna. Casca, you are the first that rears your hand.   30

Caesar. Are we all ready? What is now amiss
   That Caesar and his Senate must redress?

Metellus. Most high, most mighty, and most puissant°
      Caesar,
   Metellus Cimber throws before thy seat
   An humble heart.   *[Kneeling.]*

18 *makes to* heads for   19 *sudden* swift   19 *prevention* being forestalled   21 *turn back* i.e., return alive   22 *constant* calm   24 *change*
change his expression   28 *presently prefer* immediately present   29
addressed ready   33 *puissant* powerful

35 *Caesar.*   I must prevent thee, Cimber.
   These couchings° and these lowly courtesies°
   Might fire the blood of ordinary men,
   And turn preordinance and first decree°
   Into the law of children. Be not fond°
40 To think that Caesar bears such rebel blood°
   That will be thawed from the true quality°
   With that° which melteth fools—I mean sweet words,
   Low-crookèd curtsies, and base spaniel° fawning.
   Thy brother by decree is banishèd.
45 If thou dost bend and pray and fawn for him,
   I spurn thee like a cur out of my way.
   Know, Caesar doth not wrong, nor without cause
   Will he be satisfied.

 Metellus. Is there no voice more worthy than my own,
50 To sound more sweetly in great Caesar's ear
   For the repealing° of my banished brother?

 Brutus. I kiss thy hand, but not in flattery, Caesar,
   Desiring thee that Publius Cimber may
   Have an immediate freedom of repeal.°

 Caesar. What, Brutus?

55 *Cassius.*   Pardon, Caesar; Caesar, pardon!
   As low as to thy foot doth Cassius fall
   To beg enfranchisement° for Publius Cimber.

 Caesar. I could be well moved, if I were as you;
   If I could pray to move,° prayers would move me;
60 But I am constant as the Northern Star,°
   Of whose true-fixed and resting° quality

---

36 *couchings* low bowings 36 *lowly courtesies* humble obeisances
38 *preordinance and first decree* customs and laws established from an-
tiquity 39 *fond* so foolish as 40 *bears such rebel blood* has such un-
controlled emotions 41 *true quality* proper quality (i.e., firmness)
42 *With that* by those things 43 *spaniel* doglike, cringing 51 *repeal-
ing* recalling 54 *freedom of repeal* permission to be recalled from
exile 57 *enfranchisement* recall, freedom 59 *pray to move* i.e., beg
others to change their minds 60 *constant as the Northern Star* un-
changing as the polestar 61 *resting* changeless

There is no fellow° in the firmament.
The skies are painted with unnumb'red° sparks,
They are all fire and every one doth shine;
But there's but one in all doth hold° his place.   65
So in the world; 'tis furnished well with men,
And men are flesh and blood, and apprehensive;°
Yet in the number I do know but one
That unassailable holds on his rank,°
Unshaked of motion;° and that I am he,   70
Let me a little show it, even in this—
That I was constant° Cimber should be banished,
And constant do remain to keep him so.

Cinna. O Caesar——

Caesar.   Hence! Wilt thou lift up Olympus?°

Decius. Great Caesar——

Caesar.   Doth not Brutus bootless° kneel?   75

Casca. Speak hands for me!   *They stab Caesar.*

Caesar. Et tu, Brutè?° Then fall Caesar.   *Dies.*

Cinna. Liberty! Freedom! Tyranny is dead!
Run hence, proclaim, cry it about the streets.

Cassius. Some to the common pulpits,° and cry out   80
"Liberty, freedom, and enfranchisement!"

Brutus. People, and senators, be not affrighted.
Fly not; stand still; ambition's debt is paid.°

Casca. Go to the pulpit, Brutus.

Decius.   And Cassius too.

---

62 *fellow* equal   63 *unnumb'red* innumerable   65 *hold* keep   67 *apprehensive* capable of reason   69 *holds on his rank* maintains his position
70 *Unshaked of motion* i.e., unmoved by internal or external forces
72 *constant* firmly determined   74 *Olympus* a mountain in Greece
where the gods lived and held court   75 *bootless* in vain   77 *Et tu,
Brutè* and you (too), Brutus   80 *pulpits* platforms for public speakers
83 *ambition's debt is paid* ambition has received what was due to it

85 *Brutus.* Where's Publius?°

Cinna. Here, quite confounded with this mutiny.°

Metellus. Stand fast together, lest some friend of Caesar's
    Should chance——

Brutus. Talk not of standing.° Publius, good cheer;
90   There is no harm intended to your person,
    Nor to no Roman else. So tell them, Publius.

Cassius. And leave us, Publius, lest that the people
    Rushing on us should do your age some mischief.

Brutus. Do so; and let no man abide° this deed
95   But we the doers.

                Enter Trebonius.

Cassius. Where is Antony?

Trebonius.   Fled to his house amazed.°
    Men, wives, and children stare, cry out and run,
    As° it were doomsday.

Brutus.   Fates, we will know your pleasures.
    That we shall die, we know; 'tis but the time,
100   And drawing days out, that men stand upon.°

Casca. Why, he that cuts off twenty years of life
    Cuts off so many years of fearing death.

Brutus. Grant that, and then is death a benefit.
    So are we Caesar's friends, that have abridged
105   His time of fearing death. Stoop, Romans, stoop,
    And let us bathe our hands in Caesar's blood
    Up to the elbows, and besmear our swords.
    Then walk we forth, even to the market place,°
    And waving our red weapons o'er our heads,

---

85 *Publius* an old senator, too infirm to flee   86 *confounded with this
mutiny* overwhelmed by this uproar   89 *Talk not of standing* i.e., don't
worry about making a stand organizing resistance   94 *abide* bear the
consequences of   96 *amazed* utterly confused   98 *As* as if   100 *drawing . . . upon* (hope of) prolonging life, that men are concerned about
108 *the market place* the Roman Forum, center of business and public
affairs

Let's all cry "Peace, freedom, and liberty!"

Cassius. Stoop then, and wash. How many ages hence
　Shall this our lofty scene be acted over
　In states unborn and accents yet unknown!

Brutus. How many times shall Caesar bleed in sport,°
　That now on Pompey's basis° lies along°　　　115
　No worthier than the dust!

Cassius.　　　　　　　　　So oft as that shall be,
　So often shall the knot° of us be called
　The men that gave their country liberty.

Decius. What, shall we forth?

Cassius.　　　　　　　　Ay, every man away.
　Brutus shall lead, and we will grace° his heels　　120
　With the most boldest and best hearts of Rome.

　　　　　　　Enter a Servant.

Brutus. Soft,° who comes here? A friend of Antony's.

Servant. Thus, Brutus, did my master bid me kneel;
　Thus did Mark Antony bid me fall down;
　And, being prostrate, thus he bade me say:　　125
　Brutus is noble, wise, valiant, and honest;°
　Caesar was mighty, bold, royal,° and loving.
　Say I love Brutus and I honor him;
　Say I feared Caesar, honored him, and loved him.
　If Brutus will vouchsafe that Antony　　130
　May safely come to him and be resolved°
　How Caesar hath deserved to lie in death,
　Mark Antony shall not love Caesar dead
　So well as Brutus living; but will follow
　The fortunes and affairs of noble Brutus　　135
　Thorough° the hazards of this untrod state°

---

114 *in sport* for entertainment, i.e., as part of a play　115 *basis*
pedestal of statue　115 *along* stretched out　117 *knot* closely bound
group　120 *grace* do honor to　122 *Soft* wait a moment　126 *honest*
honorable　127 *royal* of princely generosity　131 *be resolved* have it
explained to his satisfaction　136 *Thorough* through　136 *untrod*
state new and uncertain state of affairs

With all true faith. So says my master Antony.

Brutus. Thy master is a wise and valiant Roman;
I never thought him worse.
140 Tell him, so° please him come unto this place,
He shall be satisfied and, by my honor,
Depart untouched.

Servant.   I'll fetch him presently.°

Exit Servant.

Brutus. I know that we shall have him well to friend.°

Cassius. I wish we may. But yet have I a mind
145 That fears him much; and my misgiving still
Falls shrewdly to the purpose.°

Enter Antony.

Brutus. But here comes Antony. Welcome, Mark
Antony.

Antony. O mighty Caesar! Dost thou lie so low?
Are all thy conquests, glories, triumphs, spoils,
150 Shrunk to this little measure? Fare thee well.
I know not, gentlemen, what you intend,
Who else must be let blood,° who else is rank.°
If I myself, there is no hour so fit
As Caesar's death's hour, nor no instrument
155 Of half that worth as those your swords, made rich
With the most noble blood of all this world.
I do beseech ye, if you bear me hard,°
Now, whilst your purpled° hands do reek and smoke,°
Fulfill your pleasure. Live° a thousand years,

160 I shall not find myself so apt° to die;

---

140 *so* if it should   142 *presently* immediately   143 *well to friend* as a
good friend   145–46 *misgiving . . . purpose* my forebodings always
turn out to be justified   152 *let blood* (1) bled, purged (common
Elizabethan practice of drawing blood to cure those swollen with disease) (2) put to death   152 *rank* (1) swollen with disease (2) over-
grown, i.e., too powerful   157 *bear me hard* have a grudge against me
158 *purpled* (1) made scarlet (with blood) (2) made royal (?)   158 *reek
and smoke* i.e., steam (with freshly shed warm blood)   159 *Live*
though I live   160 *apt* prepared

No place will please me so, no mean° of death,
As here by Caesar, and by you cut off,
The choice and master spirits of this age.

Brutus. O Antony, beg not your death of us!
Though now we must appear bloody and cruel,   165
As by our hands and this our present act
You see we do, yet see you but our hands
And this the bleeding business they have done.
Our hearts you see not; they are pitiful;°
And pity to the general wrong of Rome—   170
As fire drives out fire, so pity pity°—
Hath done this deed on Caesar. For your part,
To you our swords have leaden° points, Mark An-
    tony:
Our arms in strength of malice, and our hearts
Of brothers' temper,° do receive you in   175
With all kind love, good thoughts, and reverence.

Cassius. Your voice° shall be as strong as any man's
In the disposing of new dignities.°

Brutus. Only be patient till we have appeased
The multitude, beside themselves with fear,   180
And then we will deliver° you the cause
Why I, that did love Caesar when I struck him,
Have thus proceeded.

Antony.   I doubt not of your wisdom.
Let each man render me his bloody hand.
First, Marcus Brutus, will I shake with you;   185
Next, Caius Cassius, do I take your hand;
Now, Decius Brutus, yours; now yours, Metellus;
Yours, Cinna; and, my valiant Casca, yours;
Though last, not least in love, yours, good Trebonius.
Gentlemen all—alas, what shall I say?   190
My credit° now stands on such slippery ground

---

161 *mean* manner   169 *pitiful* full of pity   171 *pity pity* pity for
Rome's subjection drove out pity for Caesar   173 *leaden* blunt   174–
75 *Our arms . . . temper* our arms, strong with the might inspired by
enmity, and our hearts, full of brotherly feeling   177 *voice* vote   178
dignities offices   181 *deliver* communicate to   191 *credit* reputation

That one of two bad ways you must conceit° me,
Either a coward or a flatterer.
That I did love thee, Caesar, O, 'tis true!
195 If then thy spirit look upon us now,
Shall it not grieve thee dearer° than thy death
To see thy Antony making his peace,
Shaking the bloody fingers of thy foes,
Most noble, in the presence of thy corse?°
200 Had I as many eyes as thou hast wounds,
Weeping as fast as they stream forth thy blood,
It would become me better than to close°
In terms of friendship with thine enemies.
Pardon me, Julius! Here wast thou bayed,° brave
    hart;°
205 Here didst thou fall, and here thy hunters stand,
Signed in thy spoil° and crimsoned in thy lethe.°
O world, thou wast the forest to this hart;
And this indeed, O world, the heart of thee.
How like a deer, stroken° by many princes,
210 Dost thou here lie!

Cassius. Mark Antony——

Antony.   Pardon me, Caius Cassius.
The enemies of Caesar shall say this;
Then, in a friend, it is cold modesty.°

Cassius. I blame you not for praising Caesar so;
215 But what compact mean you to have with us?
Will you be pricked in number° of our friends,
Or shall we on,° and not depend on you?

---

192 *conceit* judge   196 *dearer* more deeply   199 *corse* corpse
202 *close* make an agreement   204 *bayed* brought to bay   204 *hart*
(1) deer (2) heart   206 *Signed in thy spoil* marked with the signs of
your slaughter   206 *lethe* (dissyllabic; the river of oblivion from which
the dead drank in Hades; here, by extension, "stream of death," or
"lifeblood")   209 *stroken* struck down   213 *modesty* moderation
216 *pricked in number* marked down (the modern "ticks off names";
the Roman made small holes in his wax-covered tablets)   217 *on* proceed

Antony. Therefore I took your hands, but was indeed
    Swayed from the point by looking down on Caesar.
    Friends am I with you all, and love you all,   220
    Upon this hope, that you shall give me reasons
    Why, and wherein, Caesar was dangerous.

Brutus. Or else were this a savage spectacle.
    Our reasons are so full of good regard°
    That were you, Antony, the son of Caesar,   225
    You should be satisfied.

Antony.   That's all I seek;
    And am moreover suitor that I may
    Produce° his body to the market place,
    And in the pulpit, as becomes a friend,
    Speak in the order° of his funeral.   230

Brutus. You shall, Mark Antony.

Cassius.   Brutus, a word with you.
    [*Aside to Brutus*] You know not what you do; do not
        consent
    That Antony speak in his funeral.
    Know you how much the people may be moved
    By that which he will utter?

Brutus.   By your pardon: 235
    I will myself into the pulpit first,
    And show the reason of our Caesar's death.
    What Antony shall speak, I will protest°
    He speaks by leave and by permission,
    And that we are contented Caesar shall   240
    Have all true° rites and lawful ceremonies.
    It shall advantage° more than do us wrong.°

Cassius. I know not what may fall;° I like it not.

Brutus. Mark Antony, here, take you Caesar's body.
    You shall not in your funeral speech blame us,   245
    But speak all good you can devise of Caesar,
    And say you do't by our permission;

224 *good regard* sound considerations   228 *Produce* bring forth
230 *order* course of ceremonies   238 *protest* declare   241 *true* proper
242 *advantage* benefit   242 *wrong* harm   243 *fall* happen

Else shall you not have any hand at all
About his funeral. And you shall speak
250 In the same pulpit whereto I am going,
After my speech is ended.

Antony.   Be it so;
I do desire no more.

Brutus. Prepare the body then, and follow us.
                    Exeunt. Manet Antony.

Antony. O pardon me, thou bleeding piece of earth,
255 That I am meek and gentle with these butchers!
Thou art the ruins of the noblest man
That ever livèd in the tide of times.°
Woe to the hand that shed this costly blood!
Over thy wounds now do I prophesy
260 (Which like dumb mouths do ope their ruby lips
To beg the voice and utterance of my tongue),
A curse shall light upon the limbs of men;
Domestic fury and fierce civil strife
Shall cumber° all the parts of Italy;
265 Blood and destruction shall be so in use,°
And dreadful objects so familiar,
That mothers shall but smile when they behold
Their infants quartered with the hands of war,
All pity choked with custom of fell deeds;°
270 And Caesar's spirit, ranging° for revenge,
With Atè° by his side come hot from hell,
Shall in these confines° with a monarch's voice
Cry "Havoc,"° and let slip° the dogs of war,
That this foul deed shall smell above the earth
275 With carrion° men, groaning for burial.

Enter Octavius' Servant.

You serve Octavius Caesar, do you not?

---

257 *tide of times* course (ebb and flow) of history   264 *cumber* burden,
oppress   265 *in use* customary   269 *custom of fell deeds* habituation
to cruel acts   270 *ranging* roving widely in search of prey   271 *Atè*
Greek goddess of discord and vengeance   272 *confines* boundaries,
regions   273 *Cry "Havoc"* give the signal for unrestricted slaughter
and looting   273 *let slip* unleash   275 *carrion* dead and rotting

Servant. I do, Mark Antony.

Antony. Caesar did write for him to come to Rome.

Servant. He did receive his letters and is coming,
And bid me say to you by word of mouth—   280
O Caesar!   [*Seeing the body.*]

Antony. Thy heart is big;° get thee apart and weep.
Passion,° I see, is catching, for mine eyes,
Seeing those beads of sorrow stand in thine,
Began to water. Is thy master coming?   285

Servant. He lies tonight within seven leagues of Rome.

Antony. Post° back with speed, and tell him what hath
    chanced.°
Here is a mourning Rome, a dangerous Rome,
No Rome° of safety for Octavius yet.
Hie° hence and tell him so. Yet stay awhile;   290
Thou shalt not back till I have borne this corse
Into the market place; there shall I try°
In my oration how the people take
The cruel issue° of these bloody men;
According to the which, thou shalt discourse   295
To young Octavius of the state of things.
Lend me your hand.   *Exeunt.*

282 *big* swollen (with grief)   283 *Passion* intense emotion, grief
287 *Post* ride post (with relays of horses), hasten   287 *chanced* happened   289 *Rome* (another play on the pronunciation "room";
cf. I.ii.156)   290 *Hie* hurry   292 *try* test   294 *cruel issue* outcome of
the cruelty

[Scene II. *The Forum.*]

Enter Brutus and goes into the pulpit, and Cassius,
with the Plebeians.

Plebeians. We will be satisfied!° Let us be satisfied!

Brutus. Then follow me, and give me audience, friends.
Cassius, go you into the other street
And part the numbers.°
5   Those that will hear me speak, let 'em stay here;
Those that will follow Cassius, go with him;
And public reasons shall be renderèd
Of Caesar's death.

First Plebeian.   I will hear Brutus speak.

Second Plebeian. I will hear Cassius, and compare their
reasons,
10   When severally° we hear them renderèd.
        [*Exit Cassius, with some of the Plebeians.*]

Third Plebeian. The noble Brutus is ascended. Silence!

Brutus. Be patient till the last.°
Romans, countrymen, and lovers,° hear me for my
cause, and be silent, that you may hear. Believe me
15   for mine honor, and have respect° to mine honor,
that you may believe. Censure° me in your wisdom,
and awake your senses,° that you may the better
judge. If there be any in this assembly, any dear friend
of Caesar's, to him I say that Brutus' love to Caesar
20   was no less than his. If then that friend demand why

III.ii.1 *will be satisfied* want a full explanation   4 *part the numbers* divide the crowd   10 *severally* separately   12 *last* conclusion (of my
speech)   13 *lovers* dear friends   15 *respect* regard   16 *Censure* judge
17 *senses* powers of understanding, reason

Brutus rose against Caesar, this is my answer: Not
that I loved Caesar less, but that I loved Rome more.
Had you rather Caesar were living, and die all slaves,
than that Caesar were dead, to live all free men? As
Caesar loved me, I weep for him, as he was fortunate,   25
I rejoice at it; as he was valiant, I honor him; but,
as he was ambitious, I slew him. There is tears, for
his love; joy, for his fortune; honor, for his valor;
and death, for his ambition. Who is here so base,
that would be a bondman?° If any, speak, for him   30
have I offended. Who is here so rude,° that would not
be a Roman? If any, speak, for him have I offended.
Who is here so vile, that will not love his country?
If any, speak; for him have I offended. I pause for a
reply.   35

All. None, Brutus, none!

Brutus. Then none have I offended. I have done no
more to Caesar than you shall do° to Brutus. The
question of his death is enrolled° in the Capitol, his
glory not extenuated,° wherein he was worthy, nor   40
his offenses enforced,° for which he suffered death.

Enter Mark Antony, with Caesar's body.

Here comes his body, mourned by Mark Antony,
who, though he had no hand in his death, shall receive
the benefit of his dying, a place° in the commonwealth, as which of you shall not? With this I depart,   45
that, as I slew my best lover° for the good of Rome,
I have the same dagger for myself, when it shall
please my country to need my death.

All. Live, Brutus! Live, live!

First Plebeian. Bring him with triumph home unto his
house.   50

30 *bondman* slave   31 *rude* barbarous   38 *shall do* i.e., if I should
become equally tyrannical   38–39 *The question . . . enrolled* the considerations that made necessary his death are recorded   40 *extenuated*
depreciated   41 *enforced* exaggerated   44 *place* i.e., as a free citizen
46 *lover* friend

Second Plebeian. Give him a statue with his ancestors.

Third Plebeian. Let him be Caesar.

Fourth Plebeian.   Caesar's better parts°
  Shall be crowned in Brutus.

First Plebeian. We'll bring him to his house with shouts
  and clamors.

Brutus. My countrymen——

55 *Second Plebeian.*   Peace! Silence! Brutus speaks.

First Plebeian. Peace, ho!
Brutus. Good countrymen, let me depart alone,
  And, for my sake, stay here with Antony.
  Do grace to Caesar's corpse, and grace his speech°
60   Tending° to Caesar's glories, which Mark Antony
  By our permission, is allowed to make.
  I do entreat you, not a man depart,
  Save I alone, till Antony have spoke.   *Exit.*

First Plebeian. Stay, ho! And let us hear Mark Antony.

65 *Third Plebeian.* Let him go up into the public chair;°
  We'll hear him. Noble Antony, go up.

Antony. For Brutus' sake, I am beholding° to you.

Fourth Plebeian. What does he say of Brutus?

Third Plebeian.   He says, for Brutus' sake,
  He finds himself beholding to us all.

Fourth Plebeian. 'Twere best he speak no harm of Brutus
70   here!

First Plebeian. This Caesar was a tyrant.

Third Plebeian.   Nay, that's certain.
  We are blest that Rome is rid of him.

---

52 *parts* qualities   59 *Do . . . speech* show respect to dead Caesar and
listen respectfully to Antony's speech   60 *Tending* relating   65 *public chair* pulpit, rostrum   67 *beholding* beholden, indebted

Second Plebeian. Peace! Let us hear what Antony can
　　say.

Antony. You gentle Romans——

All.　　　　　　　　　　　Peace, ho! Let us hear him.

Antony. Friends, Romans, countrymen, lend me your
　　ears;　　　　　　　　　　　　　　　　　　　　　　　75
　I come to bury Caesar, not to praise him.
　The evil that men do lives after them,
　The good is oft interrèd with their bones;
　So let it be with Caesar. The noble Brutus
　Hath told you Caesar was ambitious.　　　　　　　80
　If it were so, it was a grievous fault,
　And grievously hath Caesar answered° it.
　Here, under leave of Brutus and the rest
　(For Brutus is an honorable man,
　So are they all, all honorable men),　　　　　　　85
　Come I to speak in Caesar's funeral.
　He was my friend, faithful and just to me;
　But Brutus says he was ambitious,
　And Brutus is an honorable man.
　He hath brought many captives home to Rome,　　90
　Whose ransoms did the general coffers° fill;
　Did this in Caesar seem ambitious?
　When that the poor have cried, Caesar hath wept;
　Ambition should be made of sterner stuff.
　Yet Brutus says he was ambitious;　　　　　　　95
　And Brutus is an honorable man.
　You all did see that on the Lupercal
　I thrice presented him a kingly crown,
　Which he did thrice refuse. Was this ambition?
　Yet Brutus says he was ambitious;　　　　　　　100
　And sure he is an honorable man.
　I speak not to disprove what Brutus spoke,
　But here I am to speak what I do know.
　You all did love him once, not without cause;
　What cause withholds you then to mourn for him?　105
　O judgment, thou art fled to brutish beasts,

82 *answered* paid the penalty for　91 *general coffers* public treasury

And men have lost their reason! Bear with me;
My heart is in the coffin there with Caesar,
And I must pause till it come back to me.

First Plebeian. Methinks there is much reason in his
110   sayings.

Second Plebeian. If thou consider rightly of the matter,
Caesar has had great wrong.

Third Plebeian.   Has he, masters?
I fear there will a worse come in his place.

Fourth Plebeian. Marked ye his words? He would not
take the crown,
115   Therefore 'tis certain he was not ambitious.

First Plebeian. If it be found so, some will dear abide it.°

Second Plebeian. Poor soul, his eyes are red as fire with
weeping.

Third Plebeian. There's not a nobler man in Rome than
Antony.

Fourth Plebeian. Now mark him, he begins again to
speak.

120 *Antony.* But yesterday the word of Caesar might
Have stood against the world; now lies he there,
And none so poor to° do him reverence.
O masters! If I were disposed to stir
Your hearts and minds to mutiny and rage,
125   I should do Brutus wrong and Cassius wrong,
Who, you all know, are honorable men.
I will not do them wrong; I rather choose
To wrong the dead, to wrong myself and you,
Than I will wrong such honorable men.
130   But here's a parchment with the seal of Caesar;
I found it in his closet;° 'tis his will.
Let but the commons° hear this testament,
Which, pardon me, I do not mean to read,

116 *dear abide it* pay dearly for it   122 *so poor to* so low in rank as to
131 *closet* study (?) desk (?)   132 *commons* plebeians

And they would go and kiss dead Caesar's wounds,
And dip their napkins° in his sacred blood;   135
Yea, beg a hair of him for memory,
And dying, mention it within their wills,
Bequeathing it as a rich legacy
Unto their issue.°

Fourth Plebeian. We'll hear the will; read it, Mark
Antony.   140

All. The will, the will! We will hear Caesar's will!

Antony. Have patience, gentle friends, I must not read it.
It is not meet° you know how Caesar loved you.
You are not wood, you are not stones, but men;
And being men, hearing the will of Caesar,   145
It will inflame you, it will make you mad.
'Tis good you know not that you are his heirs;
For if you should, O, what would come of it?

Fourth Plebeian. Read the will! We'll hear it, Antony!
You shall read us the will, Caesar's will!   150

Antony. Will you be patient? Will you stay° awhile?
I have o'ershot myself° to tell you of it.
I fear I wrong the honorable men
Whose daggers have stabbed Caesar; I do fear it.

Fourth Plebeian. They were traitors. Honorable men!   155

All. The will! The testament!

Second Plebeian. They were villains, murderers! The
will! Read the will!

Antony. You will compel me then to read the will?
Then make a ring about the corpse of Caesar,   160
And let me show you him that made the will.
Shall I descend? And will you give me leave?

All. Come down.

Second Plebeian. Descend.   [*Antony comes down.*]

---

135 *napkins* handkerchiefs   139 *issue* heirs   143 *meet* fitting   151
stay wait   152 *o'ershot myself* gone further than I intended

165 *Third Plebeian.* You shall have leave.

Fourth Plebeian. A ring! Stand round.

First Plebeian. Stand from the hearse, stand from the
body!

Second Plebeian. Room for Antony, most noble Antony!

Antony. Nay, press not so upon me; stand far° off.

170 *All.* Stand back! Room! Bear back.

Antony. If you have tears, prepare to shed them now.
    You all do know this mantle;° I remember
    The first time ever Caesar put it on:
    'Twas on a summer's evening, in his tent,
175   That day he overcame the Nervii.°
    Look, in this place ran Cassius' dagger through;
    See what a rent the envious° Casca made;
    Through this the well-belovèd Brutus stabbed,
    And as he plucked his cursèd steel away,
180   Mark how the blood of Caesar followed it,
    As° rushing out of doors, to be resolved°
    If Brutus so unkindly° knocked, or no;
    For Brutus, as you know, was Caesar's angel.°
    Judge, O you gods, how dearly Caesar loved him!
185   This was the most unkindest° cut of all;
    For when the noble Caesar saw him stab,
    Ingratitude, more strong than traitors' arms,
    Quite vanquished him. Then burst his mighty heart;
    And, in his mantle muffling up his face,
190   Even at the base° of Pompey's statue°
    (Which all the while ran blood) great Caesar fell.
    O, what a fall was there, my countrymen!
    Then I, and you, and all of us fell down,
    Whilst bloody treason flourished° over us.

169 *far* farther   172 *mantle* cloak (here, the toga)   175 *Nervii* (a fierce
tribe decisively conquered by Caesar in 57 B.C.)   177 *envious* spiteful
181 *As* as though   181 *to be resolved* to learn for certain   182 *un-
kindly* (1) cruelly (2) unnaturally   183 *angel* favorite (i.e., considered
incapable of evil)   185 *most unkindest* most cruel and unnatural
190 *base* pedestal   190 *statue* (pronounced "stat-u-a")   194 *flour-
ished* (1) swaggered (2) brandished a sword in triumph

O, now you weep, and I perceive you feel   195
The dint° of pity; these are gracious drops.
Kind souls, what° weep you when you but behold
Our Caesar's vesture° wounded? Look you here,
Here is himself, marred° as you see with° traitors.

First Plebeian. O piteous spectacle!   200

Second Plebeian. O noble Caesar!

Third Plebeian. O woeful day!

Fourth Plebeian. O traitors, villains!

First Plebeian. O most bloody sight!

Second Plebeian. We will be revenged.   205

[*All.*] Revenge! About!° Seek! Burn! Fire! Kill! Slay!
Let not a traitor live!

Antony. Stay, countrymen.

First Plebeian. Peace there! Hear the noble Antony.

Second Plebeian. We'll hear him, we'll follow him, we'll 210
die with him!

Antony. Good friends, sweet friends, let me not stir you
up
To such a sudden flood of mutiny.
They that have done this deed are honorable.
What private griefs° they have, alas, I know not,   215
That made them do it. They are wise and honorable,
And will, no doubt, with reasons answer you.
I come not, friends, to steal away your hearts;
I am no orator, as Brutus is;
But (as you know me all) a plain blunt man   220
That love my friend, and that they know full well
That gave me public leave to speak° of him.
For I have neither writ, nor words, nor worth,

196 *dint* stroke 197 *what* why 198 *vesture* clothing 199 *marred*
mangled 199 *with* by 206 *About* let's go 215 *private griefs* personal grievances 222 *public leave to speak* permission to speak in
public

Action, nor utterance,° nor the power of speech
225 To stir men's blood; I only speak right on.°
I tell you that which you yourselves do know,
Show you sweet Caesar's wounds, poor poor dumb
mouths,
And bid them speak for me. But were I Brutus,
And Brutus Antony, there were an Antony
230 Would ruffle up° your spirits, and put a tongue
In every wound of Caesar that should move
The stones of Rome to rise and mutiny.

All. We'll mutiny.

First Plebeian.   We'll burn the house of Brutus.

Third Plebeian. Away, then! Come, seek the conspirators.

235 *Antony.* Yet hear me, countrymen. Yet hear me speak.

All. Peace, ho! Hear Antony, most noble Antony!

Antony. Why, friends, you go to do you know not what:
Wherein hath Caesar thus deserved your loves?
Alas, you know not; I must tell you then:
240 You have forgot the will I told you of.

All. Most true, the will! Let's stay and hear the will.

Antony. Here is the will, and under Caesar's seal.
To every Roman citizen he gives,
To every several° man, seventy-five drachmas.

Second Plebeian. Most noble Caesar! We'll revenge his
245 death!

Third Plebeian. O royal° Caesar!

Antony. Hear me with patience.

All. Peace, ho!

223–24 *neither . . . utterance* neither a written speech, nor fluency, nor
reputation, nor (an orator's) gestures, nor good delivery (perhaps *writ*
should be emended to *wit,* "intellectual cleverness")   225 *right on*
directly, without premeditation   230 *ruffle up* incite to rage   244 *several* individual   246 *royal* nobly generous

Antony. Moreover, he hath left you all his walks,°
His private arbors, and new-planted orchards,°   250
On this side Tiber; he hath left them you,
And to your heirs forever: common pleasures,°
To walk abroad and recreate yourselves.
Here was a Caesar! When comes such another?

First Plebeian. Never, never! Come, away, away!   255
We'll burn his body in the holy place,
And with the brands fire the traitors' houses.
Take up the body.

Second Plebeian. Go fetch fire.

Third Plebeian. Pluck down benches.   260

Fourth Plebeian. Pluck down forms, windows,° anything!   *Exeunt Plebeians* [*with the body*].

Antony. Now let it work:° Mischief, thou art afoot,
Take thou what course thou wilt.

Enter Servant.

How now, fellow?

Servant. Sir, Octavius is already come to Rome.   265

Antony. Where is he?

Servant. He and Lepidus are at Caesar's house.

Antony. And thither will I straight° to visit him;
He comes upon a wish.° Fortune is merry,
And in this mood will give us anything.   270

Servant. I heard him say, Brutus and Cassius
Are rid° like madmen through the gates of Rome.

Antony. Belike° they had some notice of° the people,
How I had moved them. Bring me to Octavius.
Exeunt.

249 *walks* parks   250 *orchards* gardens   252 *common pleasures* public
places of recreation   261 *forms, windows* long benches (and) shutters
263 *work* (1) ferment (as yeast) (2) work itself out   268 *will I straight*
will I (go) at once   269 *upon a wish* just as I wished   272 *Are rid* have
ridden   273 *Belike* probably   273 *notice of* news about

[Scene III. *A street.*]

Enter Cinna the Poet, and after him the Plebeians.

Cinna. I dreamt tonight° that I did feast with Caesar,
And things unluckily charge my fantasy.°
I have no will to wander forth° of doors,
Yet something leads me forth.

5 *First Plebeian.* What is your name?

Second Plebeian. Whither are you going?

Third Plebeian. Where do you dwell?

Fourth Plebeian. Are you a married man or a bachelor?

Second Plebeian. Answer every man directly.°

10 *First Plebeian.* Ay, and briefly.

Fourth Plebeian. Ay, and wisely.

Third Plebeian. Ay, and truly, you were best.

Cinna. What is my name? Whither am I going? Where
do I dwell? Am I a married man or a bachelor? Then,
15 to answer every man directly and briefly, wisely and
truly: wisely I say, I am a bachelor.

Second Plebeian. That's as much as to say, they are
fools that marry; you'll bear me a bang° for that, I
fear. Proceed directly.

20 *Cinna.* Directly, I am going to Caesar's funeral.

First Plebeian. As a friend or an enemy?

III.iii.1 *tonight* last night   2 *things . . . fantasy* events give ominous
weight to my imaginings   3 *forth* out   9 *directly* straightforwardly
18 *bear me a bang* get a blow from me

Cinna. As a friend.

Second Plebeian. That matter is answered directly.

Fourth Plebeian. For your dwelling, briefly.

Cinna. Briefly, I dwell by the Capitol.   25

Third Plebeian. Your name, sir, truly.

Cinna. Truly, my name is Cinna.

First Plebeian. Tear him to pieces! He's a conspirator.

Cinna. I am Cinna the poet! I am Cinna the poet!

Fourth Plebeian. Tear him for his bad verses! Tear him   30
  for his bad verses!

Cinna. I am not Cinna the conspirator.

Fourth Plebeian. It is no matter, his name's Cinna;
  pluck but his name out of his heart, and turn him
  going.°   35

Third Plebeian. Tear him, tear him! [*They attack him.*]
  Come, brands, ho! Firebrands! To Brutus', to Cas-
  sius'! Burn all! Some to Decius' house, and some to
  Casca's; some to Ligarius'! Away, go!
                    Exeunt all the Plebeians [*with Cinna*].

34–35 *turn him going* dispatch him

ACT IV

[Scene I. *A house in Rome.*]

Enter Antony, Octavius, and Lepidus.

Antony. These many then shall die; their names are
pricked.°

Octavius. Your brother too must die; consent you, Lepidus?

Lepidus. I do consent——

Octavius. Prick him down, Antony.

Lepidus. Upon condition Publius shall not live,
5 Who is your sister's son, Mark Antony.

Antony. He shall not live; look, with a spot I damn him.°
But, Lepidus, go you to Caesar's house;
Fetch the will hither, and we shall determine
How to cut off some charge° in legacies.

10 *Lepidus.* What, shall I find you here?

Octavius. Or° here or at the Capitol. *Exit Lepidus.*

IV.i.1 *pricked* ticked off, marked on the list   6 *with a spot I damn him*
with a dot (on the wax tablet) I condemn him   9 *cut off some charge* re-
duce expenses (by altering the amount left in bequests)   11 *Or* either

100

Antony. This is a slight unmeritable° man,
  Meet° to be sent on errands; is it fit,
  The threefold world° divided, he should stand
  One of the three to share it?

Octavius.   So you thought him,   15
  And took his voice° who should be pricked to die
  In our black sentence° and proscription.°

Antony. Octavius, I have seen more days° than you;
  And though we lay these honors on this man,
  To ease ourselves of divers sland'rous loads,°   20
  He shall but bear them as the ass bears gold,
  To groan and sweat under the business,°
  Either led or driven, as we point the way;
  And having brought our treasure where we will,
  Then take we down his load, and turn him off,°   25
  (Like to the empty° ass) to shake his ears
  And graze in commons.°

Octavius.   You may do your will;
  But he's a tried and valiant soldier.°

Antony. So is my horse, Octavius, and for that
  I do appoint him store° of provender.   30
  It is a creature that I teach to fight,
  To wind,° to stop, to run directly on,
  His corporal° motion governed by my spirit.°
  And, in some taste,° is Lepidus but so.°
  He must be taught, and trained, and bid go forth.   35
  A barren-spirited° fellow; one that feeds

---

12 *slight unmeritable* insignificant and undeserving   13 *Meet* fit   14 *threefold world* three areas of the Roman empire, Europe, Asia, and Africa   16 *voice* vote   17 *black sentence* sentence of death   17 *proscription* condemnation to death or exile   18 *have seen more days* am older (and more experienced)   20 *divers sland'rous loads* blame which will be laid upon us for our various actions   22 *business* hard labor   25 *turn him off* drive him away   26 *empty* unburdened   27 *in commons* on public pasture   28 *soldier* (trisyllabic)   30 *appoint him store* allot him a supply   32 *wind* turn   33 *corporal* physical   33 *spirit* mind   34 *taste* measure   34 *so* the same   36 *barren-spirited* lacking initiative or ideas of his own

On objects, arts, and imitations,°
Which, out of use and staled° by other men,
Begin his fashion.° Do not talk of him
40 But as a property.° And now, Octavius,
Listen great things. Brutus and Cassius
Are levying powers;° we must straight make head.°
Therefore let our alliance be combined,
Our best friends made,° our means stretched;°
45 And let us presently° go sit in council
How covert matters may be best disclosed,
And open perils surest answerèd.°

Octavius. Let us do so; for we are at the stake,°
And bayed about with many enemies;
50 And some that smile have in their hearts, I fear,
Millions of mischiefs.°   *Exeunt.*

[Scene II. *Camp near Sardis.*]

*Drum. Enter Brutus, Lucilius, [Lucius,] and the Army.
Titinius and Pindarus meet them.*

Brutus. Stand ho!

Lucilius. Give the word, ho! and stand.

Brutus. What now, Lucilius, is Cassius near?

37 *objects, arts, and imitations* curiosities, artifices, and fashions (or
styles)   38 *staled* made common   39 *Begin his fashion* i.e., he is
always far behind the times   40 *property* mere tool (a thing rather
than a person)   42 *powers* armed forces   42 *straight make head* immediately gather troops   44 *Our best friends made* let our closest allies
be selected   44 *stretched* be used to the fullest advantage   45 *presently* immediately   46–47 *How . . . answerèd* to decide how hidden
dangers may best be discovered and open dangers most safely en-
countered   48 *at the stake* (metaphor derived from Elizabethan sport
of bearbaiting) i.e., like a bear tied to a stake and set upon by many
dogs   51 *mischiefs* plans to injure us

Lucilius. He is at hand, and Pindarus is come
  To do you salutation from his master.   5

Brutus. He greets me well.° Your master, Pindarus,
  In his own change, or by ill officers,°
  Hath given me some worthy° cause to wish
  Things done undone; but if he be at hand,
  I shall be satisfied.°

Pindarus.   I do not doubt   10
  But that my noble master will appear
  Such as he is, full of regard° and honor.

Brutus. He is not doubted. A word, Lucilius,
  How he received you; let me be resolved.°

Lucilius. With courtesy and with respect enough,   15
  But not with such familiar instances,°
  Nor with such free and friendly conference°
  As he hath used of old.

Brutus.   Thou hast described
  A hot friend cooling. Ever note, Lucilius,
  When love begins to sicken and decay   20
  It useth an enforcèd ceremony.°
  There are no tricks in plain and simple faith;
  But hollow° men, like horses hot at hand,°
  Make gallant show and promise of their mettle;°
                   Low march within.
  But when they should endure the bloody spur,   25
  They fall their crests,° and like deceitful jades°
  Sink in the trial.° Comes his army on?

Lucilius. They mean this night in Sardis to be quartered;

IV.ii.6 *He greets me well* he sends greetings by a very good man   7 *In his . . . officers* either from a change in his feelings toward me or through the actions of bad subordinates   8 *worthy* substantial   10 *be satisfied* receive a satisfactory explanation   12 *full of regard* worthy of respect   14 *resolved* fully informed   16 *familiar instances* marks of friendship   17 *conference* conversation   21 *enforcèd ceremony* strained formality   23 *hollow* insincere   23 *hot at hand* overspirited at the start   24 *mettle* quality, courage   26 *fall their crests* let fall the ridges of their necks   26 *jades* nags   27 *Sink in the trial* fail when put to the test

The greater part, the horse in general,°
Are come with Cassius.

Enter Cassius and his Powers.

30   *Brutus.*   Hark! He is arrived.
March gently° on to meet him.

Cassius. Stand, ho!

Brutus. Stand, ho! Speak the word along.

[*First Soldier.*] Stand!

35   [*Second Soldier.*] Stand!

[*Third Soldier.*] Stand!

Cassius. Most noble brother, you have done me wrong.

Brutus. Judge me, you gods! Wrong I mine enemies?
And if not so, how should I wrong a brother.

40   *Cassius.* Brutus, this sober form° of yours hides wrongs;
And when you do them——

Brutus.   Cassius, be content.°
Speak your griefs° softly; I do know you well.
Before the eyes of both our armies here
(Which should perceive nothing but love from us)
45   Let us not wrangle. Bid them move away;
Then in my tent, Cassius, enlarge° your griefs,
And I will give you audience.

Cassius.   Pindarus,
Bid our commanders lead their charges° off
A little from this ground.

50   *Brutus.* Lucilius, do you the like, and let no man
Come to our tent till we have done our conference.
Let Lucius and Titinius guard our door.
                    Exeunt. Mane[n]t Brutus and Cassius.

---

29 *the horse in general* all the cavalry   31 *gently* slowly   40 *sober form* staid manner   41 *be content* keep calm   42 *griefs* grievances   46 *enlarge* freely express   48 *charges* troops

[handwritten: Brutus vs. Cassius]

[handwritten: Cassius wrote B. and defended Lucius]

[Scene III. *Brutus' tent.*]

Cassius. That you have wronged me doth appear in this:
　　You have condemned and noted° Lucius Pella　*[handwritten: supporter]*
　　For taking bribes here of the Sardians;
　　Wherein my letters, praying on his side,°　*[handwritten: for army $]*
　　Because I knew the man, was slighted off.°　5

Brutus. You wronged yourself to write in such a case.

Cassius. In such a time as this it is not meet　*[handwritten: shouldn't have written - not]*
　　That every nice offense should bear his comment.°　*[handwritten: honor-able]*

Brutus. Let me tell you, Cassius, you yourself
　　Are much condemned to have an itching palm,°　10　*[handwritten: greed]*
　　To sell and mart° your offices for gold
　　To undeservers.　*[handwritten: mtn. of mole-hill]*

Cassius.　　　　　　I an itching palm?
　　You know that you are Brutus that speaks this,
　　Or, by the gods, this speech were else your last.

Brutus. The name of Cassius honors° this corruption,　15
　　And chastisement doth therefore hide his head.

Cassius. Chastisement!

Brutus. Remember March, the ides of March remember.
　　Did not great Julius bleed for justice' sake?
　　What villain touched his body, that did stab,　20
　　And not° for justice? What, shall one of us,
　　That struck the foremost man of all this world

[handwritten: that's what he thought]

IV.iii.2. *noted* publicly disgraced　4 *praying on his side* appealing on
his behalf　5 *was slighted off* was contemptuously disregarded ("letters" takes a singular verb because of its singular meaning)　8 *nice
. . . comment* trivial fault should receive criticism (*his* = its)　10
condemned . . . palm accused of being mercenary　11 *mart* traffic
in　15 *honors* lends an air of respectability　21 *And not* except

But for supporting robbers,° shall we now
Contaminate our fingers with base bribes,
25　And sell the mighty space of our large honors°
For so much trash° as may be graspèd thus?°
I had rather be a dog, and bay° the moon,
Than such a Roman.

Cassius.　　　　　　　　　　Brutus, bait° not me;
I'll not endure it. You forget yourself
30　To hedge me in.° I am a soldier, I,
Older in practice, abler than yourself
To make conditions.°

Brutus.　　　　　　　　Go to! You are not, Cassius.

Cassius. I am.

Brutus. I say you are not.

35　*Cassius.* Urge° me no more, I shall forget myself;
Have mind upon your health;° tempt° me no farther.

Brutus. Away, slight° man!

Cassius. Is't possible?

Brutus.　　　　　　　　Hear me, for I will speak.
Must I give way and room to your rash choler?°
40　Shall I be frighted when a madman stares?°

Cassius. O ye gods, ye gods! Must I endure all this?

---

23 *supporting robbers* i.e., protecting dishonest officials (a point made
by Plutarch but mentioned only now by Shakespeare)　25 *mighty
. . . honors* vast capacity to be honorable and magnanimous (with sug-
gestion of potentiality for making other men free, and honorable in
office)　26 *trash* rubbish, i.e., money　26 *graspèd thus* (the small con-
fined area of the closed fist contrasts with the "mighty space" gained
by their honorable deeds in abolishing injustice and corruption)
27 *bay* howl at　28 *bait* harass and worry (as a bear tied to a stake is
baited by dogs)　30 *hedge me in* limit my freedom of action　32 *make
conditions* manage practical matters　35 *Urge* drive, bully　36 *health*
safety　36 *tempt* provoke　37 *slight* insignificant　39 *give . . .
choler* let your hasty temper have free vent and run its course un-
checked　40 *stares* glares

Brutus. All this? Ay, more: fret till your proud heart break.
>   Go show your slaves how choleric you are,
>   And make your bondmen tremble. Must I budge?°
>   Must I observe° you? Must I stand and crouch°   45
>   Under your testy humor?° By the gods,
>   You shall digest the venom° of your spleen,° *temper*
>   Though it do split you; for, from this day forth,
>   I'll use you for my mirth, yea, for my laughter,
>   When you are waspish.

Cassius.   Is it come to this?   50

Brutus. You say you are a better soldier:
>   Let it appear so; make your vaunting° true,
>   And it shall please me well. For mine own part,
>   I shall be glad to learn of° noble men.

Cassius. You wrong me every way; you wrong me, Brutus;   55
>   I said, an elder soldier, not a better.
>   Did I say, better?

Brutus.   If you did, I care not.

Cassius. When Caesar lived, he durst not thus have moved° me.

Brutus. Peace, peace, you durst not so have tempted° him.

Cassius. I durst not?   60

Brutus. No.

Cassius. What? Durst not tempt him?

Brutus.   For your life you durst not.

---

44 *budge* defer to it   45 *observe* wait on   45 *crouch* bow   46 *testy humor* irritability   47 *digest the venom* swallow the poison   47 *spleen* (considered the source of sudden passions) i.e., fiery temper   52 *vaunting* boasting   54 *learn of* (1) hear about the exploits of (2) take lessons from   58 *moved* exasperated   59 *tempted* provoked

Cassius. Do not presume too much upon my love;
    I may do that I shall be sorry for.

65 *Brutus.* You have done that you should be sorry for.
    There is no terror, Cassius, in your threats;
    For I am armed so strong in honesty°
    That they pass by me as the idle wind,
    Which I respect° not. I did send to you
70 For certain sums of gold, which you denied me;
    For I can raise no money by vile means.
    By heaven, I had rather coin my heart
    And drop my blood for drachmas than to wring
    From the hard hands of peasants their vile trash
75 By any indirection.° I did send
    To you for gold to pay my legions,
    Which you denied me. Was that done like Cassius?
    Should I have answered Caius Cassius so?
    When Marcus Brutus grows so covetous
80 To lock such rascal counters° from his friends,
    Be ready, gods, with all your thunderbolts,
    Dash him to pieces!

Cassius.   I denied you not.

Brutus. You did.

Cassius.   I did not. He was but a fool
    That brought my answer back. Brutus hath rived°
    my heart.
85 A friend should bear his friend's infirmities;
    But Brutus makes mine greater than they are.

Brutus. I do not, till you practice them on me.

Cassius. You love me not.

Brutus.   I do not like your faults.

Cassius. A friendly eye could never see such faults.

---

67 *honesty* integrity   69 *respect* heed   75 *indirection* irregular methods   80 *rascal counters* base (and worthless) coins   84 *rived* broken

Brutus. A flatterer's would not, though they do appear   90
　　As huge as high Olympus.

Cassius. Come, Antony, and young Octavius, come,
　　Revenge yourselves alone° on Cassius,
　　For Cassius is aweary of the world:
　　Hated by one he loves; braved° by his brother;   95
　　Checked° like a bondman; all his faults observed,
　　Set in a notebook, learned and conned by rote°
　　To cast into my teeth.° O, I could weep
　　My spirit from mine eyes! There is my dagger,
　　And here my naked breast; within, a heart   100
　　Dearer than Pluto's mine,° richer than gold;
　　If that thou be'st a Roman, take it forth.
　　I, that denied thee gold, will give my heart.
　　Strike as thou didst at Caesar; for I know,
　　When thou didst hate him worst, thou lovedst him
　　　better   105
　　Than ever thou lovedst Cassius.

Brutus.　　　　　　　　　　Sheathe your dagger.
　　Be angry when you will, it shall have scope.°
　　Do what you will, dishonor shall be humor.°
　　O Cassius, you are yokèd with a lamb
　　That carries anger as the flint bears fire,   110
　　Who, much enforcèd,° shows a hasty spark,
　　And straight° is cold again.

Cassius.　　　　　　　　　Hath Cassius lived
　　To be but mirth and laughter to his Brutus
　　When grief and blood ill-tempered° vexeth him?

Brutus. When I spoke that, I was ill-tempered too.   115

93 *alone* only 95 *braved* defied 96 *Checked* rebuked 97 *conned
by rote* learned by heart 98 *cast into my teeth* i.e., throw in my face
101 *Dearer than Pluto's mine* more precious than all the riches in the
earth (Pluto, god of the underworld, and Plutus, god of riches, were
frequently confused) 107 *shall have scope* (your anger) shall have
free play 108 *dishonor shall be humor* insults shall be regarded as
quirks of temperament 111 *much enforcèd* greatly provoked 112
straight immediately 114 *blood ill-tempered* i.e., a "black mood"

Cassius. Do you confess so much? Give me your hand.

Brutus. And my heart too.

Cassius.   O Brutus!

Brutus.   What's the matter?

Cassius. Have not you love enough to bear with me
    When that rash humor° which my mother gave me
    Makes me forgetful?

120 *Brutus.*   Yes, Cassius, and from henceforth,
    When you are over-earnest with your Brutus,
    He'll think your mother° chides, and leave you so.°

Enter a Poet, [followed by Lucilius, Titinius, and Lucius].

Poet. Let me go in to see the generals;
    There is some grudge° between 'em; 'tis not meet
125   They be alone.

Lucilius. You shall not come to them.

Poet. Nothing but death shall stay me.

Cassius. How now. What's the matter?

Poet. For shame, you generals! What do you mean?
130   Love, and be friends, as two such men should be;
    For I have seen more years, I'm sure, than ye.

Cassius. Ha, ha! How vilely doth this cynic° rhyme!

Brutus. Get you hence, sirrah! Saucy° fellow, hence!

Cassius. Bear with him, Brutus, 'tis his fashion.

135 *Brutus.* I'll know his humor when he knows his time.°
    What should the wars do with these jigging° fools?
    Companion,° hence!

---

119 *rash humor* hasty temperament   122 *your mother* i.e., your inherited temperament   122 *leave you so* leave it at that   124 *grudge*
bad feeling   132 *cynic* rude fellow   133 *Saucy* impertinent   135 *I'll
. . . time* I'll accept his eccentricity when he can judge the suitable time
for it   136 *jigging* doggerel-writing, rhyming   137 *Companion* base
fellow

Cassius.   Away, away, be gone!

                              Exit Poet.

Brutus. Lucilius and Titinius, bid the commanders
Prepare to lodge their companies tonight.

Cassius. And come yourselves, and bring Messala with
   you   140
   Immediately to us.   [*Exeunt Lucilius and Titinius.*]

Brutus.   Lucius, a bowl of wine.

                              [*Exit Lucius.*]

Cassius. I did not think you could have been so angry.

Brutus. O Cassius, I am sick of many griefs.

Cassius. Of your philosophy you make no use,
   If you give place° to accidental evils.°   145

Brutus. No man bears sorrow better. Portia is dead.

Cassius. Ha? Portia?

Brutus. She is dead.

Cassius. How scaped I killing when I crossed° you so?
   O insupportable and touching° loss!   150
   Upon° what sickness?

Brutus.   Impatient of° my absence,
   And grief that young Octavius with Mark Antony
   Have made themselves so strong—for with her death
   That tidings came°—with this she fell distract,°
   And (her attendants absent) swallowed fire.°   155

Cassius. And died so?

Brutus.   Even so.

---

145 *place* way   145 *accidental evils* misfortunes brought on by chance
(Brutus seems not to be behaving as a Stoic philosopher should)
149 *crossed* contradicted   150 *touching* wounding, grievous   151
Upon as a result of   151 *Impatient of* unable to endure   153–54
for . . . came i.e., news of her death came at the same time as news
of their strength   154 *fell distract* became distraught   155 *swallowed
fire* (according to Plutarch she choked herself by putting hot coals into
her mouth)

Cassius.   O ye immortal gods!

Enter Boy [Lucius], with wine and tapers.

Brutus. Speak no more of her. Give me a bowl of wine.
In this I bury all unkindness, Cassius.   *Drinks.*

Cassius. My heart is thirsty for that noble pledge.
160   Fill, Lucius, till the wine o'erswell the cup;
I cannot drink too much of Brutus' love.
                         [*Drinks. Exit Lucius.*]

Enter Titinius and Messala.

Brutus. Come in, Titinius! Welcome, good Messala.
Now sit we close about this taper here,
And call in question° our necessities.

Cassius. Portia, art thou gone?

165   *Brutus.*   No more, I pray you.
Messala, I have here receivèd letters
That young Octavius and Mark Antony
Come down upon us with a mighty power,°
Bending their expedition° toward Philippi.

170   *Messala.* Myself have letters of the selfsame tenure.°

Brutus. With what addition?

Messala. That by proscription° and bills of outlawry°
Octavius, Antony, and Lepidus
Have put to death an hundred senators.

175   *Brutus.* Therein our letters do not well agree.
Mine speak of seventy senators that died
By their proscriptions, Cicero being one.

Cassius. Cicero one?

Messala.   Cicero is dead,
And by that order of proscription.
180   Had you your letters from your wife, my lord?

---

164 *call in question* consider   168 *power* army   169 *Bending their
expedition* directing their rapid march   170 *tenure* tenor, general
meaning   172 *proscription* proclamation of the death sentence   172
bills of outlawry lists of those proscribed

Brutus. No, Messala.

Messala. Nor nothing in your letters writ of her?

Brutus. Nothing, Messala.

Messala.   That methinks is strange.

Brutus. Why ask you? Hear you aught of her in yours?

Messala. No, my lord.   *185*

Brutus. Now as you are a Roman, tell me true.

Messala. Then like a Roman bear the truth I tell,
   For certain she is dead, and by strange manner.

Brutus. Why, farewell, Portia. We must die, Messala.
   With meditating that she must die once,°   *190*
   I have the patience to endure it now.

Messala. Even so great men great losses should endure.

Cassius. I have as much of this in art° as you,
   But yet my nature could not bear it so.°

Brutus. Well, to our work alive.° What do you think   *195*
   Of marching to Philippi presently?°

Cassius. I do not think it good.

Brutus.   Your reason?

Cassius.   This it is:
   'Tis better that the enemy seek us;
   So shall he waste his means, weary his soldiers,
   Doing himself offense,° whilst we, lying still,   *200*
   Are full of rest, defense, and nimbleness.

Brutus. Good reasons must of force° give place to better.
   The people 'twixt Philippi and this ground

190 *once* at some time   193 *this in art* i.e., this Stoicism in theory
180–94 *Had . . . so* (some editors suggest that this was the original
version of Shakespeare's account of Portia's death and that he later
deleted this and wrote in lines 142–57, preferring to demonstrate
Brutus' humanity rather than his Stoicism; the Folio printer then set
up both versions by mistake. Line 158 would follow 141—as 195 would
follow 179—neatly enough to make this an attractive theory)
195 *alive* as men still living   196 *presently* immediately   200 *offense*
harm   202 *force* necessity

Do stand but in a forced affection;°
205   For they have grudged us contribution.
The enemy, marching along by them,
By them shall make a fuller number up,
Come on refreshed, new-added° and encouraged;
From which advantage shall we cut him off
210   If at Philippi we do face him there,
These people at our back.

Cassius.   Hear me, good brother.

Brutus. Under your pardon.° You must note beside
That we have tried the utmost of our friends,
Our legions are brimful, our cause is ripe.
215   The enemy increaseth every day;
We, at the height, are ready to decline.
There is a tide in the affairs of men
Which, taken at the flood, leads on to fortune;
Omitted,° all the voyage of their life
220   Is bound in° shallows and in miseries.
On such a full sea are we now afloat,
And we must take the current when it serves,
Or lose our ventures.°

on a roll

Cassius.   Then, with your will,° go on;
We'll along ourselves and meet them at Philippi.

225   *Brutus.* The deep of night is crept upon our talk,
And nature must obey necessity,
Which we will niggard with a little rest.°
There is no more to say?

Cassius.   No more. Good night.
Early tomorrow will we rise and hence.°

Enter Lucius.

204 *Do . . . affection* i.e., support us only under compulsion   208 *new-added* reinforced   212 *Under your pardon* excuse me   219 *Omitted* neglected   220 *bound in* limited to   223 *ventures* shipping trade, i.e., risks   223 *with your will* as you wish   227 *niggard with a little rest* i.e., put off with the shortest possible sleep   229 *hence* leave this place

Brutus. Lucius, my gown.°   *Exit Lucius.*
                        Farewell, good Messala.   230
   Good night, Titinius. Noble, noble Cassius,
   Good night, and good repose.

Cassius.   O my dear brother,
   This was an ill beginning of the night.
   Never come° such division 'tween our souls!
   Let it not, Brutus.

          Enter Lucius, with the gown.

Brutus.   Everything is well.   235

Cassius. Good night, my lord.

Brutus.   Good night, good brother.

Titinius, Messala. Good night, Lord Brutus.

Brutus.   Farewell, every one.
                              Exeunt.
   Give me the gown. Where is thy instrument?°

Lucius. Here in the tent.

Brutus.   What, thou speak'st drowsily?
   Poor knave,° I blame thee not; thou art o'erwatched.° 240
   Call Claudius and some other of my men;
   I'll have them sleep on cushions in my tent.

Lucius. Varro and Claudius!

          Enter Varro and Claudius.

Varro. Calls my lord?

Brutus. I pray you, sirs, lie in my tent and sleep.   245
   It may be I shall raise° you by and by
   On business to my brother Cassius.

Varro. So please you, we will stand and watch your
      pleasure.°

---

230 *gown* dressing gown   234 *Never come* may there never again come
238 *instrument* (probably a lute)   240 *knave* boy   240 *o'erwatched*
tired out from lack of sleep   246 *raise* rouse   248 *watch your
pleasure* be on the watch for your command

Brutus. I will not have it so; lie down, good sirs;
250   It may be I shall otherwise bethink me.°

                       [Varro and Claudius lie down.]

Look, Lucius, here's the book I sought for so;
I put it in the pocket of my gown.

Lucius. I was sure your lordship did not give it me.

Brutus. Bear with me, good boy, I am much forgetful.
255   Canst thou hold up thy heavy eyes awhile,
And touch° thy instrument a strain° or two?

Lucius. Ay, my lord, an't° please you.

Brutus.   It does, my boy.
I trouble thee too much, but thou art willing.

Lucius. It is my duty, sir.

260   *Brutus.* I should not urge thy duty past thy might;
I know young bloods° look for a time of rest.

Lucius. I have slept, my lord, already.

Brutus. It was well done, and thou shalt sleep again;
I will not hold thee long. If I do live,
265   I will be good to thee.

                Music, and a song.

This is a sleepy tune. O murd'rous° slumber!
Layest thou thy leaden° mace° upon my boy,
That plays thee music? Gentle knave, good night;
I will not do thee so much wrong to wake thee.
270   If thou dost nod, thou break'st thy instrument;
I'll take it from thee; and, good boy, good night.
Let me see, let me see; is not the leaf turned down
Where I left reading? Here it is, I think.

            Enter the Ghost of Caesar.

---

250 *otherwise bethink me* change my mind   256 *touch* play on   256
strain tune   257 *an't* if it   261 *young bloods* youthful constitutions
266 *murd'rous* deathlike   267 *leaden* heavy (association also with
death, for lead was used in coffinmaking)   267 *mace* staff of office
(with which a man was touched on the shoulder when arrested)

How ill this taper burns.° Ha! Who comes here?
I think it is the weakness of mine eyes   275
That shapes this monstrous apparition.
It comes upon° me. Art thou anything?
Art thou some god, some angel, or some devil,
That mak'st my blood cold, and my hair to stare?°
Speak to me what thou art.   280

Ghost. Thy evil spirit, Brutus.

Brutus.   Why com'st thou?

Ghost. To tell thee thou shalt see me at Philippi.

Brutus. Well; then I shall see thee again?

Ghost. Ay, at Philippi.

Brutus. Why, I will see thee at Philippi then.   285
                                        [*Exit Ghost.*]
Now I have taken heart thou vanishest.
Ill spirit, I would hold more talk with thee.
Boy! Lucius! Varro! Claudius! Sirs, awake!
Claudius!

Lucius. The strings, my lord, are false.°   290

Brutus. He thinks he still is at his instrument.
Lucius, awake!

Lucius. My lord?

Brutus. Didst thou dream, Lucius, that thou so criedst
out?

Lucius. My lord, I do not know that I did cry.   295

Brutus. Yes, that thou didst. Didst thou see anything?

Lucius. Nothing, my lord.

Brutus. Sleep again, Lucius. Sirrah Claudius!
[*To Varro*] Fellow thou, awake!

---

274 *How . . . burns* (lights allegedly burned dimly or blue in the presence of a supernatural being)   277 *upon* toward   279 *stare* stand on end   290 *false* out of tune

300 *Varro.* My lord?

Claudius. My lord?

Brutus. Why did you so cry out, sirs, in your sleep?

Both. Did we, my lord?

Brutus.   Ay. Saw you anything?

Varro. No, my lord, I saw nothing.

Claudius.   Nor I, my lord.

305 *Brutus.* Go and commend me° to my brother Cassius;
      Bid him set on his pow'rs betimes before,°
      And we will follow.

Both.   It shall be done, my lord.

                                              Exeunt.

ACT V

[Scene I. *The plains of Philippi.*]

Enter Octavius, Antony, and their Army.

Octavius. Now, Antony, our hopes are answerèd;
   You said the enemy would not come down,
   But keep the hills and upper regions.
   It proves not so; their battles° are at hand;
   They mean to warn° us at Philippi here,   5
   Answering before we do demand° of them.

Antony. Tut, I am in their bosoms,° and I know
   Wherefore they do it. They could be content
   To visit other places,° and come down
   With fearful° bravery,° thinking by this face°   10
   To fasten in our thoughts° that they have courage;
   But 'tis not so.

               Enter a Messenger.

Messenger.   Prepare you, generals,
   The enemy comes on in gallant show;
   Their bloody sign° of battle is hung out,

V.i.4 *battles* armies   5 *warn* challenge   6 *Answering . . . demand* appearing in opposition before we force a meeting   7 *I am in their
bosoms* I understand their inmost thoughts   8–9 *They could . . . places*
they would prefer to be somewhere else   10 *fearful* (1) frightened
(2) awe-inspiring   10 *bravery* bravado (and show of splendor)
10 *face* appearance   11 *fasten in our thoughts* persuade us   14 *bloody
sign* red flag

119

15   And something to be done immediately.

Antony. Octavius, lead your battle softly° on
    Upon the left hand of the even° field.

Octavius. Upon the right hand I; keep thou the left.

Antony. Why do you cross° me in this exigent?°

20   *Octavius.* I do not cross you; but I will do so.   *March.*

Drum. Enter Brutus, Cassius, and their Army; [Lucilius,
        Titinius, Messala, and others].

Brutus. They stand, and would have parley.

Cassius. Stand fast, Titinius, we must out and talk.

Octavius. Mark Antony, shall we give sign of battle?

25   *Antony.* No, Caesar, we will answer on their charge.°
    Make forth;° the generals would have some words.

Octavius. Stir not until the signal.

Brutus. Words before blows; is it so, countrymen?

Octavius. Not that we love words better, as you do.

Brutus. Good words are better than bad strokes, Octa-
    vius.

Antony. In your bad strokes, Brutus, you give good
30   words;
    Witness the hole you made in Caesar's heart,
    Crying "Long live! Hail, Caesar!"

Cassius.   Antony,
    The posture° of your blows are yet unknown;
    But for your words, they rob the Hybla° bees,
    And leave them honeyless.

35   *Antony.*   Not stingless too.

---

16 *battle softly* army slowly   17 *even* level   19 *cross* oppose, con-
tradict   19 *exigent* crisis   24 *answer on their charge* meet them when
they attack   25 *Make forth* go forward   33 *posture* nature, quality
34 *Hybla* a Sicilian town famous for its sweet honey

Brutus. O, yes, and soundless too;
 For you have stol'n their buzzing, Antony,
 And very wisely threat before you sting.

Antony. Villains! You did not so, when your vile daggers
 Hacked one another in the sides of Caesar. 40
 You showed your teeth° like apes, and fawned like
  hounds,
 And bowed like bondmen, kissing Caesar's feet;
 Whilst damnèd Casca, like a cur, behind
 Struck Caesar on the neck. O you flatterers!

Cassius. Flatterers! Now, Brutus, thank yourself; 45
 This tongue had not offended so today,
 If Cassius might have ruled.°

Octavius. Come, come, the cause.° If arguing make us
  sweat,
 The proof° of it will turn to redder drops.
 Look, 50
 I draw a sword against conspirators.
 When think you that the sword goes up° again?
 Never, till Caesar's three and thirty wounds
 Be well avenged; or till another Caesar°
 Have added slaughter to° the sword of traitors. '55

Brutus. Caesar, thou canst not die by traitors' hands,
 Unless thou bring'st them with thee.

Octavius.   So I hope.
 I was not born to die on Brutus' sword.

Brutus. O, if thou wert the noblest of thy strain,°
 Young man, thou couldst not die more honorable. 60

---

41 *showed your teeth* grinned 47 *ruled* had his way (i.e., in urging that
Antony be slain) 48 *cause* business at hand 49 *proof* test 52 *up*
into the sheath 54 *another Caesar* i.e., Octavius himself 55 *Have
added slaughter to* has also been killed by 59 *strain* family, line of
descent

Cassius. A peevish° schoolboy, worthless° of such honor,
Joined with a masker and a reveler.°

Antony. Old Cassius still!

Octavius.   Come, Antony; away!
Defiance, traitors, hurl we in your teeth.
65   If you dare fight today, come to the field;
If not, when you have stomachs.°

                    Exit Octavius, Antony, and Army.

Cassius. Why, now blow wind, swell billow, and swim
   bark!
The storm is up, and all is on the hazard.°

Brutus. Ho, Lucilius, hark, a word with you.
                    Lucilius and Messala stand forth.

Lucilius.   My lord?
        [*Brutus and Lucilius converse apart.*]

Cassius. Messala.

Messala.   What says my general?

70   *Cassius.*   Messala,
This is my birthday; as this very day
Was Cassius born. Give me thy hand, Messala:
Be thou my witness that against my will
(As Pompey was)° am I compelled to set°
75   Upon one battle all our liberties.
You know that I held Epicurus strong,°
And his opinion; now I change my mind,
And partly credit things that do presage.°
Coming from Sardis, on our former° ensign

61 *peevish* childish (Octavius was 21)   61 *worthless* unworthy
62 *masker and a reveler* i.e., that dissipated Antony, who loved par-
ticipating in masques and wild parties (cf. I.ii.203–04, II.i.189,
II.ii.116)   66 *stomachs* inclination, appetite   68 *on the hazard* at
stake   74 *As Pompey was* (at Pharsalus where, having been persuaded to give battle against his will, he was decisively defeated and
later murdered)   74 *set* stake   76 *held Epicurus strong* believed
strongly in the philosophy of Epicurus (a materialist who believed that
because the gods were not interested in human affairs omens were to
be discounted)   78 *presage* foretell the future   79 *former* foremost

Two mighty eagles fell,° and there they perched,   80
Gorging and feeding from our soldiers' hands,
Who to Philippi here consorted° us.
This morning are they fled away and gone,
And in their steads do ravens, crows, and kites°
Fly o'er our heads and downward look on us   85
As we were sickly° prey; their shadows seem
A canopy most fatal,° under which
Our army lies, ready to give up the ghost.

Messala. Believe not so.

Cassius.   I but believe it partly,
For I am fresh of spirit and resolved   90
To meet all perils very constantly.°

Brutus. Even so, Lucilius.

Cassius.   Now, most noble Brutus,
The gods today stand friendly, that we may,
Lovers° in peace, lead on our days to age!
But since the affairs of men rests still incertain,°   95
Let's reason with the worst that may befall.°
If we do lose this battle, then is this
The very last time we shall speak together.
What are you then determinèd to do?

Brutus. Even by the rule of that philosophy°   100
By which I did blame Cato for the death
Which he did give himself; I know not how,
But I do find it cowardly and vile,
For fear of what might fall,° so to prevent°
The time° of life, arming myself with patience   105
To stay the providence° of some high powers
That govern us below.

fate

80 *fell* swooped down   82 *consorted* accompanied   84 *ravens, crows,
and kites* (scavengers; traditionally, they know when a battle is pending
and accompany the armies)   86 *sickly* ready for death   87 *fatal*
presaging death   91 *constantly* resolutely   94 *Lovers* devoted friends
95 *rests still incertain* always stand in doubt   96 *reason . . . befall*
consider what must be done if the worst happens   100 *that philosophy*
i.e., Stoicism   104 *fall* befall   104 *prevent* anticipate   105 *time* term,
natural end   106 *stay the providence* await the ordained fate

Cassius.   Then, if we lose this battle,
You are contented to be led in triumph°
Thorough the streets of Rome?

110 *Brutus.* No, Cassius, no; think not, thou noble Roman,
That ever Brutus will go bound to Rome;
He bears too great a mind. But this same day
Must end that work the ides of March begun;
And whether we shall meet again I know not.
115 Therefore our everlasting farewell take.
Forever, and forever, farewell, Cassius!
If we do meet again, why, we shall smile;
If not, why then this parting was well made.

Cassius. Forever, and forever, farewell, Brutus!
120 If we do meet again, we'll smile indeed;
If not, 'tis true this parting was well made.

Brutus. Why then, lead on. O, that a man might know
The end of this day's business ere it come!
But it sufficeth that the day will end,
125 And then the end is known. Come, ho! Away! *Exeunt.*

agree to kill themselves

[Scene II. *The field of battle.*]

Alarum.° Enter Brutus and Messala.

Brutus. Ride, ride, Messala, ride, and give these bills°
Unto the legions on the other side.°   *Loud alarum.*
Let them set on at once; for I perceive
But cold demeanor° in Octavius' wing,
5 And sudden push° gives them the overthrow.
Ride, ride, Messala! Let them all come down. *Exeunt.*

---

108 *in triumph* (as a captive) in the victor's procession   V.ii.1 s.d. *Alarum*
call to arms (drums or trumpets)   1 *bills* written orders   2 *side* wing
(commanded by Cassius)   4 *But cold demeanor* marked lack of spirit
in fighting   5 *push* attack

[Scene III. *The field of battle.*]

Alarums. Enter Cassius and Titinius.

Cassius. O, look, Titinius, look, the villains° fly!
  Myself have to mine own° turned enemy.
  This ensign° here of mine was turning back;
  I slew the coward, and did take it° from him.

Titinius. O Cassius, Brutus gave the word too early,   5
  Who, having some advantage on Octavius,
  Took it too eagerly; his soldiers fell to spoil,°
  Whilst we by Antony are all enclosed.

Enter Pindarus.

Pindarus. Fly further off, my lord, fly further off!
  Mark Antony is in your tents, my lord.   10
  Fly, therefore, noble Cassius, fly far° off!

Cassius. This hill is far enough. Look, look, Titinius!
  Are those my tents where I perceive the fire?

Titinius. They are, my lord.

Cassius.   Titinius, if thou lovest me,
  Mount thou my horse and hide thy spurs in him   15
  Till he have brought thee up to yonder troops
  And here again, that I may rest assured
  Whether yond troops are friend or enemy.

Titinius. I will be here again even with a thought.°
                           Exit.

Cassius. Go, Pindarus, get higher on that hill;   20

V.iii.1 *villains* i.e., cowardly soldiers of his own side 2 *mine own* my
own men 3 *ensign* standard-bearer 4 *it* i.e., the standard 7 *spoil*
looting 11 *far* farther 19 *even with a thought* as quickly as thought

My sight was ever thick.° Regard Titinius,
And tell me what thou not'st about the field.

[*Exit Pindarus.*]

This day I breathèd first. Time is come round,
And where I did begin, there shall I end.
25   My life is run his compass.° Sirrah, what news?

Pindarus. (*Above*)° O my lord!

Cassius. What news?

Pindarus. [*Above*] Titinius is enclosèd round about
With horsemen that make to him on the spur;°
30   Yet he spurs on. Now they are almost on him.
Now, Titinius! Now some light.° O, he lights too!
He's ta'en!° (*Shout.*) And, hark! They shout for joy.

Cassius. Come down; behold no more.
O, coward that I am, to live so long,
35   To see my best friend ta'en before my face!

Enter Pindarus.

Come hither, sirrah.
In Parthia did I take thee prisoner;
And then I swore thee, saving of° thy life,
That whatsoever I did bid thee do,
40   Thou shouldst attempt it. Come now, keep thine oath.
Now be a freeman, and with this good sword,
That ran through Caesar's bowels, search° this bosom.
Stand° not to answer. Here, take thou the hilts,
And when my face is covered, as 'tis now,
45   Guide thou the sword—Caesar, thou art revenged,
Even with the sword that killed thee.   [*Dies.*]

Pindarus. So, I am free; yet would not so have been,
Durst I have done my will. O Cassius!
Far from this country Pindarus shall run,
50   Where never Roman shall take note of him.   [*Exit.*]

21 *My ... thick* I have always been nearsighted   25 *is run his compass*
has completed its circuit   26 s.d. *Above* on the upper stage   29 *make
... spur* ride toward him at top speed   31 *light* dismount   32 *ta'en*
taken, captured   38 *swore ... of* made you swear, when I spared
42 *search* penetrate   43 *Stand* delay

Enter Titinius and Messala.

Messala. It is but change,° Titinius; for Octavius
  Is overthrown by noble Brutus' power,
  As Cassius' legions are by Antony.

Titinius. These tidings will well comfort Cassius.

Messala. Where did you leave him?

Titinius.   All disconsolate,   55
  With Pindarus his bondman, on this hill.

Messala. Is not that he that lies upon the ground?

Titinius. He lies not like the living. O my heart!

Messala. Is not that he?

Titinius.   No, this was he, Messala,
  But Cassius is no more. O setting sun,   60
  As in thy red rays thou dost sink to night,
  So in his red blood Cassius' day is set.
  The sun of Rome is set. Our day is gone;
  Clouds, dews,° and dangers come; our deeds are done!
  Mistrust of° my success hath done this deed.   65

Messala. Mistrust of good success hath done this deed.
  O hateful Error, Melancholy's child,°
  Why dost thou show to the apt° thoughts of men
  The things that are not? O Error, soon conceived,
  Thou never com'st unto a happy birth,   70
  But kill'st the mother° that engend'red thee!

Titinius. What, Pindarus! Where art thou, Pindarus?

Messala. Seek him, Titinius, whilst I go to meet
  The noble Brutus, thrusting this report
  Into his ears. I may say "thrusting" it;   75

51 *change* exchange (of fortune)   64 *dews* (considered unwholesome)
65 *Mistrust of* lack of confidence in   67 *Melancholy's child* (i.e., those
of despondent temperament are liable to be introspective and full of
imaginary fears)   68 *apt* easily impressed   71 *mother* i.e., the melancholy person, Cassius, who conceived the error

For piercing steel and darts envenomèd
Shall be as welcome to the ears of Brutus
As tidings of this sight.

Titinius.   Hie° you, Messala,
And I will seek for Pindarus the while.

                           [Exit Messala.]

80   Why didst thou send me forth, brave° Cassius?
Did I not meet thy friends, and did not they
Put on my brows this wreath of victory,
And bid me give it thee? Didst thou not hear their
     shouts?
Alas, thou hast misconstrued everything!
85   But hold thee,° take this garland on thy brow;
Thy Brutus bid me give it thee, and I
Will do his bidding. Brutus, come apace,°
And see how I regarded° Caius Cassius.
By your leave,° gods. This is a Roman's part:°
90   Come, Cassius' sword, and find Titinius' heart.   *Dies.*

Alarum. Enter Brutus, Messala, young Cato, Strato,
         Volumnius, and Lucilius.

Brutus. Where, where, Messala, doth his body lie?

Messala. Lo, yonder, and Titinius mourning it.

Brutus. Titinius' face is upward.

Cato.   He is slain.

Brutus. O Julius Caesar, thou art mighty yet!
95   Thy spirit walks abroad, and turns our swords
In our own proper° entrails.   *Low alarums.*

Cato.   Brave° Titinius!
Look, whe'r° he have not crowned dead Cassius.

Brutus. Are yet two Romans living such as these?
The last of all the Romans, fare thee well!

---

78 *Hie* hasten   80 *brave* noble   85 *hold thee* wait a moment   87
apace quickly   88 *regarded* honored   89 *By your leave* with your
permission (because he is ending his life before the time appointed by
the gods)   89 *part* role, duty   96 *own proper* (emphatic) very own
96 *Brave* noble   97 *whe'r* whether

It is impossible that ever Rome　　　　　　　　　　*100*
Should breed thy fellow.° Friends, I owe moe° tears
To this dead man than you shall see me pay.
I shall find time, Cassius; I shall find time.
Come, therefore, and to Thasos° send his body;
His funerals shall not be in our camp,　　　　　　　*105*
Lest it discomfort us.° Lucilius, come,
And come, young Cato; let us to the field.
Labeo and Flavius set our battles° on.
'Tis three o'clock; and, Romans, yet ere night
We shall try fortune in a second fight.　　*Exeunt.*　*110*

[Scene IV. *The field of battle.*]

*Alarum. Enter Brutus, Messala, [young] Cato, Lucilius,
and Flavius.*

Brutus. Yet, countrymen, O, yet hold up your heads!
　　　　　　　　　　　　[*Exit, with followers.*]
Cato. What bastard° doth not? Who will go with me?
I will proclaim my name about the field.
I am the son of Marcus Cato,° ho!
A foe to tyrants, and my country's friend.　　　　　*5*
I am the son of Marcus Cato, ho!

　　　　　　Enter Soldiers and fight.

Lucilius.° And I am Brutus, Marcus Brutus, I;
Brutus, my country's friend; know me for Brutus!
　　　　　　　　　　[*Young Cato falls.*]

101 *fellow* equal　　101 *moe* more　　104 *Thasos* an island near Philippi
106 *discomfort us* dishearten our troops　　108 *battles* armies　　V.iv.2
What bastard who is such a low fellow that he　　4 *son of Marcus
Cato* son of Cato of Utica, hence, brother of Brutus' wife　　7 *Lucilius*
(the Folio fails to provide a speech prefix for lines 7–8, but because it is
clear from Plutarch and from line 14 that Lucilius impersonates Brutus
it is plausible to attribute 7–8 to Lucilius)

O young and noble Cato, art thou down?
10 Why, now thou diest as bravely as Titinius,
And mayst be honored, being Cato's son.

[*First*] *Soldier*. Yield, or thou diest.

Lucilius.   Only I yield to die°.
There is so much° that thou wilt kill me straight;°
Kill Brutus, and be honored in his death.

15 [*First*] *Soldier*. We must not. A noble prisoner!

Enter Antony.

Second Soldier. Room, ho! Tell Antony, Brutus is ta'en.

First Soldier. I'll tell thee news. Here comes the general.
Brutus is ta'en, Brutus is ta'en, my lord.

Antony. Where is he? *not really—Lucilius is lying + [illegible]*

20 *Lucilius*. Safe, Antony; Brutus is safe enough.
I dare assure thee that no enemy
Shall ever take alive the noble Brutus.
The gods defend him from so great a shame!
When you do find him, or alive or dead,
25 He will be found like Brutus, like himself.°

Antony. This is not Brutus, friend, but, I assure you,
A prize no less in worth. Keep this man safe;
Give him all kindness. I had rather have
Such men my friends than enemies. Go on,
30 And see whe'r Brutus be alive or dead,
And bring us word unto Octavius' tent
How everything is chanced.°   *Exeunt.*

thinks Brutus captured

---

12 *Only I yield to die* I yield only to die   13 *so much* so great an induce-
ment, i.e., gaining great honor by killing Brutus (?), so much to be
blamed for(?), a sum of money (offered to the soldier) (?)   13 *straight*
immediately   25 *like himself* i.e., behaving in accordance with his
noble nature   32 *is chanced* has turned out

[Scene V. *The field of battle.*]

Enter Brutus, Dardanius, Clitus, Strato, and Volumnius.

Brutus. Come, poor remains° of friends, rest on this
   rock.

Clitus. Statilius showed the torchlight,° but, my lord,
   He came not back; he is or ta'en or slain.

Brutus. Sit thee down, Clitus. Slaying is the word;
   It is a deed in fashion. Hark thee, Clitus.   5
                                   [*Whispers.*]

Clitus. What, I, my lord? No, not for all the world!

Brutus. Peace then, no words.

Clitus.   I'll rather kill myself.

Brutus. Hark thee, Dardanius.   [*Whispers.*]

Dardanius.   Shall I do such a deed?

Clitus. O Dardanius!

Dardanius. O Clitus!   10

Clitus. What ill request did Brutus make to thee?

Dardanius. To kill him, Clitus. Look, he meditates.

Clitus. Now is that noble vessel° full of grief,
   That it runs over even at his eyes.

V.v.1 *poor remains* wretched survivors   2 *showed the torchlight*
(Statilius had volunteered to see if Cassius' camp was occupied by the
enemy; he signaled on arrival there but was obviously captured thereafter)   13 *vessel* (figurative for "human being." Also an allusion to
the small jars of tears offered to the dead)

15   *Brutus.* Come hither, good Volumnius; list° a word.

Volumnius. What says my lord?

Brutus.   Why, this, Volumnius:
    The ghost of Caesar hath appeared to me
    Two several° times by night; at Sardis once,
    And this last night here in Philippi fields.
    I know my hour is come.

20   *Volumnius.*   Not so, my lord.

Brutus. Nay, I am sure it is, Volumnius.
    Thou seest the world, Volumnius, how it goes;
    Our enemies have beat us to the pit.°   *Low alarums.*
    It is more worthy to leap in ourselves
25   Than tarry till they push us. Good Volumnius,
    Thou know'st that we two went to school together;
    Even for that our love of old, I prithee
    Hold thou my sword-hilts whilst I run on it.

Volumnius. That's not an office for a friend, my lord.
                                Alarum still.°

30   *Clitus.* Fly, fly, my lord, there is no tarrying here.

Brutus. Farewell to you; and you; and you, Volumnius.
    Strato, thou hast been all this while asleep;
    Farewell to thee too, Strato. Countrymen,
    My heart doth joy that yet in all my life
35   I found no man but he was true to me.
    I shall have glory by this losing day
    More than Octavius and Mark Antony
    By this vile conquest° shall attain unto.
    So fare you well at once,° for Brutus' tongue
40   Hath almost ended his life's history.
    Night hangs upon mine eyes; my bones would rest,

15 *list* hear   18 *several* separate   23 *pit* (1) trap for capturing wild
animals (2) grave   29 s.d. *still* continuing   38 *vile conquest* i.e., overthrow of the revolution against tyranny   39 *at once* without further
delay

That have but labored to attain this hour.°
     Alarum. Cry within, "Fly, fly, fly!"

Clitus. Fly, my lord, fly!

Brutus.   Hence! I will follow.
 [*Exeunt Clitus, Dardanius, and Volumnius.*]
I prithee, Strato, stay thou by thy lord,
Thou art a fellow of a good respect.°   45
Thy life hath had some smatch° of honor in it;
Hold then my sword, and turn away thy face,
While I do run upon it. Wilt thou, Strato?

Strato. Give me your hand first. Fare you well, my lord.

Brutus. Farewell, good Strato—Caesar, now be still; 50
I killed not thee with half so good a will.   *Dies.*

 Alarum. Retreat. Enter Antony, Octavius, Messala,
    Lucilius, and the Army.

Octavius. What man is that?

Messala. My master's man.° Strato, where is thy master?

Strato. Free from the bondage you are in, Messala;
The conquerors can but make a fire of him.   55
For Brutus only overcame himself,°
And no man else hath honor by his death.

Lucilius. So Brutus should be found. I thank thee,
  Brutus,
That thou hast proved Lucilius' saying° true.

Octavius. All that served Brutus, I will entertain° them. 60
Fellow, wilt thou bestow° thy time with me?

Strato. Ay, if Messala will prefer° me to you.

Octavius. Do so, good Messala.

---

42 *but . . . hour* i.e., worked hard only to reach this goal of death
(which brings, for a Stoic, rest from life's trials) 45 *respect* reputation
46 *smatch* smack, taste 53 *man* servant 56 *Brutus only overcame
himself* only Brutus overcame Brutus 59 *saying* (see V.iv.21–25)
60 *entertain* take into service 61 *bestow* spend 62 *prefer* recommend

Messala. How died my master, Strato?

65 *Strato.* I held the sword, and he did run on it.

Messala. Octavius, then take him to follow thee,
That did the latest° service to my master.

Antony. This was the noblest Roman of them all.
All the conspirators save only he
70 Did that they did in envy of great Caesar;
He, only in a general honest thought
And common good to all, made one of them.°
His life was gentle,° and the elements°
So mixed° in him that Nature might stand up
And say to all the world, "This was a man!"

Octavius. According to his virtue,° let us use° him
With all respect and rites of burial.
Within my tent his bones tonight shall lie,
Most like a soldier ordered honorably.°
80 So call the field° to rest, and let's away
To part° the glories of this happy day.   *Exeunt omnes.*

FINIS

---

67 *latest* last   71–72 *He only . . . them* he, moved only by impersonal motives directed to the good of the community, joined the conspirators   73 *gentle* noble   73 *elements* (the four opposed elements, of which all nature was thought to be composed, were represented in the human body by the four liquids, bile, phlegm, blood, and choler; the dominance of one of these determined a man's temperament—melancholic, phlegmatic, sanguine, or choleric)   74 *So mixed* i.e., so well-balanced   76 *virtue* excellence   76 *use* treat   79 *ordered honorably* arrayed (and treated) with all honor   80 *field* army   81 *part* divide

Textual Note

The First Folio of 1623 provides us with the text for *Julius Caesar;* there are no early quarto editions. In setting this play for the press, the printer's compositors probably worked from the playhouse promptbook, for the Folio text contains remarkably few misprints, serious errors in punctuation, or misattribution of speeches. The stage directions, unusually numerous and detailed, also suggest a stage manager's prompt copy; stage directions like "Alarum still" and "Enter Boy with wine and tapers" are obviously closely connected with actual performance.

In the present edition, the names of characters have been normalized so that *Marullus* appears for the Folio Murellus (and Murrellus), *Casca* for Caska, *Lucilius* for Lucillius. Occasionally the Folio uses the forms "Antonio" (I.ii.3, 4, 6, 190; I.iii.37), "Claudio" (IV.iii.241, 243, 243 s.d., 288), "Flavio," "Labio" (V.iii.108), "Octavio" (III.i.275 s.d., V.ii.4), "Varrus" (IV.iii.243, 243 s.d., 288); these are standardized, appearing as *Antonius, Claudius, Flavius, Labeo, Octavius,* and *Varro.* The present edition modernizes spelling and punctuation, corrects a few obvious misprints, translates the act divisions from Latin into English, expands the speech prefixes, and alters the lineation of a few passages. The only other substantial departures from the Folio are listed below, the present reading in italics and then the Folio's reading in roman.

I.iii.129 *In favor's* Is Fauors
II.i.40. *ides* first   213 *eighth* eight

II.ii.19 *fought* fight   23 *did neigh* do neigh   46 *are* heare

III.i.39 *law* lane   113 *states* State   115 *lies* lye   283 *for* from

III.ii.106 *art* are

IV.iii.253 *not* it not

V.i.41 *teeth* teethes

V.iii.104 *Thasos* Tharsus

V.iv.7 *Lucilius* [F omits, and prints "Lucilius" as the prefix to line 9]

The Source of "Julius Caesar"

Shakespeare's main source for *Julius Caesar* was Sir Thomas North's translation of Plutarch's *The Lives of the Noble Grecians and Romans*, printed in 1579 and again in 1595. A classicist might be somewhat alarmed to learn that North translated not from the Greek of Plutarch but the French translation of Jacques Amyot. A student, unaware of the practice of Elizabethan dramatists, might be taken aback by Shakespeare's close adherence to various sources in writing his plays. Indeed, Shakespeare's use of Plutarch is detailed, literal, and incontrovertible. Sometimes he seems to versify directly from the book; at other times he selects, cuts, compresses, and amalgamates events from the full range of Plutarch's material dealing with the history of Julius Caesar. A complete understanding of his skill can be gained only by reading through Plutarch's comparisons of Demetrius and Antony, Dion and Brutus, and more particularly, the chapters on Julius Caesar, Brutus, and Antony, where we sometimes find three variant accounts of the same event, from each of which Shakespeare has taken some details to construct his own version.

Since it was impossible to give a complete selection of versions for each event of the play, let alone indicate all the historical events that Shakespeare does not use, we present one version of each happening—the one that seems closest to Shakespeare's own dramatization—and arrange these to read as a connected story. In addition, we add some brief selections to give a fuller view of each main character in the story. This use of extracts has inevitably led to some omissions and overlapping; however, we hope that readers will be stimulated to go to the sources themselves.

A number of other sources, besides Plutarch, have been suggested for this play, and those who are interested will find comprehensive discussions of this subject in the introduction to the New Arden edition of *Julius Caesar*, edited by T. S. Dorsch, and in Kenneth Muir's book, *Shakespeare's Sources* (Vol. I). Although Shakespeare must of course have used a sixteenth-century edition of North's Plutarch, because the 1612 edition—reprinted in modernized spelling by Walter W. Skeat, *Shakespeare's Plutarch* (Macmillan, 1875)—is the only one readily available to most readers, the selections below have been drawn from Skeat, and Skeat's page numbers have been given. In these selections the 1612 edition has no additions or subtractions in matters of substance; the only differences are trivial ones (e.g., "O Ligarius" vs. "Ligarius") that do not affect the study of Shakespeare's use of Plutarch.

Selections from *The Lives of the Noble Grecians and Romans*

CAESAR OVERCOMES THE SONS OF POMPEY

After all these things were ended, he was chosen Consul the fourth time, and went into Spain to make war with the sons of Pompey: who were yet but very young, but had notwithstanding raised a marvelous great army together and showed they had manhood and courage worthy to command such an army, insomuch as they put Caesar himself in great danger of his life. The greatest battle that was fought between them in all this war was by the city of Munda. For then Caesar, seeing his men sorely distressed, and having their hands full of their enemies, he ran into the press among his men that fought, and cried out unto them: "What, are ye not ashamed to be beaten and taken prisoners, yielding yourselves with your own hands to these young boys?" And so, with all the force he could make, having with much ado put his enemies to flight, he slew above thirty thousand of them in the field, and lost of his own men a thousand of the best he had. After this battle he went into his tent and told his friends that he had often before fought for victory, but, this last time now, that he had fought for the safety of his own life. He won this battle on the very feast day of the Bacchanalians, in the which men say that Pompey the Great went out of Rome, about four years before, to begin this civil war. For his sons, the younger scaped from the battle; but, within few days after, Didius brought the head of the elder. This was the last war that Caesar made. But the triumph he made into Rome for the same did as much offend the Romans, and more, than anything that ever he had done before: because he had not overcome captains that were strangers, nor barbarous kings, but had destroyed the sons of the noblest man of Rome, whom fortune had overthrown. And because he had plucked up his race by the roots, men did not think it meet for him to triumph so for the calamities of his country, rejoicing at a thing for the which he had but one excuse to allege in his defense unto the gods and men, that he was compelled to do that he did. And the rather they thought it not meet, because he had never before sent letters nor messengers unto the commonwealth at Rome, for any victory that he had ever won in all the civil wars: but did always for shame refuse the glory of it. [*The Life of Julius Caesar*, pp. 91–92.]

CAESAR IS GIVEN DICTATORIAL POWERS

This notwithstanding, the Romans, inclining to Caesar's prosperity and taking the bit in the mouth, supposing that to be ruled by one man alone, it would be a good mean for them to take breath a little, after so many troubles and miseries as they had abidden in these civil wars, they chose him perpetual Dictator. This was a plain tyranny: for to this absolute power of Dictator, they added this, never to be afraid to be deposed. Cicero pronounced before the Senate, that they should give him such honors as were meet for a man: howbeit others afterwards added too honors beyond all reason. For men striving who should most honor him, they made him hateful and troublesome to themselves that most favored him, by reason of the unmeasurable greatness and honors which they gave him. Thereupon it is reported, that even they that most hated him were no less favorers and furtherers of his honors than they that most flattered him, because they might have greater occasions to rise, and that it might appear they had just cause and color to attempt that they did against him. And now for himself, after he had ended his civil wars, he did so honorably behave himself, that there was no fault to be found in him: and therefore methinks, amongst other honors they gave him, he rightly deserved this, that they should build him a temple of Clemency, to thank him for his courtesy he had used unto them in his victory. For he pardoned many of them that had borne arms against him, and furthermore, did prefer some of them to honor and office in the commonwealth: as, amongst others, Cassius and Brutus, both the which were made Praetors. And, where Pompey's images had been thrown down, he caused them to be set up again: whereupon Cicero said then, that, Caesar setting up Pompey's images again, he made his own to stand the surer. And when some of his friends did counsel him to have a guard for the safety of his person, and some also did offer themselves to serve him, he would never consent to it, but said: "It was better to die once than always to be afraid of death." [*The Life of Julius Caesar*, p. 92.]

CAESAR'S AMBITION

But the chiefest cause that made him mortally hated was the covetous desire he had to be called king: which first gave the people just cause, and next his secret enemies honest color, to bear him ill will. This notwithstanding, they that procured him this honor and dignity gave it out among the people that it was written in the Sibylline prophecies, "how the Romans might overcome the Parthians, if they made war with them and were led by a king, but otherwise that they were unconquerable." And furthermore they were so bold besides, that, Caesar returning to Rome from the city of Alba, when they came to salute him, they called him king. But the people being offended, and Caesar also angry, he said he was not called king, but Caesar. Then every man keeping silence, he went his way heavy and sorrowful. When they had decreed divers honors for him in the Senate, the Consuls and Praetors, accompanied with the whole assembly of the Senate, went unto him in the market place, where he was set by the pulpit for orations, to tell him what honors they had decreed for him in his absence. But he, sitting still in his majesty, disdaining to rise up unto them when they came in, as if they had been private men, answered them: "that his honors had more need to be cut off than enlarged." This did not only offend the Senate but the common people also, to see that he should so lightly esteem of the magistrates of the commonwealth: insomuch as every man that might lawfully go his way departed thence very sorrowfully. Thereupon also Caesar rising departed home to his house, and tearing open his doublet collar, making his neck bare, he cried out aloud to his friends, "that his throat was ready to offer to any man that would come and cut it." Notwithstanding it is reported that afterwards, to excuse his folly, he imputed it to his disease, saying, "that their wits are not perfect which have this disease of the falling evil, when standing on their feet they speak to the common people, but are soon troubled with a trembling of their body, and a sudden dimness and giddiness." But that was not true, for he would have risen up to the Senate, but Cornelius Balbus one of his friends (or rather a flatterer) would not let him, saying: "What, do you not remember that you are Caesar, and will you not let them reverence you and do their duties?" [*The Life of Julius Caesar*, pp. 94–95.]

CAESAR REFUSES THE CROWN

Besides these occasions and offenses, there followed also his shame and reproach, abusing the Tribunes of the people in this sort. At that time the feast *Lupercalia* was celebrated, the which in old time men say was the feast of shepherds or herdmen, and is much like unto the feast of the Lycaeans in Arcadia. But howsoever it is, that day there are divers noblemen's sons, young men (and some of them magistrates themselves that govern them), which run naked through the city, striking in sport them they meet in their way with leather thongs, hair and all on, to make them give place. And many noblewomen and gentlewomen also go of purpose to stand in their way, and do put forth their hands to be stricken, as scholars hold them out to their schoolmaster to be stricken with the ferula: persuading themselves that, being with child, they shall have good delivery; and so, being barren, that it will make them to conceive with child. Caesar sat to behold that sport upon the pulpit for orations, in a chair of gold, appareled in triumphant manner. Antonius, who was Consul at that time, was one of them that ran this holy course. So when he came into the market place, the people made a lane for him to run at liberty, and he came to Caesar, and presented him a diadem wreathed about with laurel. Whereupon there rose a certain cry of rejoicing, not very great, done only by a few appointed for the purpose. But when Caesar refused the diadem, then all the people together made an outcry of joy. [*The Life of Julius Caesar*, pp. 95–96.]

Antonius again did put it on his head: Caesar again refused it: and thus they were striving off and on a great while together. As oft as Antonius did put this laurel crown unto him, a few of his followers rejoiced at it: and as oft also as Caesar refused it, all the people together clapped their hands. And this was a wonderful thing, that they suffered all things subjects should do by commandment of their kings: and yet they could not abide the name of a king, detesting it as the utter destruction of their liberty. Caesar, in a rage, arose out of his seat, and plucking down the collar of his gown from his neck, he showed it naked, bidding any man strike off his head that would. This laurel crown was afterwards put upon the head of one of Caesar's statues or images, the which one of the tribunes plucked off. The people liked his doing therein so well that they waited on him home to his house, with great clapping of hands. Howbeit Caesar did turn them out of their offices for it. [*The Life of Marcus Antonius*, p. 164.]

ATTEMPTS TO TURN BRUTUS AGAINST CAESAR

Hereupon the people went straight unto Marcus Brutus, who from his father came of the first Brutus, and by his mother of the house of the Servilians, a noble house as any was in Rome, and was also nephew and son-in-law of Marcus Cato. Notwithstanding, the great honors and favor Caesar showed unto him kept him back that of himself alone he did not conspire nor consent to depose him of his kingdom. For Caesar did not only save his life after the battle of Pharsalia, when Pompey fled, and did at his request also save many mo of his friends besides: but furthermore, he put a marvelous confidence in him. For he had already preferred him to the Praetorship for that year, and further-more was appointed to be Consul the fourth year after that, having through Caesar's friendship obtained it before Cassius, who likewise made suit for the same: and Caesar also, as it is reported, said in this contention, "Indeed Cassius hath alleged best reason, but yet shall he not be chosen before Brutus." Some one day accusing Brutus while he practiced this conspiracy, Caesar would not hear of it, but, clapping his hand on his body, told them, "Brutus will look for this skin": meaning thereby, that Brutus for his virtue deserved to rule after him, but yet that, for ambition's sake, he would not show himself unthankful or dishonorable. Now they that desired change, and wished Brutus only their prince and governor above all other, they durst not come to him themselves to tell him what they would have him to do, but in the night did cast sundry papers into the Praetor's seat, where he gave audience, and the most of them to this effect: "Thou sleepest, Brutus, and art not Brutus indeed." Cassius, finding Brutus' ambition stirred up the more by these seditious bills, did prick him forward and egg him on the more, for a private quarrel he had conceived against Caesar: the circumstance whereof we have set down more at large in Brutus' life. Caesar also had Cassius in great jealousy, and suspected him much: whereupon he said on a time to his friends, "What will Cassius do, think ye? I like not his pale looks." Another time when Caesar's friends complained unto him of Antonius and Dolabella, that they pretended some mischief towards him: he answered them again, "As for those fat men and smooth-combed heads," quoth he, "I never reckon of them; but these pale-visaged and carrion-lean people, I fear them most," meaning Brutus and Cassius. [*The Life of Julius Caesar*, pp. 96–97.]

The Conspiracy Is Formed

Now when Cassius felt his friends, and did stir them up against Caesar: they all agreed, and promised to take part with him, so Brutus were the chief of their conspiracy. For they told him that so high an enterprise and attempt as that, did not so much require men of manhood and courage to draw their swords, as it stood them upon to have a man of such estimation as Brutus, to make every man boldly think, that by his only presence the fact were holy and just. If he took not this course, then that they should go to it with fainter hearts; and when they had done it, they should be more fearful: because every man would think that Brutus would not have refused to have made one with them, if the cause had been good and honest. Therefore Cassius, considering this matter with himself, did first of all speak to Brutus, since they grew strange together for the suit they had for the praetorship. So when he was reconciled to him again, and that they had embraced one another, Cassius asked him if he were determined to be in the Senate House the first day of the month of March, because he heard say that Caesar's friends should move the council that day, that Caesar should be called king by the Senate. Brutus answered him, he would not be there. "But if we be sent for," said Cassius, "how then?" "For myself then," said Brutus, "I mean not to hold my peace, but to withstand it, and rather die than lose my liberty."

Cassius being bold, and taking hold of this word: "Why," quoth he, "what Roman is he alive that will suffer thee to die for thy liberty? What? Knowest thou not that thou art Brutus? Thinkest thou that they be cobblers, tapsters, or suchlike base mechanical people, that write these bills and scrolls which are found daily in thy Praetor's chair, and not the noblest men and best citizens that do it? No; be thou well assured that of other Praetors they look for gifts, common distributions amongst the people, and for common plays, and to see fencers fight at the sharp, to show the people pastime: but at thy hands they specially require (as a due debt unto them) the taking away of the tyranny, being fully bent to suffer any extremity for thy sake, so that thou wilt show thyself to be the man thou art taken for, and that they hope thou art." Thereupon he kissed Brutus and embraced him: and so each taking leave of other, they went both to speak with their friends about it. Now amongst Pompey's friends, there was one called Caius Ligarius, who had been accused unto Caesar for taking part with Pompey, and Caesar discharged him. But Ligarius thanked not Caesar so much for his discharge, as he was offended with him for that he was brought in danger by his tyrannical power; and therefore in his heart he was always his mortal enemy, and was besides very familiar with Brutus, who went to see him being sick in his bed, and said unto him: "Ligarius, in what a time art thou sick?" Ligarius rising up in his bed, and taking him by the right hand, said unto him: "Brutus," said he, "if thou hast any great enterprise in hand worthy of thyself, I am whole."

After that time they began to feel all their acquaintance whom they trusted, and laid their heads together, consulting upon it, and did not only pick out their friends, but all those also whom they thought stout enough to attempt any desperate matter, and that were not afraid to lose their lives. For this cause they durst not acquaint Cicero with their conspiracy, although he was a man whom they loved dearly, and trusted best: for they were afraid that he being a coward by nature, and age also having increased his fear, he would quite turn and alter all their purpose, and quench the heat of their enterprise (the which specially required hot and earnest execution), seeking by persuasion to bring all things to such safety, as there should be no peril. Brutus also did let other of his friends alone, as Statilius Epicurian, and Faonius, that made profession to follow Marcus Cato: because that, having cast out words afar off, disputing together in philosophy to feel their minds, Faonius answered, "that civil war was worse than tyrannical government usurped against the law." [*The Life of Marcus Brutus*, pp. 112–14.]

Brutus and Porcia Are Troubled

Furthermore, the only name and great calling of Brutus did bring on the most of them to give consent to this conspiracy: who having never taken oaths together, nor taken or given any caution or assurance, nor binding themselves one to another by any religious oaths, they all kept the matter so secret to themselves, and could so cunningly handle it, that notwithstanding the gods did reveal it by manifest signs and tokens from above, and by predictions of sacrifices, yet all this would not be believed. Now Brutus, who knew very well that for his sake all the noblest, valiantest, and most courageous men of Rome did venture their lives, weighing with himself the greatness of the danger: when he was out of his house, he did so frame and fashion his countenance and looks that no man could discern he had anything to trouble his mind. But when night came that he was in his own house, then he was clean changed: for either care did wake him against his will when he would have slept, or else oftentimes of himself he fell into such deep thoughts of this enterprise, casting in his mind all the dangers that might happen: that his wife, lying by him, found that there was some marvelous great matter that troubled his mind, not being wont to be in that taking, and that he could not well determine with himself.

His wife Porcia (as we have told you before) was the daughter of Cato, whom Brutus married being his cousin, not a maiden, but a young widow after the death of her first husband Bibulus, by whom she had also a young son called Bibulus, who afterwards wrote a book of the acts and gests of Brutus, extant at this present day. This young lady, being excellently well seen in philosophy, loving her husband well, and being of a noble courage, as she was also wise: because she would not ask her husband what he ailed before she had made some proof by herself: she took a little razor, such as barbers occupy to pare men's nails, and, causing her maids and women to go out of her chamber, gave herself a great gash withal in her thigh, that she was straight all of a gore blood: and incontinently after a vehement fever took her, by reason of the pain of her wound. Then perceiving her husband was marvelously out of quiet, and that he could take no rest, even in her greatest pain of all she spoke in this sort unto him: "I being, O Brutus," said she, "the daughter of Cato, was married unto thee; not to be thy bedfellow and companion in bed and at board only, like a harlot, but to be partaker also with thee of thy good and evil fortune. Now for thyself, I can find no cause of fault in thee touching our match: but for my part, how may I show my duty towards thee and how much I would do for thy sake, if I cannot constantly bear a secret mischance or grief with thee, which requireth secrecy and fidelity? I confess that a woman's wit commonly is too weak to keep a secret safely: but yet, Brutus, good education and the company of virtuous men have some power to reform the defect of nature. And for myself, I have this benefit moreover, that I am the daughter of Cato, and wife of Brutus. This notwithstanding, I did not trust to any of these things before, until that now I have found by experience that no pain or grief whatsoever can overcome me." With those words she showed him her wound on her thigh, and told him what she had done to prove herself. Brutus was amazed to hear what she said unto him, and lifting up his hands to heaven, he besought the gods to give him the grace he might bring his enterprise to so good pass, that he might be found a husband worthy of so noble a wife as Porcia: so he then did comfort her the best he could. [*The Life of Marcus Brutus*, pp. 114–16.]

OMENS AND EVENTS PRECEDING THE MURDER

Certainly destiny may easier be foreseen than avoided, considering the strange and wonderful signs that were said to be seen before Caesar's death. For, touching the fires in the element, and spirits running up and down in the night, and also the solitary birds to be seen at noondays sitting in the great market place, are not all these signs perhaps worth the noting, in such a wonderful chance as happened? But

Strabo the philosopher writeth, that divers men were seen going up and down in fire: and furthermore, that there was a slave of the soldiers that did cast a marvelous burning flame out of his hand, insomuch as they that saw it thought he had been burnt; but when the fire was out, it was found he had no hurt. Caesar self also doing sacrifice unto the gods, found that one of the beasts which was sacrificed had no heart: and that was a strange thing in nature, how a beast could live without a heart. Furthermore there was a certain soothsayer that had given Caesar warning long time afore, to take heed of the day of the Ides of March (which is the fifteenth of the month), for on that day he should be in great danger. That day being come, Caesar going unto the Senate House, and speaking merrily unto the soothsayer, told him, "The Ides of March be come": "So they be," softly answered the soothsayer, "but yet are they not past." And the very day before, Caesar, supping with Marcus Lepidus, sealed certain letters, as he was wont to do, at the board: so, talk falling out amongst them, reasoning what death was best, he, preventing their opinions, cried out aloud, "Death unlooked for." Then going to bed the same night, as his manner was, and lying with his wife Calpurnia, all the windows and doors of his chamber flying open, the noise awoke him, and made him afraid when he saw such light: but more, when he heard his wife Calpurnia, being fast asleep, weep and sigh, and put forth many fumbling lamentable speeches: for she dreamed that Caesar was slain, and that she had him in her arms. Others also do deny that she had any such dream, as, amongst other, Titus Livius writeth that it was in this sort: the Senate having set upon the top of Caesar's house, for an ornament and setting forth of the same, a certain pinnacle, Calpurnia dreamed that she saw it broken down, and that she thought she lamented and wept for it. Insomuch that, Caesar rising in the morning, she prayed him, if it were possible, not to go out of the doors that day, but to adjourn the session of the Senate until another day. And if that he made no reckoning of her dream, yet that he would search further of the soothsayers by their sacrifices, to know what should happen him that day. Thereby it seemed that Caesar likewise did fear or suspect some-

what, because his wife Calpurnia until that time was never
given to any fear and superstition: and that then he saw
her so troubled in mind with this dream she had. But much
more afterwards, when the soothsayers having sacrificed
many beasts one after another, told him that none did like
them: then he determined to send Antonius to adjourn the
session of the Senate.

But in the meantime came Decius Brutus, surnamed
Albinus, in whom Caesar put such confidence, that in his
last will and testament he had appointed him to be his next
heir, and yet was of the conspiracy with Cassius and Brutus:
he, fearing that if Caesar did adjourn the session that day,
the conspiracy would be betrayed, laughed at the soothsayers, and reproved Caesar, saying, "that he gave the
Senate occasion to mislike with him, and that they might
think he mocked them, considering that by his commandment they were assembled, and that they were ready willingly
to grant him all things, and to proclaim him king of all his
provinces of the Empire of Rome out of Italy, and that he
should wear his diadem in all other places both by sea and
land. And furthermore, that if any man should tell them
from him they should depart for that present time, and
return again when Calpurnia should have better dreams,
what would his enemies and ill-willers say, and how could
they like of his friends' words? And who could persuade
them otherwise, but that they would think his dominion a
slavery unto them and tyrannical in himself? And yet if it
be so," said he, "that you utterly mislike of this day, it is
better that you go yourself in person, and, saluting the
Senate, to dismiss them till another time." Therewithal he
took Caesar by the hand, and brought him out of his
house. Caesar was not gone far from his house, but a bondman, a stranger, did what he could to speak with him: and
when he saw he was put back by the great press and multitude of people that followed him, he went straight into his
house, and put himself into Calpurnia's hands, to be kept
till Caesar came back again, telling her that he had greater
matters to impart unto him. And one Artemidorus also,
born in the isle of Gnidos, a doctor of rhetoric in the Greek
tongue, who by means of his profession was very familiar

with certain of Brutus' confederates, and therefore knew the most part of all their practices against Caesar, came and brought him a little bill, written with his own hand, of all that he meant to tell him. He, marking how Caesar received all the supplications that were offered him, and that he gave them straight to his men that were about him, pressed nearer to him, and said: "Caesar, read this memorial to yourself, and that quickly, for they be matters of great weight, and touch you nearly." Caesar took it of him, but could never read it, though he many times attempted it, for the number of people that did salute him: but holding it still in his hand, keeping it to himself, went on withal into the Senate House. Howbeit others are of opinion, that it was some man else that gave him that memorial, and not Artemidorus, who did what he could all the way as he went to give it Caesar, but he was always repulsed by the people. For these things, they may seem to come by chance; but the place where the murder was prepared, and where the Senate were assembled, and where also there stood up an image of Pompey dedicated by himself amongst other ornaments which he gave unto the theater, all these were manifest proofs that it was the ordinance of some god that made this treason to be executed, specially in that very place. It is also reported that Cassius (though otherwise he did favor the doctrine of Epicurus) beholding the image of Pompey, before they entered into the action of their traitorous enterprise, he did softly call upon it to aid him: but the instant danger of the present time, taking away his former reason, did suddenly put him into a furious passion, and made him like a man half beside himself. [*The Life of Julius Caesar*, pp. 97–100.]

. . . One came unto Casca being a conspirator, and taking him by the hand, said unto him: "O Casca, thou keptest it close from me, but Brutus hath told me all." Casca being amazed at it, the other went on with his tale, and said: "Why, how now, how cometh it to pass thou art thus rich, that thou dost sue to be Aedilis?" Thus Casca being deceived by the other's doubtful words, he told them it was a thousand to one, he blabbed not out all the conspiracy. Another Senator, called Popilius Laena, after he had saluted Brutus and Cassius more friendly than he was wont to do, he rounded softly in their ears, and told them: "I pray the gods you may go through with that you have taken in hand; but withal, dispatch, I read you, for your enterprise is betrayed." When he had said, he presently departed from them, and left them both afraid that their conspiracy would out.

Now in the meantime, there came one of Brutus' men posthaste unto him, and told him his wife was a-dying. For Porcia, being very careful and pensive for that which was to come, and being too weak to away with so great and inward grief of mind, she could hardly keep within, but was frighted with every little noise and cry she heard, as those that are taken and possessed with the fury of the Bacchantes; asking every man that came from the market place what Brutus did, and still sent messenger after messenger, to know what news. At length Caesar's coming being prolonged (as you have heard), Porcia's weakness was not able to hold out any longer, and thereupon she suddenly swooned, that she had no leisure to go to her chamber, but was taken in the midst of her house, where her speech and senses failed her. Howbeit she soon came to herself again, and so was laid in her bed and attended by her women. When Brutus heard these news, it grieved him, as it is to be presupposed: yet he left not off the care of his country and commonwealth, neither went home to his house for any news he heard. [*The Life of Marcus Brutus*, p. 117.]

When Caesar came out of his litter, Popilius Laena (that had talked before with Brutus and Cassius, and had prayed the gods they might bring this enterprise to pass) went unto Caesar and kept him a long time with a talk. Caesar gave good ear unto him: wherefore the conspirators (if so they should be called) not hearing what he said to Caesar, but conjecturing by that he had told them a little before that his talk was none other but the very discovery of their conspiracy, they were afraid, every man of them: and, one looking in another's face, it was easy to see that they all were of a mind, that it was no tarrying for them till they were apprehended, but rather that they should kill themselves with their own hands. And when Cassius and certain other clapped their hands on their swords under their gowns to draw them, Brutus, marking the countenance and gesture of Laena, and considering that he did use himself rather like an humble and earnest suitor than like an accuser, he said nothing to his companions (because there were many amongst them that were not of the conspiracy) but with a pleasant countenance encouraged Cassius. And immediately after Laena went from Caesar, and kissed his hand; which showed plainly that it was for some matter concerning himself that he had held him so long in talk. [*The Life of Marcus Brutus*, p. 118.]

THE ASSASSINATION

Now Antonius, that was a faithful friend to Caesar, and a valiant man besides of his hands, him Decius Brutus Albinus entertained out of the Senate House, having begun a long tale of set purpose. So Caesar coming into the house, all the Senate stood up on their feet to do him honor. Then part of Brutus' company and confederates stood round about Caesar's chair, and part of them also came towards him, as though they made suit with Metellus Cimber, to call home his brother again from banishment: and thus prosecuting still their suit, they followed Caesar till he was set in his chair. Who denying their petitions, and being offended with them one after another, because the more they were denied the more they pressed upon him and were the earnester with him, Metellus at length, taking his gown with both his hands, pulled it over his neck, which was the sign given the confederates to set upon him. Then Casca, behind him, struck him in the neck with his sword; howbeit the wound was not great nor mortal, because it seemed the fear of such a devilish attempt did amaze him and take his strength from him, that he killed him not at the first blow. But Caesar, turning straight unto him, caught hold of his sword and held it hard: and they both cried out, Caesar in Latin: "O vile traitor Casca, what doest thou?" and Casca, in Greek, to his brother: "Brother, help me." At the beginning of this stir, they that were present, not knowing of the conspiracy, were so amazed with the horrible sight they saw, they had no power to fly, neither to help him, nor so much as once to make an outcry. They on the other side that had conspired his death compassed him in on every side with their swords drawn in their hands, that Caesar turned him nowhere but he was stricken at by some, and still had naked swords in his face, and was hackled and mangled among them, as a wild beast taken of hunters. For it was agreed among them that every man should give him a wound, because all their parts should be in this murder: and then Brutus himself gave him one wound about his privities. Men report also, that Caesar did still defend himself against the rest, running every way with his body: but when he saw Brutus with his sword drawn in his hand, then he pulled his gown over his head, and made no more resistance, and was driven either casually or purposedly, by the counsel of the conspirators, against the base whereupon Pompey's image stood, which ran all of a gore blood till he was slain. Thus it seemed that the image took just revenge of Pompey's enemy, being thrown down on the ground at his feet, and yielding up the ghost there, for the number of wounds he had upon him. For it is reported, that he had three-and-twenty wounds upon his body: and divers of the conspirators did hurt themselves, striking one body with so many blows. [*The Life of Julius Caesar*, pp.100–01.]

Caesar being slain in this manner, Brutus, standing in the midst of the house, would have spoken and stayed the other Senators that were not of the conspiracy, to have told them the reason why they had done this fact. But they, as men both afraid and amazed, fled one upon another's neck in haste to get out at the door, and no man followed them. For it was set down and agreed between them that they should kill no man but Caesar only, and should entreat all the rest to look to defend their liberty. All the conspirators, but Brutus, determining upon this matter, thought it good also to kill Antonius, because he was a wicked man, and that in nature favored tyranny: besides also, for that he was in great estimation with soldiers, having been conversant of long time amongst them: and especially having a mind bent to great enterprises, he was also of great authority at that time, being Consul with Caesar. But Brutus would not agree to it. First, for that he said it was not honest: secondly, because he told them there was hope of change in him. For he did not mistrust but that Antonius, being a noble-minded and courageous man (when he should know that Caesar was dead), would willingly help his country to recover her liberty, having them an example unto him to follow their courage and virtue. So Brutus by this means saved Antonius' life, who at that present time disguised himself and stole away: but Brutus and his consorts, having their swords bloody in their hands, went straight to the Capitol, persuading the Romans as they went to take their liberty again. Now at the first time, when the murder was newly done, there were sudden outcries of people that ran up and down the city, the which indeed did the more increase the fear and tumult. But when they saw they slew no man, neither did spoil or make havoc of anything, then certain of the Senators and many of the people, emboldening themselves, went to the Capitol unto them. [*The Life of Marcus Brutus*, pp. 119–20.]

PUBLIC REACTION; ANTONY GAINS CONTROL

There, a great number of men being assembled together one after another, Brutus made an oration unto them, to win the favor of the people, and to justify that they had done. All those that were by said they had done well, and cried unto them that they should boldly come down from the Capitol: whereupon Brutus and his companions came boldly down into the market place. The rest followed in troupe, but Brutus went foremost, very honorably compassed in round about with the noblest men of the city, which brought him from the Capitol, through the market place, to the pulpit for orations. When the people saw him in the pulpit, although they were a multitude of rakehells of all sorts, and had a good will to make some stir; yet, being ashamed to do it, for the reverence they bore unto Brutus, they kept silence to hear what he would say. When Brutus began to speak, they gave him quiet audience: howbeit, immediately after, they showed that they were not all contented with the murder. For when another, called Cinna, would have spoken, and began to accuse Caesar, they fell into a great uproar among them, and marvelously reviled him; insomuch that the conspirators returned again into the Capitol. There Brutus, being afraid to be besieged, sent back again the noblemen that came thither with him, thinking it no reason that they, which were no partakers of the murder, should be partakers of the danger. Then the next morning, the Senate being assembled, and held within the temple of the goddess Tellus, to wit, the Earth: and Antonius, Plancus, and Cicero, having made a motion to the Senate in that assembly that they should take an order to pardon and forget all that was past, and to establish friendship and peace again: it was decreed, that they should not only be pardoned, but also that the Consuls should refer it to the Senate, what honors should be appointed unto them. This being agreed upon, the Senate broke up; and Antonius the Consul, to put them in heart that were in the Capitol, sent them his son for a pledge. Upon this assurance, Brutus and his companions came down from the Capitol, where every man saluted and embraced each other; among the which Antonius himself did bid Cassius to supper to him, and Lepidus also bade Brutus; and so one bade another, as they had friendship and acquaintance together.

The next day following, the Senate, being called again to council, did first of all commend Antonius, for that he had wisely stayed and quenched the beginning of a civil war: then they also gave Brutus and his consorts great praises; and lastly they appointed them several governments of provinces. For unto Brutus they appointed Crete; Africa unto Cassius; Asia unto Trebonius; Bithynia unto Cimber; and unto the other, Decius Brutus Albinus, Gaul on this side of the Alps. When this was done, they came to talk of Caesar's will and testament and of his funerals and tomb. Then Antonius, thinking good his testament should be read openly, and also that his body should be honorably buried, and not in hugger-mugger, lest the people might thereby take occasion to be worse offended if they did otherwise:

Cassius stoutly spoke against it. But Brutus went with the motion, and agreed unto it; wherein it seemeth he committed a second fault. For the first fault he did, was when he would not consent to his fellow conspirators, that Antonius should be slain: and therefore he was justly accused that thereby he had saved and strengthened a strong and grievous enemy of their conspiracy. The second fault was when he agreed that Caesar's funerals should be as Antonius would have them, the which indeed marred all. For first of all, when Caesar's testament was openly read among them, whereby it appeared that he bequeathed unto every citizen of Rome 75 drachmas a man: and that he left his gardens and arbors unto the people, which he had on this side of the river Tiber, in the place where now the temple of Fortune is built: the people then loved him, and were marvelous sorry for him. Afterwards, when Caesar's body was brought into the market place, Antonius making his funeral oration in praise of the dead, according to the ancient custom of Rome, and perceiving that his words moved the common people to compassion, he framed his eloquence to make their hearts yearn the more; and taking Caesar's gown all bloody in his hand, he laid it open to the sight of them all, showing what a number of cuts and holes it had upon it. Therewithal the people fell presently into such a rage and mutiny, that there was no more order kept amongst the common people. For some of them cried out, "Kill the murderers": others plucked up forms, tables, and stalls about the market place, as they had done before at the funerals of Clodius, and having laid them all on a heap together, they set them on fire, and thereupon did put the body of Caesar, and burnt it in the midst of the most holy places. And furthermore, when the fire was throughly kindled, some here, some there, took burning firebrands, and ran with them to the murderers' houses that killed him, to set them on fire. Howbeit the conspirators, foreseeing the danger before, had wisely provided for themselves and fled.

But there was a poet called Cinna, who had been no partaker of the conspiracy, but was always one of Caesar's chiefest friends: he dreamed, the night before, that Caesar bade him to supper with him, and that, he refusing to go,

Caesar was very importunate with him, and compelled him; so that at length he led him by the hand into a great dark place, where, being marvelously afraid, he was driven to follow him in spite of his heart. This dream put him all night into a fever: and yet notwithstanding, the next morning, when he heard that they carried Caesar's body to burial, being ashamed not to accompany his funerals, he went out of his house, and thrust himself into the press of the common people that were in a great uproar. And because someone called him by his name Cinna, the people, thinking he had been that Cinna who in an oration he made had spoken very evil of Caesar, they, falling upon him in their rage, slew him outright in the market place. This made Brutus and his companions more afraid than any other thing, next unto the change of Antonius. Wherefore they got them out of Rome, and kept at the first in the city of Antium, hoping to return again to Rome, when the fury of the people was a little assuaged. The which they hoped would be quickly, considering that they had to deal with a fickle and inconstant multitude, easy to be carried, and that the Senate stood for them: who notwithstanding made no enquiry for them that had torn poor Cinna the poet in pieces, but caused them to be sought for and apprehended that went with firebrands to set fire on the conspirators' houses. [*The Life of Marcus Brutus*, pp. 120–22.]

SUPERNATURAL EVENTS FOLLOW CAESAR'S DEATH

But his great prosperity and good fortune that favored him all his lifetime, did continue afterwards in the revenge of his death, pursuing the murderers both by sea and land, till they had not left a man more to be executed, of all them that were actors or counselers in the conspiracy of his death. Furthermore, of all the chances that happen unto men upon the earth, that which came to Cassius above all other, is most to be wondered at: for he, being overcome in battle at the journey of Philippi, slew himself with the same sword with the which he struck Caesar. Again, of signs in the element, the great comet, which seven nights together was seen very bright after Caesar's death, the eighth night after was never seen more. Also the brightness of the sun was darkened, the which all that year through rose very pale and shined not out, whereby it gave but small heat: therefore the air being very cloudy and dark, by the weakness of the heat that could not come forth, did cause the earth to bring forth but raw and unripe fruit, which rotted before it could ripe. [*The Life of Julius Caesar*, p. 103.]

THE TRIUMVIRATE

Now the state of Rome standing in these terms, there fell out another change and alteration, when the young man Octavius Caesar came to Rome. He was the son of Julius Caesar's niece, whom he had adopted for his son, and made his heir, by his last will and testament. But when Julius Caesar, his adopted father, was slain, he was in the city of Apollonia (where he studied) tarrying for him, because he was determined to make war with the Parthians: but when he heard the news of his death, he returned again to Rome. Where, to begin to curry favor with the common people, he first of all took upon him his adopted father's name, and made distribution among them of the money which his father had bequeathed unto them. By this means he troubled Antonius sorely, and by force of money got a great number of his father's soldiers together, that had served in the wars with him. [*The Life of Marcus Brutus*, p. 123.]

[After much political and military maneuvering, Octavius Caesar, Antonius, and Lepidus met] in an island environed round about with a little river, and there remained three days together. Now as touching all other matters they were easily agreed, and did divide all the Empire of Rome between them, as if it had been their own inheritance. But yet they could hardly agree whom they would put to death: for every one of them would kill their enemies, and save their kinsmen and friends. Yet at length, giving place to their greedy desire to be revenged of their enemies, they spurned all reverence of blood and holiness of friendship at their feet. For Caesar left Cicero to Antonius' will, Antonius also

forsook Lucius Caesar, who was his uncle by his mother:
and both of them together suffered Lepidus to kill his own
brother Paulus. Yet some writers affirm, that Caesar and
Antonius requested Paulus might be slain, and that Lepidus
was contented with it. In my opinion there was never a more
horrible, unnatural, and crueler change than this was. For
thus changing murder for murder, they did as well kill those
whom they did forsake and leave unto others, as those also
which others left unto them to kill: but so much more was
their wickedness and cruelty great unto their friends, for
that they put them to death being innocents, and having no
cause to hate them. [*The Life of Marcus Antonius*, p. 169.]

DISAGREEMENTS BETWEEN BRUTUS AND CASSIUS

Now whilst Brutus and Cassius were together in the city
of Smyrna, Brutus prayed Cassius to let him have some
part of his money whereof he had great store; because all
that he could rap and rend of his side, he had bestowed it
in making so great a number of ships, that by means of
them they should keep all the sea at their commandment.
Cassius' friends hindered this request and earnestly dis-
suaded him from it, persuading him, that it was no reason
that Brutus should have the money which Cassius had gotten
together by sparing and levied with great evil will of the
people their subjects, for him to bestow liberally upon his
soldiers, and by this means to win their good wills, by Cassius' charge. This notwithstanding, Cassius gave him the
third part of this total sum. [*The Life of Marcus Brutus*, pp.
130–31.]

. . . [Later] Brutus sent to pray Cassius to come to the
city of Sardis, and so he did. Brutus, understanding of his
coming, went to meet him with all his friends. There both
their armies being armed, they called them both *Emperors*.
Now as it commonly happened in great affairs between two
persons, both of them having many friends and so many
captains under them, there ran tales and complaints betwixt
them. Therefore, before they fell in hand with any other
matter, they went into a little chamber together, and bade

every man avoid, and did shut the doors to them. Then they began to pour out their complaints one to the other, and grew hot and loud, earnestly accusing one another, and at length fell both a-weeping. Their friends that were without the chamber, hearing them loud within, and angry between themselves, they were both amazed and afraid also, lest it would grow to further matter: but yet they were commanded that no man should come to them. Notwithstanding, one Marcus Faonius, that had been a friend and a follower of Cato while he lived, and took upon him to counterfeit a philosopher, not with wisdom and discretion, but with a certain bedlam and frantic motion: he would needs come into the chamber, though the men offered to keep him out. But it was no boot to let Faonius, when a mad mood or toy took him in the head: for he was a hot, hasty man, and sudden in all his doings, and cared for never a Senator of them all. Now, though he used this bold manner of speech after the profession of the Cynic philosophers (as who would say, *Dogs*), yet his boldness did no hurt many times, because they did but laugh at him to see him so mad. This Faonius at that time, in despite of the doorkeepers, came into the chamber, and with a certain scoffing and mocking gesture, which he counterfeited of purpose, he rehearsed the verses which old Nestor said in Homer:

> My lords, I pray you hearken both to me,
> For I have seen moe years than suchie three.

Cassius fell a-laughing at him: but Brutus thrust him out of the chamber, and called him dog, and counterfeit Cynic. Howbeit his coming in broke their strife at that time, and so they left each other. . . . The next day after, Brutus, upon complaint of the Sardians, did condemn and note Lucius Pella for a defamed person, that had been a praetor of the Romans, and whom Brutus had given charge unto: for that he was accused and convicted of robbery and pilfery in his office. This judgment much misliked Cassius, because he himself had secretly (not many days before) warned two of his friends, attainted and convicted of the like offenses, and

openly had cleared them: but yet he did not therefore leave
to employ them in any manner of service as he did before.
And therefore he greatly reproved Brutus, for that he would
show himself so straight and severe, in such a time as was
meeter to bear a little than to take things at the worst.
Brutus in contrary manner answered, that he should remember the Ides of March, at which time they slew Julius Caesar,
who neither pilled nor polled the country, but only was a
favorer and suborner of all them that did rob and spoil, by
his countenance and authority. And if there were any
occasion whereby they might honestly set aside justice and
equity, they should have had more reason to have suffered
Caesar's friends to have robbed and done what wrong and
injury they had would than to bear with their own men.
"For then," said he, "they could but have said we had been
cowards, but now they may accuse us of injustice, beside
the pains we take, and the danger we put ourselves into."
And thus may we see what Brutus' intent and purpose was.
[*The Life of Marcus Brutus*, pp. 134–35.]

THE GHOST OF CAESAR; OMENS OF
DEFEAT AND DECISIONS OF WAR

But as they both prepared to pass over again out of Asia
into Europe, there went a rumor that there appeared a
wonderful sign unto him. Brutus was a careful man, and
slept very little, both for that his diet was moderate, as also
because he was continually occupied. He never slept in the
daytime, and in the night no longer than the time he was
driven to be alone, and when everybody else took their rest.
But now whilst he was in war, and his head ever busily
occupied to think of his affairs and what would happen,
after he had slumbered a little after supper, he spent all the
rest of the night in dispatching of his weightiest causes; and
after he had taken order for them, if he had any leisure left
him, he would read some book till the third watch of the
night, at what time the captains, petty captains, and colonels,
did use to come to him. So, being ready to go into Europe,
one night very late (when all the camp took quiet rest) as

he was in his tent with a little light, thinking of weighty matters, he thought he heard one come in to him, and casting his eye towards the door of his tent, that he saw a wonderful strange and monstrous shape of a body coming towards him, and said never a word. So Brutus boldly asked what he was, a god or a man, and what cause brought him thither? The spirit answered him, "I am thy evil spirit, Brutus: and thou shalt see me by the city of Philippi." Brutus, being no otherwise afraid, replied again unto it: "Well, then I shall see thee again." The spirit presently vanished away: and Brutus called his men unto him, who told him that they heard no noise, nor saw anything at all. Thereupon Brutus returned again to think on his matters as he did before: and when the day broke, he went unto Cassius, to tell him what vision had appeared unto him in the night. Cassius being in opinion an Epicurean, and reasoning thereon with Brutus, spoke to him touching the vision thus. "In our sect, Brutus, we have an opinion, that we do not always feel or see that which we suppose we do both see and feel, but that our senses being credulous and therefore easily abused (when they are idle and unoccupied in their own objects) are induced to imagine they see and conjecture that which in truth they do not. . . ." With these words Cassius did somewhat comfort and quiet Brutus. When they raised their camp, there came two eagles that, flying with a marvelous force, lighted upon two of the foremost ensigns, and always followed the soldiers, which gave them meat and fed them, until they came near to the city of Philippi: and there, one day only before the battle, they both flew away. . . . The Romans called the valley between both camps, the Philippian fields: and there were never seen two so great armies of the Romans, one before the other, ready to fight. In truth, Brutus' army was inferior to Octavius Caesar's in number of men; but for bravery and rich furniture, Brutus' army far excelled Caesar's. For the most part of their armors were silver and gilt, which Brutus had bountifully given them: although, in all other things, he taught his captains to live in order without excess. . . . [*The Life of Marcus Brutus*, pp. 135–37.]

Brutus . . . mustered his army, and did purify it in the

fields, according to the manner of the Romans. . . . Notwithstanding, being busily occupied about the ceremonies of this purification, it is reported that there chanced certain unlucky signs unto Cassius. For one of his sergeants that carried the rods before him, brought him the garland of flowers turned backward, the which he should have worn on his head in the time of sacrificing. Moreover it is reported also, that another time before, in certain sports and triumph where they carried an image of Cassius' victory, of clean gold, it fell by chance, the man stumbling that carried it. And yet further, there was seen a marvelous number of fowls of prey, that feed upon dead carcasses: and beehives also were found, where bees were gathered together in a certain place within the trenches of the camp: the which place the soothsayers thought good to shut out of the precinct of the camp, for to take away the superstitious fear and mistrust men would have of it. The which began somewhat to alter Cassius' mind from Epicurus' opinions, and had put the soldiers also in a marvelous fear. Thereupon Cassius was of opinion not to try this war at one battle, but rather to delay time, and to draw it out in length, considering that they were the stronger in money, and the weaker in men and armor. But Brutus, in contrary manner, did alway before, and at that time also, desire nothing more than to put all to the hazard of battle, as soon as might be possible: to the end he might either quickly restore his country to her former liberty, or rid him forthwith of this miserable world, being still troubled in following and maintaining of such great armies together. But perceiving that, in the daily skirmishes and bickerings they made, his men were always the stronger and ever had the better, that yet quickened his spirits again, and did put him in better heart. And furthermore, because that some of their own men had already yielded themselves to their enemies, and that it was suspected moreover divers others would do the like, that made many of Cassius' friends which were of his mind before (when it came to be debated in council, whether the battle should be fought or not) that they were then of Brutus' mind. . . . Thereupon it was presently determined they should fight battle the next day. So Brutus, all supper time, looked with a cheerful countenance, like a man that had good hope, and talked very wisely of philosophy, and after supper went to bed. But touching Cassius, Messala reporteth that he supped by himself in his tent with a few of his friends, and that all supper time he looked very sadly, and was full of thoughts, although it was against his nature: and that after supper he took him by the hand, and holding him fast (in token of kindness, as his manner was) told him in Greek: "Messala, I protest unto thee, and make thee my witness, that I am compelled against my mind and will (as Pompey the Great was) to jeopard the liberty of our country to the hazard of a battle. And yet we must be lively, and of good courage, considering our good fortune, whom we should wrong too much to mistrust her, although we follow evil counsel." Messala writeth, that Cassius having spoken these last words unto him, he bade him farewell, and willed him to come to supper to him the next night following, because it was his birthday. The next morning, by break of day, the signal of battle was set out in Brutus' and Cassius' camp, which was an arming scarlet coat: and both the chieftains spoke together in the midst of their armies. There Cassius began to speak first, and said: "The gods grant us, O Brutus, that this day we may win the field, and ever after to live all the rest of our life quietly one with another. But sith the gods have so ordained it, that the greatest and chiefest things amongst men are most uncertain, and that if the battle fall out otherwise today than we wish or look for, we shall hardly meet again, what art thou then determined to do, to fly or die?" Brutus answered him, being yet but a young man and not over greatly experienced in the world: "I trust (I know not how) a certain rule of philosophy, by the which I did greatly blame and reprove Cato for killing himself, as being no lawful nor godly act, touching the gods: nor concerning men, valiant; not to give place and yield to divine providence, and not constantly and patiently to take whatsoever it pleaseth him to send us, but to draw back and fly: but being now in the midst of the danger, I am of a contrary mind. For if it be not the will of God that this battle fall out fortunate for us, I will look no more for hope, neither seek to make any new supply for war again,

but will rid me of this miserable world, and content me with
my fortune. For I gave up my life for my country in the
Ides of March, for the which I shall live in another more
glorious world." Cassius fell a-laughing to hear what he
said, and embracing him, "Come on then," said he, "let us
go and charge our enemies with this mind. For either we
shall conquer, or we shall not need to fear the conquerors."
After this talk, they fell to consultation among their friends
for the ordering of the battle. Then Brutus prayed Cassius
he might have the leading of the right wing, the which men
thought was far meeter for Cassius, both because he was
the elder man, and also for that he had the better experience.
But yet Cassius gave it him, and willed that Messala (who
had charge of one of the warlikest legions they had) should
be also in that wing with Brutus. So Brutus presently sent
out his horsemen, who were excellently well appointed, and
his footmen also were as willing and ready to give charge.
[*The Life of Marcus Brutus*, pp. 138–40.]

THE BATTLE

In the meantime Brutus, that led the right wing, sent little
bills to the colonels and captains of private bands, in the
which he wrote the word of the battle; and he himself,
riding a-horseback by all the troops, did speak to them, and
encouraged them to stick to it like men. So by this means
very few of them understood what was the word of the
battle, and besides, the most part of them never tarried to
have it told them, but ran with great fury to assail the enemies; whereby, through this disorder, the legions were
marvelously scattered and dispersed one from the other.
For first of all Messala's legion, and then the next unto them,
went beyond the left wing of the enemies and did nothing,
but glancing by them overthrew some as they went; and so
going on further, fell right upon Caesar's camp, out of the
which (as himself writeth in his commentaries) he had been
conveyed away a little before, through the counsel and
advice of one of his friends called Marcus Artorius: who,
dreaming in the night, had a vision appeared unto him, that

commanded Octavius Caesar should be carried out of his camp. Insomuch as it was thought he was slain, because his litter (which had nothing in it) was thrust through and through with pikes and darts. There was great slaughter in this camp. For amongst others, there were slain 2,000 Lacedaemonians, who were arrived but even a little before, coming to aid Caesar. The other also that had not glanced by, but had given a charge full upon Caesar's battle, they easily made them fly, because they were greatly troubled for the loss of their camp; and of them there were slain by hand three legions. Then, being very earnest to follow the chase of them that fled, they ran in amongst them hand over head into their camp, and Brutus among them. But that which the conquerors thought not of, occasion showed it unto them that were overcome; and that was, the left wing of their enemies left naked and unguarded of them of the right wing, who were strayed too far off, in following of them that were overthrown. So they gave a hot charge upon them. But, notwithstanding all the force they made, they could not break into the midst of their battle, where they found them that received them and valiantly made head against them. Howbeit they broke and overthrew the left wing where Cassius was, by reason of the great disorder among them, and also because they had no intelligence how the right wing had sped. So they chased them, beating them into their camp, the which they spoiled, none of both the chieftains being present there. For Antonius, as it is reported, to fly the fury of the first charge, was gotten into the next marsh: and no man could tell what became of Octavius Caesar after he was carried out of his camp. Insomuch that there were certain soldiers that showed their swords bloodied, and said that they had slain him, and did describe his face, and showed what age he was of. Furthermore, the voward and the midst of Brutus' battle had already put all their enemies to flight that withstood them, with great slaughter: so that Brutus had conquered all on his side and Cassius had lost all on the other side. For nothing undid them but that Brutus went not to help Cassius, thinking he had overcome them as himself had done; and Cassius on the other side tarried not for Brutus, thinking he had been overthrown as himself was. And to prove that the victory fell on Brutus' side, Messala confirmeth that they won three eagles and divers other ensigns of the enemies, and their enemies won never a one of theirs. Now Brutus returning from the chase, after he had slain and sacked Caesar's men, he wondered much that he could not see Cassius' tent standing up high as it was wont, neither the other tents of his camp standing as they were before, because all the whole camp had been spoiled, and the tents thrown down, at the first coming of their enemies. But they that were about Brutus, whose sight served them better, told him that they saw a great glistering of harness, and a number of silvered targets that went and came into Cassius' camp, and were not (as they took it) the armors nor the number of men that they had left there to guard the camp; and yet that they saw not such a number of dead bodies and great overthrow as there should have been, if so many legions had been slain. This made Brutus at the first mistrust that which had happened. So he appointed a number of men to keep the camp of his enemy which he had taken, and caused his men to be sent for that yet followed the chase, and gathered them together, thinking to lead them to aid Cassius, who was in this state as you shall hear. [*The Life of Marcus Brutus*, pp. 140–42.]

THE DEATH OF CASSIUS

First of all, he was marvelous angry to see how Brutus' men ran to give charge upon their enemies, and tarried not for the word of the battle, nor commandment to give charge: and it grieved him beside that after he had overcome them, his men fell straight to spoil and were not careful to compass in the rest of the enemies behind: but with tarrying too long also, more than through the valiantness or foresight of the captains his enemies, Cassius found himself compassed in with the right wing of his enemies' army. Whereupon his horsemen broke immediately, and fled for life towards the sea. Furthermore perceiving his footmen to give ground, he did what he could to keep them from flying, and took an ensign from one of the ensign-bearers that fled, and stuck it fast at his feet: although with much ado he could scant keep his own guard together.

So Cassius himself was at length compelled to fly, with a few about him, unto a little hill, from whence they might easily see what was done in all the plain: howbeit Cassius himself saw nothing, for his sight was very bad, saving that he saw (and yet with much ado) how the enemies spoiled his camp before his eyes. He saw also a great troop of horsemen, whom Brutus sent to aid him, and thought that they were his enemies that followed him: but yet he sent Titinius, one of them that was with him, to go and know what they were. Brutus' horsemen saw him coming afar off, whom when they knew that he was one of Cassius' chiefest friends, they shouted out for joy; and they that were familiarly acquainted with him lighted from their horses, and went and embraced him. The rest compassed him in round about on horseback, with songs of victory and great rushing of their harness, so that they made all the field ring again for joy. But this marred all. For Cassius, thinking indeed that Titinius was taken of the enemies, he then spoke these words: "Desiring too much to live, I have lived to see one of my best friends taken, for my sake, before my face." After that, he got into a tent where nobody was, and took Pindarus with him, one of his bondsmen whom he reserved ever for such a pinch, since the cursed battle of the Parthians, where Crassus was slain, though he notwithstanding scaped from that overthrow: but then, casting his cloak over his head, and holding out his bare neck unto Pindarus, he gave him his head to be stricken off. So the head was found severed from the body: but after that time Pindarus was never seen more. Whereupon some took occasion to say that he had slain his master without his commandment. By and by they knew the horsemen that came towards them, and might see Titinius crowned with a garland of triumph, who came before with great speed unto Cassius. But when he perceived, by the cries and tears of his friends which tormented themselves, the misfortune that had chanced to his captain Cassius by mistaking, he drew out his sword, cursing himself a thousand times that he had tarried so long, and so slew himself presently in the field. Brutus in the meantime came forward still, and understood also that Cassius had been overthrown: but he knew nothing of his death till he came very near to his camp. So when he was come thither, after he had lamented the death of Cassius, calling him the last of all the Romans, being impossible that Rome should ever breed again so noble and valiant a man as he, he caused his body to be buried, and sent it to the city of Thasos, fearing lest his funerals within his camp should cause great disorder. [*The Life of Marcus Brutus*, pp. 142–44.]

THE EXPLOITS OF YOUNG CATO AND LUCILIUS

There was the son of Marcus Cato slain, valiantly fighting among the lusty youths. For notwithstanding that he was very weary and overharried, yet would he not therefore fly; but manfully fighting and laying about him, telling aloud his name and also his father's name, at length he was beaten down amongst many other dead bodies of his enemies, which he had slain round about him. So there were slain in the field all the chiefest gentlemen and nobility that were in his army, who valiantly ran into any danger to save Brutus' life: amongst whom there was one of Brutus' friends called Lucilius, who seeing a troop of barbarous men making no reckoning of all men else they met in their way, but going all together right against Brutus, he determined to stay them with the hazard of his life; and being left behind, told them that he was Brutus: and because they should believe him, he prayed them to bring him to Antonius, for he said he was afraid of Caesar, and that he did trust Antonius better. These barbarous men, being very glad of this good hap, and thinking themselves happy men, they carried him in the night, and sent some before unto Antonius, to tell him of their coming. He was marvelous glad of it, and went out to meet them that brought him. Others also understanding of it that they had brought Brutus prisoner, they came out of all parts of the camp to see him, some pitying his hard fortune and others saying that it was not done like himself, so cowardly to be taken alive of the barbarous people for fear of death. When they came near together, Antonius stayed a while bethinking himself how he should use Brutus. In the meantime Lucilius was brought to him, who stoutly with a bold countenance said: "Antonius, I dare assure thee, that no enemy hath taken nor shall take Marcus Brutus alive, and I beseech God keep him from that fortune: for wheresoever he be found, alive or dead, he will be found like himself. And now for myself, I am come unto thee, having deceived these men of arms here, bearing them down that I was Brutus, and do not refuse to suffer any torment thou wilt put me to." Lucilius' words made them all amazed that heard him. Antonius on the other side, looking upon all them that had brought him, said unto them: "My companions, I think ye are sorry you have failed of your purpose, and that you think this man hath done you great wrong: but I assure you, you have taken a better booty than that you followed. For instead of an enemy you have brought me a friend: and for my part, if you had brought me Brutus alive, truly I cannot tell what I should have done to him. For I had rather have such men my friends, as this man here, than mine enemies." Then he embraced Lucilius, and at that time delivered him to one of his friends in custody; and Lucilius ever after served him faithfully, even to his death. [*The Life of Marcus Brutus*, pp. 148–49.]

THE DEATH OF BRUTUS

Now Brutus having passed a little river, walled in on every side with high rocks and shadowed with great trees, being then dark night, he went no further, but stayed at the foot of a rock with certain of his captains and friends that followed him: and looking up to the firmament that was full of stars, sighing, he rehearsed two verses, of the which Volumnius wrote the one, to this effect:

Let not the wight from whom this mischief went,
O Jove, escape without due punishment:

and saith that he had forgotten the other. Within a little

while after, naming his friends that he had seen slain in battle before his eyes, he fetched a greater sigh than before, specially when he came to name Labeo and Flavius, of whom the one was his lieutenant, and the other captain of the pioneers of his camp. In the meantime one of the company being athirst, and seeing Brutus athirst also, he ran to the river for water and brought it in his sallet. At the same time they heard a noise on the other side of the river: whereupon Volumnius took Dardanus, Brutus' servant, with him, to see what it was: and returning straight again, asked if there were any water left. Brutus smiling, gently told him, "All is drunk, but they shall bring you some more." Thereupon he sent him again that went for water before, who was in great danger of being taken by the enemies, and hardly escaped, being sore hurt.

Furthermore, Brutus thought that there was no great number of men slain in battle: and to know the truth of it, there was one called Statilius that promised to go through his enemies, for otherwise it was impossible to go see their camp: and from thence, if all were well, that he would lift up a torchlight in the air and then return again with speed to him. The torchlight was lift up as he had promised, for Statilius went thither. Now Brutus seeing Statilius tarry long after that, and that he came not again, he said: "If Statilius be alive, he will come again." But his evil fortune was such that, as he came back, he lighted in his enemies' hands and was slain. Now the night being far spent, Brutus, as he sat, bowed towards Clitus, one of his men, and told him somewhat in his ear: the other answered him not, but fell a-weeping. Thereupon he proved Dardanus, and said somewhat also to him: at length he came to Volumnius himself, and speaking to him in Greek, prayed him for the studies' sake which brought them acquainted together that he would help him to put his hand to his sword, to thrust it in him to kill him. Volumnius denied his request, and so did many others: and amongst the rest, one of them said, there was no tarrying for them there, but that they must needs fly. Then Brutus, rising up, "We must fly indeed," said he, "but it must be with our hands, not with our feet." Then taking every man by the hand, he said these words unto them with a cheerful

countenance: "It rejoiceth my heart, that not one of my friends hath failed me at my need, and I do not complain of my fortune, but only for my country's sake: for as for me, I think myself happier than they that have overcome, considering that I leave a perpetual fame of virtue and honesty, the which our enemies the conquerors shall never attain unto by force or money; neither can let their posterity to say that they, being naughty and unjust men, have slain good men, to usurp tyrannical power not pertaining to them." Having so said, he prayed every man to shift for himself, and then he went a little aside with two or three only, among the which Strato was one, with whom he came first acquainted by the study of rhetoric. He came as near to him as he could, and taking his sword by the hilt with both his hands, and falling down upon the point of it, ran himself through. Others say that not he, but Strato (at his request) held the sword in his hand, and turned his head aside, and that Brutus fell down upon it, and so ran himself through, and died presently. Messala, that had been Brutus' great friend, became afterwards Octavius Caesar's friend: so, shortly after, Caesar being at good leisure, he brought Strato, Brutus' friend, unto him, and weeping said: "Caesar, behold, here is he that did the last service to my Brutus." Caesar welcomed him at that time, and afterwards he did him as faithful service in all his affairs as any Grecian else he had about him, until the battle of Actium. It is reported also that this Messala himself answered Caesar one day, when he gave him great praise before his face, that he had fought valiantly and with great affection for him at the battle of Actium (notwithstanding that he had been his cruel enemy before, at the battle of Philippi, for Brutus' sake): "I ever loved," said he, "to take the best and justest part."
[*The Life of Marcus Brutus*, pp. 149–51.]

Antonius having found Brutus' body after this battle, blaming him much for the murder of his brother Caius, whom he had put to death in Macedon for revenge of Cicero's cruel death, and yet laying the fault more in Hortensius than in him, he made Hortensius to be slain on his brother's tomb. Furthermore he cast his coat-armor

(which was wonderful rich and sumptuous) upon Brutus'
body, and gave commandment to one of his slaves enfranchised, to defray the charge of his burial. But afterwards
Antonius hearing that his enfranchised bondman had not
burnt his coat-armor with his body, because it was very rich
and worth a great sum of money, and that he had also kept
back much of the ready money appointed for his funeral
and tomb, he also put him to death. [*The Life of Marcus
Antonius*, p. 171.]

THE DEATH OF PORCIA

And for Porcia, Brutus' wife, Nicolaus the Philosopher
and Valerius Maximus do write that she, determining to kill
herself (her parents and friends carefully looking to her to
keep her from it), took hot burning coals and cast them into
her mouth, and kept her mouth so close that she choked
herself. There was a letter of Brutus found written to his
friends, complaining of their negligence, that his wife being
sick, they would not help her, but suffered her to kill herself;
choosing to die, rather than to languish in pain. Thus it
appeareth that Nicolaus knew not well that time, sith the
letter (at the least if it were Brutus' letter) doth plainly
declare the disease and love of this lady, and also the manner
of her death. [*The Life of Marcus Brutus*, pp. 151–52.]

THE CHARACTER OF CAESAR

Furthermore, they did not wonder so much at his valiantness in putting himself at every instant in such manifest
danger, and in taking so extreme pains as he did, knowing
that it was his greedy desire of honor that set him on fire,
and pricked him forward to do it: but that he always continued all labor and hardness, more than his body could
bear, that filled them all with admiration. For, concerning
the constitution of his body, he was lean, white, and soft-
skinned, and often subject to headache, and otherwhile to
the falling sickness (the which took him the first time, as it

is reported, in Corduba, a city of Spain) but yet therefore yielded not to the disease of his body, to make it a cloak to cherish him withal, but contrarily, took the pains of war as a medicine to cure his sick body, fighting always with his disease, traveling continually, living soberly, and commonly lying abroad in the field. [*The Life of Julius Caesar*, p. 57.]

Furthermore, Caesar being born to attempt all great enterprises, and having an ambitious desire besides to covet great honors, the prosperous good success he had of his former conquests bred no desire in him quietly to enjoy the fruits of his labors; but rather gave him the hope of things to come, still kindling more and more in him thoughts of greater enterprises and desire of new glory, as if that which he had present were stale and nothing worth. This humor of his was no other but an emulation with himself as with another man, and a certain contention to overcome the things he prepared to attempt. [*The Life of Julius Caesar*, p. 93.]

In this journey it is reported, that passing over the mountains of the Alps, they came through a little poor village that had not many households, and yet poor cottages. There his friends that did accompany him asked him merrily, if there were any contending for offices in that town, and whether there were any strife there amongst the noblemen for honor. Caesar, speaking in good earnest, answered: "I cannot tell that," said he, "but for my part I had rather be the chiefest man here than the second person in Rome." Another time also when he was in Spain, reading the history of Alexander's acts, when he had read it, he was sorrowful a good while after, and then burst out in weeping. His friends seeing that, marveled what should be the cause of his sorrow. He answered them, "Do ye not think," said he, "that I have good cause to be heavy, when King Alexander, being no elder than myself is now, had in old time won so many nations and countries: and that I hitherunto have done nothing worthy of myself?" [*The Life of Julius Caesar*, p. 52.]

But the time of the great armies and conquests he made afterwards, and of the war in the which he subdued all the

Gauls (entering into another course of life far contrary unto the first) made him to be known for as valiant a soldier and as excellent a captain to lead men, as those that afore him had been counted the wisest and most valiant generals that ever were, and that by their valiant deeds had achieved great honor. [*The Life of Julius Caesar*, p. 55.]

Now Caesar immediately won many men's good wills at Rome, through his eloquence in pleading of their causes, and the people loved him marvelously also, because of the courteous manner he had to speak to every man, and to use them gently, being more ceremonious therein than was looked for in one of his years. Furthermore, he ever kept a good board, and fared well at his table, and was very liberal besides: the which indeed did advance him forward, and brought him in estimation with the people. . . . Thereupon Cicero, like a wise shipmaster that feareth the calmness of the sea, was the first man that, mistrusting his manner of dealing in the commonwealth, found out his craft and malice, which he cunningly cloaked under the habit of outward courtesy and familiarity. "And yet," said he, "when I consider how finely he combeth his fair bush of hair, and how smooth it lieth, and that I see him scratch his head with one finger only, my mind gives me then, that such a kind of man should not have so wicked a thought in his head, as to overthrow the state of the commonwealth." But this was long time after that. [*The Life of Julius Caesar*, p. 45.]

THE CHARACTERS OF BRUTUS AND CASSIUS

Marcus Brutus came of that Junius Brutus, for whom the ancient Romans made his statue of brass to be set up in the Capitol, with the images of the kings, holding a naked sword in his hand: because he had valiantly put down the Tarquins from the kingdom of Rome. But that Junius Brutus, being of a sour, stern nature not softened by reason, being like unto sword blades of too hard a temper, was so subject to his choler and malice he bore unto the tyrants, that for their sakes he caused his own sons to be executed. But this Marcus Brutus in contrary manner, whose life we presently write, having framed his manners of life by the rules of virtue and study of philosophy, and having employed his wit, which was gentle and constant, in attempting of great things, methinks he was rightly made and framed unto virtue. So that his very enemies which wish him most hurt, because of his conspiracy against Julius Caesar, if there were any noble attempt done in all this conspiracy, they refer it wholly unto Brutus; and all the cruel and violent acts unto Cassius, who was Brutus' familiar friend, but not so well given and conditioned as he. [*The Life of Marcus Brutus*, pp. 105–06.]

He was properly learned in the Latin tongue, and was able to make long discourse in it: beside that he could also plead very well in Latin. But for the Greek tongue, they do note in some of his Epistles that he counterfeited that brief compendious manner of speech of the Lacedaemonians. As, when the war was begun, he wrote unto the Pergamenians in this sort: "I understand you have given Dolabella money: if you have done it willingly, you confess you have offended me; if against your wills, show it then by giving me willingly." Another time again unto the Samians: "Your councils be long, your doings be slow, consider the end." And in another Epistle he wrote unto the Patareians: "The Xanthians, despising my good will, have made their country a grave of despair; and the Patareians, that put themselves into my protection, have lost no jot of their liberty: and therefore, whilst you have liberty, either choose the judgment of the Patareians, or the fortune of the Xanthians." These were Brutus' manner of letters, which were honored for their briefness. [*The Life of Marcus Brutus*, p. 107.]

They say also that Caesar said, when he heard Brutus plead: "I know not," said he, "what this young man would; but what he would, he willeth it vehemently." For as Brutus' gravity and constant mind would not grant all men their requests that sued unto him, but, being moved with reason and discretion, did always incline to that which was good and honest: even so, when it was moved to follow any matter, he used a kind of forcible and vehement persuasion, that calmed not till he had obtained his desire. For by flattering

of him a man could never obtain anything at his hands, nor
make him to do that which was unjust. Further, he thought
it not meet for a man of calling and estimation, to yield
unto the requests and entreaties of a shameless and importunate suitor, requesting things unmeet: the which notwithstanding some men do for shame, because they dare
deny nothing: and therefore he was wont to say, "that he
thought them evil brought up in their youth, that could
deny nothing." [*The Life of Marcus Brutus*, pp. 109–10.]

And surely (in my opinion), I am persuaded that Brutus
might indeed have come to have been the chiefest man of
Rome, if he could have contented himself for a time to have
been next unto Caesar, and to have suffered his glory and
authority, which he had gotten by his great victories, to
consume with time. But Cassius, being a choleric man, and
hating Caesar privately more than he did the tyranny
openly, he incensed Brutus against him. It is also reported,
that Brutus could evil away with the tyranny, and that
Cassius hated the tyrant: making many complaints for the
injuries he had done him; and amongst others, for that he
had taken away his lions from him. Cassius had provided
them for his sports when he should be aedilis; and they
were found in the city of Megara, when it was won by
Calenus: and Caesar kept them. The rumor went, that these
lions did marvelous great hurt to the Megarians: for when
the city was taken, they broke their cages where they were
tied up and turned them loose, thinking they would have
done great mischief to the enemies, and have kept them
from setting upon them: but the lions (contrary to expectation) turned upon themselves that fled unarmed, and did so
cruelly tear some in pieces, that it pitied their enemies to see
them. And this was the cause (as some do report) that made
Cassius conspire against Caesar. But this holdeth no water:
for Cassius, even from his cradle, could not abide any
manner of tyrants; as it appeared when he was but a boy,
and went unto the same school that Faustus, the son of Sulla,
did. And Faustus, bragging among other boys, highly
boasted of his father's kingdom: Cassius rose up on his feet,
and gave him two good wirts on the ear. Faustus' governors
would have put this matter in suit against Cassius: but

Pompey would not suffer them, but caused the two boys to be brought before him and asked them how the matter came to pass. Then Cassius (as it is written of him) said unto the other: "Go to, Faustus, speak again, and thou darest, before this nobleman here, the same words that made me angry with thee, that my fists may walk once again about thine ears." Such was Cassius' hot stirring nature. [*The Life of Marcus Brutus*, pp.111–12.]

Now Cassius would have done Brutus much honor, as Brutus did unto him, but Brutus most commonly prevented him and went first unto him, both because he was the elder man as also for that he was sickly of body. And men reputed him commonly to be very skillful in wars, but otherwise marvelous choleric and cruel, who sought to rule men by fear rather than with lenity: and on the other side, he was too familar with his friends, and would jest too broadly with them. But Brutus, in contrary manner, for his virtue and valiantness, was well beloved of the people and his own, esteemed of noblemen, and hated of no man, not so much as of his enemies; because he was a marvelous lowly and gentle person, noble-minded, and would never be in any rage, nor carried away with pleasure and covetousness, but had ever an upright mind with him and would never yield to any wrong or injustice; the which was the chiefest cause of his fame, of his rising, and of the good will that every man bore him: for they were all persuaded that his intent was good. For they did not certainly believe that, if Pompey himself had overcome Caesar, he would have resigned his authority to the law, but rather they were of opinion that he would still keep the sovereignty and absolute government in his hands, taking only, to please the people, the title of Consul, or Dictator, or of some other more civil office. And as for Cassius, a hot, choleric, and cruel man, that would oftentimes be carried away from justice for gain, it was certainly thought that he made war and put himself into sundry dangers, more to have absolute power and authority than to defend the liberty of his country. For they that will also consider others that were elder men than they, as Cinna, Marinus, and Carbo, it is out of doubt that the end and hope of their victory was to be the lords of their country, and in manner they did all confess that they fought for the tyranny and to be lords of the Empire of Rome. And in contrary manner, his enemies themselves did never reprove Brutus for any such change or desire. For it was said that Antonius spoke it openly divers times, that he thought, that of all them that had slain Caesar, there was none but Brutus only that was moved to do it, as thinking the act commendable of itself: but that all the other conspirators did conspire his death for some private malice or envy that they otherwise did bear unto him. [*The Life of Marcus Brutus*, pp. 129–30.]

THE CHARACTER OF ANTONY

Now Antonius being a fair young man, and in the prime of his youth, he fell acquainted with Curio, whose friendship and acquaintance (as it is reported) was a plague unto him. For he was a dissolute man, given over to all lust and insolency, who, to have Antonius the better at his commandment, trained him on into great follies and vain expenses upon women, in rioting and banqueting: so that in short time he brought Antonius into a marvelous great debt, and too great for one of his years, to wit, of two hundred and fifty talents, for all which sum Curio was his surety. His father, hearing of it, did put his son from him and forbade him his house. Then he fell in with Clodius, one of the desperatest and most wicked tribunes at that time in Rome. Him he followed for a time in his desperate attempts, who bred great stir and mischief in Rome: but at length he forsook him, being weary of his rashness and folly, or else for that he was afraid of them that were bent against Clodius.

Thereupon he left Italy, and went into Greece, and there bestowed the most part of his time, sometime in wars, and otherwhile in the study of eloquence. He used a manner of phrase in his speech called "Asiatic," which carried the best grace and estimation at that time and was much like to his manners and life: for it was full of ostentation, foolish bravery, and vain ambition. [*The Life of Marcus Antonius*, pp. 154–55.]

So was his great courtesy also much commended of all, the which he showed unto Archelaus: for having been his very friend, he made war with him against his will while he lived; but after his death he fought for his body, and gave it honorable burial. For these respects he won himself great fame of them of Alexandria, and he was also thought a worthy man of all the soldiers in the Romans' camp. But besides all this, he had a noble presence, and showed a countenance of one of a noble house: he had a goodly thick beard, a broad forehead, crooked-nosed, and there appeared such a manly look in his countenance, as is commonly seen in Hercules' pictures, stamped or graven in metal. Now it had been a speech of old time, that the family of the Antonii were descended from one Anton, the son of Hercules, whereof the family took name. This opinion did Antonius seek to confirm in all his doings: not only resembling him in the likeness of his body, as we have said before, but also in the wearing of his garments. For when he would openly show himself abroad before many people, he would always wear his cassock girt down low upon his hips, with a great sword hanging by his side and upon that some ill-favored cloak. Furthermore, things that seem intolerable in other men, as to boast commonly, to jest with one or other, to drink like a good fellow with everybody, to sit with the soldiers when they dine, and to eat and drink with them soldierlike, it is incredible what wonderful love it won him amongst them. And furthermore, being given to love, that made him the more desired, and by that means he brought many to love him. For he would further every man's love, and also would not be angry that men should merrily tell him of those he loved. But besides all this, that which most procured his rising and advancement was his liberality, who gave all to the soldiers and kept nothing for himself: and when he was grown to great credit, then was his authority and power also very great, the which notwithstanding himself did overthrow by a thousand other faults he had. [*The Life of Marcus Antonius*, pp. 156–57.]

But then in contrary manner, he purchased divers other men's evil wills, because that through negligence he would not do them justice that were injured, and dealt very churlishly with them that had any suit unto him: and besides all this, he had an ill name to entice men's wives. [*The Life of Marcus Antonius*, p. 159.]

Now after that Caesar had gotten Rome at his commandment, and had driven Pompey out of Italy, he purposed first to go into Spain against the legions Pompey had there, and in the meantime to make provision for ships and marine preparation, to follow Pompey. In his absence, he left Lepidus, that was praetor, governor of Rome; and Antonius, that was tribune, he gave him charge of all the soldiers and of Italy. . . . To conclude, Caesar's friends, that governed under him, were cause why they hated Caesar's government (which indeed in respect of himself was no less than tyranny) by reason of the great insolencies and outrageous parts that were committed: amongst whom Antonius, that was of greatest power, and that also committed greatest faults, deserved most blame. But Caesar, notwithstanding, when he returned from the wars of Spain, made no reckoning of the complaints that were put up against him: but contrarily, because he found him a hardy man, and a valiant captain, he employed him in his chiefest affairs, and was no whit deceived in his opinion of him. [*The Life of Marcus Antonius*, pp. 158–59.]

Commentaries

MAYNARD MACK

Teaching "Julius Caesar"

It is easy to see . . . [in the first twenty-five lines of I.ii., with Caesar, Calpurnia, Antony, and the Soothsayer] how a first-rate dramatic imagination works. There is no hint of any procession in Plutarch, Shakespeare's source. "Caesar," says Plutarch, "*sat* to behold." There is no mention of Calpurnia in Plutarch's account of the Lupercalian race, and there is no mention anywhere of her sterility. Shakespeare, in nine lines, has given us an unforgettable picture of a man who would like to be emperor pathetically concerned that he lacks an heir, and determined, even at the cost of making his wife a public spectacle, to establish that this is owing to no lack of virility in him. The first episode thus dramatizes instantaneously the oncoming theme of the play: that a man's will is not enough; that there are other matters to be reckoned with, like the infertility of one's wife, or one's own affliction of the falling sickness which

Essays on the Teaching of English, ed. Edward J. Gordon and Edward S. Noyes. New York: Appleton-Century Crofts, 1960. Published for the National Council of Teachers of English.

spoils everything one hoped for just at the instant when one had it almost in one's hand. Brutus will be obliged to learn this lesson too.

In the second episode the theme develops. We see again the uneasy rationalism that everybody in this play affects; we hear it reverberate in the faint contempt—almost a challenge—of Brutus' words as he turns to Caesar: "A soothsayer bids you beware the ides of March." Yet underneath, in the soothsayer's presence and his sober warning, Shakespeare allows us to catch a hint of something else, something far more primitive and mysterious, from which rationalism in this play keeps trying vainly to cut itself away: "He is a dreamer. Let us leave him. Pass." Only we in the audience are in a position to see that the dreamer has foretold the path down which all these reasoners will go to that fatal encounter at the Capitol.

Meantime, in these same two episodes, we have learned something about the character of Caesar. In the first, it was the Caesar of human frailties who spoke to us, the husband with his hopeful superstition. In the second, it was the marble superman of state, impassive, impervious, speaking of himself in the third person: "Speak! Caesar is turn'd to hear." He even has the soothsayer brought before his face to repeat the message, as if he thought that somehow, in awe of the marble presence, the message would falter and dissolve: how can a superman need to beware the ides of March?

We hardly have time to do more than glimpse here a man of divided selves, when he is gone. But in his absence, the words of Cassius confirm our glimpse. Cassius' description of him exhibits the same duality that we had noticed earlier. On the one hand, an extremely ordinary man whose stamina in the swimming match was soon exhausted, who, when he had a fever once in Spain, shook and groaned like a sick girl, who even now, as we soon learn, is falling down with epilepsy in the marketplace. On the other hand, a being who has somehow become a god, who "bears the palm alone," who "bestrides the narrow world like a colossus." When the procession returns, no longer festive now, but angry, tense, there is the same effect once more. Our one Caesar shows a normal man's suspicion of his enemies, voices some shrewd human observations about Cassius, says to Antony, "Come on my right hand, for this ear is deaf." Our other Caesar says, as if he were suddenly reminded of something he had forgotten, "I rather tell thee what is to be feared/Than what I fear, for always I am Caesar."

Whenever Caesar appears hereafter, we shall find this singular division in him, and nowhere more so than in the scene in which he receives the conspirators at his house. Some aspects of this scene seem calculated for nothing else than to fix upon our minds the superman conception, the Big Brother of Orwell's *1984*, the great resonant name echoing down the halls of time. Thus at the beginning of the scene:

> the things that threatened me
> Ne'er looked but on my back; when they shall see
> The face of Caesar, they are vanished.

And again later:

> danger knows full well
> That Caesar is more dangerous than he:
> We are two lions littered in one day,
> And I the elder and more terrible.

And again still later: "Shall Caesar send a lie?" And again: "The cause is in my will: I will not come." Other aspects, including his concern about Calpurnia's dreams, his vacillation about going to the senate house, his anxiety about the portents of the night, plainly mark out his human weaknesses. Finally, as is the habit in this Rome, he puts the irrational from him that his wife's intuitions and her dream embody; he accepts the rationalization of the irrational that Decius skillfully manufactures, and, as earlier at the Lupercalia, hides from himself his own vivid sense of forces that lie beyond the will's control by attributing it to her:

How foolish do your fears seem now, Calpurnia!
I am ashamed I did yield to them.
Give me my robe, for I will go.

So far in our consideration of the implications of I.ii, we have been looking at Caesar, the title personage of the play, and its historical center. It is time now to turn to Brutus, the play's tragic center, whom we also find to be a divided man—"poor Brutus," to use his own phrase, "with himself at war." The war, we realize as the scene progresses is a conflict between a quiet essentially domestic and loving nature, and a powerful integrity expressing itself in a sense of honorable duty to the commonweal. This duality in Brutus seems to be what Cassius is probing at in his long disquisition about the mirror. The Brutus looking into the glass that Cassius figuratively holds up to him, the Brutus of this moment, now, in Rome, is a grave studious private man, of a wonderfully gentle temper, as we shall see again and again later on, very slow to passion, as Cassius' ill-concealed disappointment in having failed to kindle him to immediate response reveals, a man whose sensitive nature recoils at the hint of violence lurking in some of Cassius' speeches, just as he has already recoiled at going on with Caesar to the market place, to witness the mass hysteria of clapping hands, sweaty nightcaps, and stinking breath. This is the present self that looks into Cassius' mirror.

The image that looks back out, that Cassius wants him to see, the potential Brutus, is the man of public spirit, worried already by the question of Caesar's intentions, the lineal descendant of an earlier Brutus who drove a would-be monarch from the city, a man whose body is visibly stiffening in our sight at each huzza from the Forum, and whose anxiety, though he makes no reply to Cassius' inflammatory language, keeps bursting to the surface: "What means this shouting? I do fear the people/Choose Caesar for their king." The problem at the tragic center of the play, we begin to sense, is to be the tug of private versus public, the individual versus a world he never made, any citizen anywhere versus the selective service greetings that history is always mailing out to each of us. And this problem is to be traversed by that other tug this scene presents, of the irrational versus the rational, the destiny we think we can control versus the destiny that sweeps all before it.

Through I.ii, Brutus' public self, the self that responds to these selective service greetings, is no more than a reflection in a mirror, a mere anxiety in his own brain, about which he refuses to confide, even to Cassius. In II.i, we see the public self making further headway. First, there is Brutus' argument with himself about the threat of Caesar, and in his conclusion that Caesar must be killed we note how far his private self—he is, after all, one of Caesar's closest friends—has been invaded by the self of public spirit. From here on, the course of the invasion accelerates. The letter comes, tossed from the public world into the private world, into Brutus' garden, and addressing, as Cassius had, that public image reflected in the mirror: "Brutus, thou sleep'st: awake and see thyself." Then follows the well-known brief soliloquy (which Shakespeare was to expand into the whole play of *Macbeth*), showing us that Brutus' mind has moved on now from the phase of decision to the inquietudes that follow decision:

> Between the acting of a dreadful thing
> And the first motion, all the interim is
> Like a phantasma, or a hideous dream.

What is important to observe is that these lines stress once again the gulf that separates motive from action, that which is interior in man and controllable by his will from that which, once acted, becomes independent of him and moves with a life of its own. This gulf is a no man's land, a phantasma, a hideous dream.

Finally, there arrives in such a form that no audience can miss it the actual visible invasion itself, as this peaceful garden quiet is broken in on by knocking, like the knocking of fate in Beethoven's fifth symphony, and by men with faces hidden in their cloaks. Following this, a lovely interlude with Portia serves to emphasize how much the

private self, the private world has been shattered. We have
something close to discord here—as much of a discord as
these very gentle people are capable of—and though there
is a reconciliation at the end and Brutus' promise to confide in her soon, this division in the family is an omen.
So is that knock of the latecomer, Caius Ligarius, which
reminds us once again of the intrusions of the public life.
And when Ligarius throws off his sick man's kerchief on
learning that there is an honorable exploit afoot, we may
see in it an epitome of the whole scene, a graphic visual
renunciation, like Brutus', of the private good to the public; and we may see this also in Brutus' own exit a few
lines later, not into the inner house where Portia waits for
him, but out into the thunder and lightning of the public
life of Rome. It is perhaps significant that at our final view
of Portia, two scenes later, she too stands outside the
privacy of the house, her mind wholly occupied with
thoughts of what is happening at the Capitol, and trying to
put on a public self for Brutus' sake: "Run, Lucius, and
commend me to my Lord/Say I am merry. . . ."

Meantime, up there by the Capitol, the tragic center and
the historical center meet. The suspense is very great as
Caesar, seeing the Soothsayer in the throng, reminds him
that the ides of March are come, and receives in answer,
"Ay, Caesar, but not gone." More suspense as Artemidorus presses forward with the paper that we know contains a full discovery of the plot. Decius, apprehensive,
steps quickly into the breach with another paper, a petition from Trebonius. More suspense still as Popilius sidles
past Cassius with the whisper, "I wish your enterprise
today may thrive," and then moves on to Caesar's side,
where he engages him in animated talk. But they detect no
telltale change in Caesar's countenance; Trebonius steps
into his assignment and takes Antony aside; Metellus
Cimber throws himself at Caesar's feet; Brutus gives the
signal to "press near and second him," and Caesar's "Are
we all ready?" draws every eye to Caesar's chair. One by
one they all kneel before this demigod—an effective tab-
leau which gives a coloring of priestlike ritual to what they

are about to do. Caesar is to bleed, but, as Brutus has said, they will sublimate the act into a sacrifice:

> Let's kill him boldly but not wrathfully;
> Let's carve him as a dish fit for the gods,
> Not hew him as a carcass fit for hounds.

Everything in the scene must underscore this ceremonial attitude, in order to bring out the almost fatuous cleavage between the spirit of this enterprise and its bloody purpose.

The Caesar that we are permitted to see while all this ceremony is preparing is almost entirely the superman, for obvious reasons. To give a color of justice to Brutus' act and so to preserve our sense of his nobility even if we happen to think the assassination a mistake, as an Elizabethan audience emphatically would, Caesar has to appear in a mood of superhumanity at least as fatuous as the conspirators' mood of sacrifice. Hence Shakespeare makes him first of all insult Metellus Cimber: "If thou dost bend and pray and fawn for him,/I spurn thee like a cur"; then comment with intolerable pomposity, and, in fact, blasphemy, on his own iron resolution, for he affects to be immovable even by prayer and hence superior to the very gods. Finally, Shakespeare puts into his mouth one of those supreme arrogances that will remind us of the destroying *hubris* which makes men mad in order to ruin them. "Hence!" Caesar cries, "Wilt thou lift up Olympus?" It is at just this point, when the colossus Caesar drunk with self-love is before us, that Casca strikes. Then they all strike, with a last blow that brings out for the final time the other, human side of this double Caesar: "Et tu, Brute?"

And now this little group of men has altered history. The representative of the evil direction it was taking toward autocratic power lies dead before them. The direction to which it must be restored becomes emphatic in Cassius' cry of "Liberty, freedom, and enfranchisement." Solemnly, and again like priests who have just sacrificed a victim, they kneel together and bathe their hands and swords in Caesar's blood. Brutus exclaims:

> Then walk we forth, even to the market place;
> And waving our red weapons o'er our heads,
> Let's all cry, "Peace, freedom, and liberty!"

If the conjunction of those red hands and weapons with this slogan is not enough to bring an audience up with a start, the next passage will be, for now the conspirators explicitly invoke the judgment of history on their deed. On the stages of theaters the world over, so they anticipate, this lofty incident will be reenacted, and

> So oft as that shall be.
> So often shall the knot of us be called
> The men that gave their country liberty.

We, the audience, recalling what actually did result in Rome—the civil wars, the long line of despotic emperors —cannot miss the irony of their prediction, an irony that insists on our recognizing that this effort to control history is going to fail. Why does it fail?

One reason why is shown us in the next few moments. The leader of this assault on history is, like many another reformer, a man of high idealism, who devoutly believes that the rest of the world is like himself. It was just to kill Caesar—so he persuades himself—because he was a great threat to freedom. It would not have been just to kill Antony, and he vetoed the idea. Even now, when the consequence of that decision has come back to face him in the shape of Antony's servant, kneeling before him, he sees no reason to reconsider it. There are good grounds for what they have done, he says; Antony will hear them, and be satisfied. With Antony, who shortly arrives in person, he takes this line again:

> Our reasons are so full of good regard
> That were you, Antony, the son of Caesar
> You should be satisfied.

With equal confidence in the rationality of man, he puts by Cassius' fears of what Antony will do if allowed to address the people: "By your pardon; I will myself into the pulpit first/And show the reason of our Caesar's death." Here is a man so much a friend of Caesar's that he is still speaking of him as "our Caesar," so capable of rising to what he takes to be his duty that he has taken on the leadership of those who intend to kill him, so trusting of common decency that he expects the populace will respond to reason, and Antony to the obligation laid on him by their permitting him to speak. At such a man, one hardly knows whether to laugh or cry.

The same mixture of feelings is likely to be stirring in us as Brutus speaks to the people in III.ii. As everybody knows, this is a speech in what used to be called the great liberal tradition, the tradition that assumed, as our American founding fathers did, that men in the mass are reasonable. It has therefore been made a prose oration, spare and terse in diction, tightly patterned in syntax so that it requires close attention, and founded, with respect to its argument, on three elements: the abstract sentiment of duty to the state (because he endangered Rome, Caesar had to be slain); the abstract sentiment of political justice (because he was ambitious, Caesar deserved his fall); and the moral authority of the man Brutus. As long as that moral authority is concretely before them in Brutus' presence, the populace is impressed. But since they are not trained minds, and only trained minds respond accurately to abstractions, they do not understand the content of his argument at all, as one of them indicates by shouting, "Let him be Caesar!" What moves them is the obvious sincerity and the known integrity of the speaker; and when he finishes, they are ready to carry him off on their shoulders on that account alone, leaving Antony a vacant Forum. The fair-mindedness of Brutus is thrilling but painful to behold as he calms this triumphal surge in his favor, urges them to stay and hear Antony, and then, in a moment very impressive dramatically as well as symbolically, walks off the stage, alone. We see then, if we have not seen before, the first answer to the question why the attack on history failed. It was blinded, as it so often has been, by the very idealism that impelled it.

When Antony takes the rostrum, we begin to get a second answer. It has been said by somebody that in a school for demagogues this speech should be the whole curriculum. Antony himself describes its method when he observes in the preceding scene, apropos of the effect of Caesar's dead body on the messenger from Octavius, "Passion, I see, is catching." This is a statement that cannot be made about reason, as many a school teacher learns to his cost. I have not time at my disposal to do anything like justice to Antony's speech, but I should like to make the following summary points.

First, Brutus formulates from the outset positive propositions about Caesar and about his own motives, on no other authority than his own. Because of his known integrity, Brutus can do this. Antony takes the safer alternative of concealing propositions in questions, by which the audience's mind is then guided to conclusions which seem its own:

> He hath brought many captives to Rome,
> Whose ransoms did the general coffers fill:
> Did this in Caesar seem ambitious?

* * *

> You all did see that on the Lupercal
> I thrice presented him a kingly crown,
> Which he did thrice refuse: was this ambition?

How well Shakespeare knew his crowds can be seen in the replies to Antony. Brutus, appealing to their reason, was greeted with wild outbursts of uncomprehending emotion: "Let him be Caesar!" Antony appeals only to their emotions and their pockets, but now they say, "Methinks there is much reason in his sayings," and chew upon it seriously.

Second, Antony stirs up impulses and then thwarts them. He appeals to their curiosity and their greed in the matter of the will, but then he doesn't come clean on it. In the same manner, he stirs up their rage against the conspirators, yet always pretends to hold them back: "I

fear I wrong the honorable men/Whose daggers have
stabbed Caesar; I do fear it." Third, and this is largely the
technical means by which he accomplishes the stirring up,
his speech is baited with irony. The passage just quoted is
a typical specimen. So is the famous refrain, "For Brutus
is an honorable man." Now the rhetorical value of irony is
that it stimulates the mind to formulate the contrary, that
is, the intended meaning. It stimulates what the psycholo-
gists of propaganda nowadays call the assertive factor.
"Are you the one man in seven who shaves daily?" "Did
your husband forget to kiss you this morning?" The ad-
vertiser's technique is not, of course, ironical, but it illus-
trates the effect.

Finally, Antony rests his case, not, like Brutus, on abstractions centering in the state and political justice, but
on emotions centering in the individual listener. The first
great crescendo of the speech, which culminates in the
passage on Caesar's wounds, appeals first to pity and then
to indignation. The second one, culminating in the reading
of Caesar's will, appeals first to curiosity and greed and
then to gratitude. The management of the will is particularly cunning: it is an item more concrete than any words
could be, an actual tantalizing document that can be
flashed before the eye, after the manner of the senator
mentioned in my preamble. It is described, at first vaguely,
as being of such a sort that they would honor Caesar for
it. Then, closer home, as something which would show
"how Caesar loved you." Then, with an undisguised appeal to self-interest, as a testament that will make them his
"heirs." The emotions aroused by this news enable Antony
to make a final test of his ironical refrain about the "honorable men," and finding the results all that he had hoped,
he can come down now amoug the crowd as one of them,
and appeal directly to their feelings by appealing to his
own: "If you have tears to shed, prepare to shed them
now."

The success of this direct appeal to passion can be seen
at its close. Where formerly we had a populace, now we
have a mob. Since it is a mob, its mind can be sealed
against any later seepage of rationality back into it by the

insinuation that reasoning is always false anyway—simply a surface covering up private grudges, like the "reason" they have heard from Brutus; whereas from Antony himself, the plain blunt friend of Caesar, they are getting the plain blunt truth and (a favorite trick of politicians) only what they already know to be the truth.

But also, since it is a mob and therefore will eventually cool off, it must be called back one final time to hear the will. Antony no longer needs this as an incentive to riot; the mingled rage and pity he has aroused will take care of that. But when the hangover comes, and you are remembering how that fellow looked swaying a little on the rope's end, with his eyes bugging out and the veins knotted at his temples, then it is good to have something really reasonable to cling to, like seventy-five drachmas (or even thirty pieces of silver) and some orchards along a river.

At about this point, it becomes impossible not to see that a second reason for the failure of the attack on history is what it left out of account—what all these Romans from the beginning, except Antony, have been trying to leave out of account: the phenomenon of feeling, the nonrational factor in men, in the world, in history itself—of which this blind infuriated mob is one kind of exemplification. Too secure in his own fancied suppression of the subrational, Brutus has failed altogether to reckon with its power. Thus he could seriously say to Antony in the passage I quoted earlier: Antony, even if you were "the son of Caesar/You should be satisfied," as if the feeling of a son for a murdered father could ever be "satisfied" by reasons. And thus, too, he could walk off the stage alone, urging the crowd to hear Antony, the very figure of embodied "reason," unaware that only the irrational is catching.

Meantime, the scene of the mob tearing Cinna the Poet to pieces simply for having the same name as one of the conspirators (III.iii) gives us our first taste of the chaos invoked by Antony when he stood alone over Caesar's corpse. And as we consider that prediction and this mob, we are bound to realize that there is a third reason why the attack on history failed. As we have seen already, history is only partly responsive to noble motives, only partly responsive to rationality. Now we see—what Shakespeare hinted in the beginning with those two episodes of Calpurnia and the soothsayer—that it is only partly responsive to human influence of any sort. With all their reasons, the conspirators and Caesar only carried out what the soothsayer foreknew. There is, in short, a determination in history, whether we call it natural or providential, which at least *helps* to shape our ends, "rough hew them how we will." One of the names of that factor in this play is Caesarism. Brutus put the point, all unconsciously, in that scene when the conspirators were gathered at his house. He said:

> We all stand up against the spirit of Caesar:
> And in the spirit of men there is no blood:
> O that we then could come by Caesar's spirit,
> And not dismember Caesar! But, alas,
> Caesar must bleed for it.

Then Caesar did bleed for it; but his spirit, as Brutus' own remark should have told him, proved to be invulnerable. It was only set free by his assassination, and now, as Antony says, "ranging for revenge, . . . Shall in these confines with a monarch's voice/Cry 'Havoc' and let slip the dogs of war."

The rest of the play, I think, is self-explanatory. It is clear all through Acts IV and V that Brutus and Cassius are defeated before they begin to fight. Antony knows it and says so at V.i. Cassius knows it too. Cassius, an Epicurean in philosophy, and therefore one who has never heretofore believed in omens, now mistrusts his former rationalism: he suspects there may be something after all in those ravens, crows, and kites that wheel overhead. Brutus too mistrusts *his* rationalism. As a Stoic, his philosophy requires him to repudiate suicide, but he admits to Cassius that if the need comes he will repudiate philosophy instead. This, like Cassius' statement, is an unconscious admission of the force of unreason in human affairs, an unreason that makes its presence felt again and again

during the great battle. Cassius, for instance, fails to
realize that Octavius "Is overthrown by noble Brutus'
power," becomes the victim of a mistaken report of Titinius' death, runs on his sword crying, "Caesar, thou art
reveng'd," and is greeted, dead, by Brutus, in words that
make still clearer their defeat by history: "O Julius
Caesar, thou art mighty yet!/Thy spirit walks abroad, and
turns our swords/In our own proper entrails." In the same
vein, when it is Brutus' turn to die, we learn that the ghost
of Caesar has reappeared, and he thrusts the sword home,
saying, "Caesar, now be still."

To come then to a brief summary. Though I shouldn't
care to be dogmatic about it, it seems clear to me that
Shakespeare's primary theme in *Julius Caesar* has to do
with the always ambiguous impact between man and history. During the first half of the play, what we are chiefly
conscious of is the human will as a force in history—men
making choices, controlling events. Our typical scenes are
I.ii, where a man is trying to make up his mind; or II.i,
where a man first reaches a decision and then, with his
fellows, lays plans to implement it; or II.ii, where we have
Decius Brutus persuading Caesar to decide to go to the
senate house; or III.i and ii, where up through the assassination, and even up through Antony's speech, men are
still, so to speak, impinging on history, molding it to their
conscious will.

But then comes a change. Though we still have men in
action trying to mold their world (or else we would have
no play at all), one senses a real shift in the direction of
the impact. We begin to feel the insufficiency of noble
aims, for history is also consequences; the insufficiency of
reason and rational expectation, for the ultimate consequences of an act in history are unpredictable, and usually,
by all human standards, illogical as well; and finally, the
insufficiency of the human will itself, for there is always
something to be reckoned with that is nonhuman and in-
scrutable—Nemesis, Moira, Fortuna, the Parcae, Providence, Determinism: men have had many names for it,
but it is always there. Accordingly, in the second half of
the play, our typical scenes are those like III.iii, where

Antony has raised something that is no longer under his control; or like IV.i, where we see men acting as if, under the control of expediency or necessity or call it what you will, they no longer had wills of their own but prick down the names of nephews and brothers indiscriminately for slaughter; or like IV.iii and all the scenes thereafter, where we are constantly made to feel that Cassius and Brutus are in the hands of something bigger than they know.

In this light, we can see readily enough why it is that Shakespeare gave Julius Caesar that double character. The human Caesar who has human ailments and is a human friend is the Caesar that can be killed. The marmoreal Caesar, the everlasting Big Brother—the Napoleon, Mussolini, Hitler, Franco, Peron, Stalin, Kruschev, to mention only a handful of his more recent incarnations—that Caesar is the one who must repeatedly be killed but never dies, because he is in you, and you, and you, and me. Every classroom is a Rome, and there is no reason for any pupil, when he studies *Julius Caesar,* to imagine that this is ancient history.

ERNEST SCHANZER

The Problem of "Julius Caesar"

Julius Caesar is one of Shakespeare's most perplexing plays. Its stylistic simplicity, coupled with an absence of bawdy lines, has made it a favorite school text, and this has led some critics to believe that it ought to be a simple play, a belief which has easily ripened into the conviction that it *is* a simple play. Others have acknowledged its perplexities. Professor Allardyce Nicoll calls it one of Shakespeare's "most difficult plays rightly to assess,"[1] and Mr. Wilson Knight remarks that "to close analysis it reveals subtleties and complexities which render interpretation difficult."[2] There is widespread disagreement among critics about who is the play's principal character or whether it has a principal character, on whether it is a tragedy and if so whose, on whether Shakespeare wants us to consider the assassination as damnable or praiseworthy, while of all the chief characters in the play violently contradictory interpretations have been offered. To illustrate this polarity of views it will be sufficient to refer to two eminent critics. Professor Dover Wilson tells us that in this play Shakespeare adopted the traditional Renaissance view of Caesar, derived from Lucan, which regarded him as "a Roman Tamburlaine of illimitable ambition and ruthless irresisti-

---

From *Shakespeare Quarterly*, VI (Summer, 1955), pp. 297–308. Reprinted by permission of *Shakespeare Quarterly* and Ernest Schanzer.
[1] Allardyce Nicoll, *Shakespeare*, p. 134.
[2] G. Wilson Knight, *The Imperial Theme*, p. 63.

ble genius; a monstrous tyrant who destroyed his country and ruined 'the mightiest and most flourishing commonwealth that the world will ever see.' "[3] "The play's theme is the single one, Liberty versus Tyranny" (p. xxi). The assassination is wholly laudable, the conspirators are unselfish champions of freedom, while Brutus' tragedy consists in his vain struggle against the destiny of Rome, which lies in the establishment of Caesarism (p. xxii).

When we turn from this to Sir Mark Hunter's interpretation of the play, we are told that "there can be no doubt that to Shakespeare's way of thinking, however much he extends sympathy to the perpetrators of the deed, the murder of Julius was the foulest crime in secular history." Of Caesar we learn, "When put to the test of the stage the personality of Julius 'moves before us as something right royal,' a character sufficiently great to render the impassioned eulogy of Antony and the calm tribute of Brutus not inconsistent with what we have actually heard and seen of the object of their praise." Of the conspirators we are told, "Brutus excepted, there is no sign anywhere that the enemies of the Dictator, though they have all the political catchwords at command—Liberty, Enfranchisement, etc —care one jot for the welfare of anyone outside their own order." And of Brutus, "Noble-hearted and sincere beyond question, Brutus is intellectually dishonest," he is self-righteous, pathetically inconsistent, a "befogged and wholly mischievous politician."[4]

Thus, while Dover Wilson roots the play in the dominant literary tradition of the Renaissance, which is overwhelmingly hostile to Caesar, Sir Mark Hunter, with equal confidence, places it in the dominant medieval tradition, which is wholly eulogistic. In this he is supported by so great an authority as W. W. Fowler, who tells us that Shakespeare's idea of Caesar "was simply an inheritance from the education of the Middle Ages," when the textbook for Roman History was that of Orosius, who brings out the greatness and moderation of Caesar and the cruel injustice of the

[3] *Julius Caesar* (New Cambridge edition), p. xxv.
[4] *Trans. Royal Soc. Lit.*, X (1931), 136 ff.

assassination.[5] The reader of Shakespeare's play is thus faced with a difficult choice. Is he to throw in his lot with Professor Dover Wilson and Cassius, and regard Shakespeare's Caesar as a boastful tyrant, strutting blindly to his well-merited doom, and the assassination as a glorious act of liberation, or is he to follow Sir Mark Hunter and Mark Antony, and look at him as "the noblest man that ever lived in the tide of times," and at the assassination as a hideous crime? Fortunately for the less resolute spirits there is a third tradition in relation to which the play may be viewed, made up of writers whose reaction to Caesar and the conspiracy is not simple and undivided, like that of Lucan and Orosius, but of a complex and sometimes bafflingly contradictory nature.

Among these writers are above all Plutarch, Shakespeare's main source; Appian, with whose *Roman History* Shakespeare was probably acquainted in the 1578 translation; Suetonius; Dante; and a number of Renaissance writers, among them the author of the anonymous play entitled *Caesar's Revenge*, which, as I have argued elsewhere,[6] was probably one of the chief formative influences upon Shakespeare's play. The reasons for their divided attitude to the Caesar story vary, of course, a good deal among the different writers. With Plutarch it seems to result largely from a personal dislike of Caesar's character, coupled with a belief in him as the Man of Destiny "whom God had ordained of special grace to be Governor of the Empire of Rome, and to set all things again at quiet stay, the which required the counsel and authority of an absolute Prince."[7] And much the same seems to me to hold true of Dante's attitude. Plutarch's view of the conspirators is also complicated by a desire to show "his angel" Brutus as the only just man among the wicked, joined with a reluctance to accept the conclusion that Brutus chose other than honest men for his associates. Plutarch is thus driven to alternate between blackening and whitewashing the character of Brutus'

[5] W. W. Fowler, *Roman Essays and Interpretations*, p. 273.
[6] *Notes and Queries*, New Series, I, 5 (1954).
[7] *Tudor Translations*, ed. W. E. Henley, XII, 237. ("Comparison of Dion with Brutus.")

fellow conspirators. Appian's divided attitude seems to arise mainly from a mingling of admiration for Brutus and Cassius, "two most noble and illustrious Romans, and of incomparable virtue, but for one crime," and an abhorrence of their foul deed of murder. "Yet by these men the act against Caesar was done, contrary in all thing, being no simple work, nor in no small matter, for it was against their friend, contrary to reason, and against their well doer, unthankfully, whom he had saved in the war, and against the chief ruler, injustly in the Senate house, and against an holy man, having on an holy vesture; and such an officer, as never was the like, so profitable to all men and to his country and Empire. The which God did punish in them, and many times gave tokens of it."[8] (Had Shakespeare this passage at the back of his mind when he made Macbeth, contemplating the murder of Duncan, recoil at the threefold violation of sacred relationships, that of kinsman, subject, and host, and declare that Duncan had been "So clear in his great office, that his virtues/Will plead like angels, trumpet-tongued, against/The deep damnation of his taking-off"? [I.vii]) The divided attitude in *Caesar's Revenge* issues largely from the author's attempt to combine Appian's presentation of the Caesar story, which seems to have served as his chief source, with that of the French Senecan plays of Muret, Garnier, and Grévin, which makes him both depict Caesar as a thrasonical, infatuated world-conqueror, and show Brutus driven to despair and suicide through the burden of guilt incurred by having murdered his friend and benefactor.

It is to this tradition of a divided, complex, and often ambiguous response to the Caesar story that Shakespeare's play belongs. But with Shakespeare, as I hope to show, this ambiguity and divided response, however much it may also be a reflection of his own feelings, is used as a deliberate dramatic device, and is no mere accidental inheritance from his sources. It seems highly likely that Shakespeare's own attitude to the Caesar story underwent a complete change as a result of his reading of Plutarch. His earlier response

[8] Appian, *Roman History*, 1578 translation, p. 303.

appears to have been much like that of his medieval ancestors and was probably also that of the great mass of the
people of England who had heard of Caesar at all. To them
he was one of the Nine Worthies, the great warrior hero,
and his murderers were damnable villains. This view is
above all expressed in the *Henry VI* plays.

> A far more glorious star thy soul will make
> Than Julius Caesar or bright——

Bedford says of the dead Henry V (*1 Henry VI*, I.i):

> They that stabb'd Caesar shed no blood at all,
> Did not offend, nor were not worthy blame,
> If this foul deed were by to equal it

Queen Margaret exclaims at the murder of her son (*3 Henry
VI*, V.v); while Suffolk tells his assassins:

> Great men oft die by vile besonians:
> A Roman sworder and banditto slave
> Murder'd sweet Tully; Brutus' bastard hand
> Stabb'd Julius Caesar.
>
> > (*2 Henry VI*, IV.i.)

Added to this popular view of Caesar we find the knowledge
of him as the writer of commentaries, a man of learning and
wit. "Kent, in the commentaries Caesar wrote,/Is term'd
the civil'st place," we learn in *2 Henry VI*, IV.vii. And in
Richard III Prince Edward admiringly exclaims,

> That Julius Caesar was a famous man;
> With what his valor did enrich his wit,
> His wit set down to make his valor live:
> Death makes no conquest of this conqueror;
> For now he lives in fame, though not in life.
>
> > (III.i.)

After this the tone and content of the Caesar references
change. In *As You Like It* Rosalind speaks jestingly of
"Caesar's thrasonical brag of 'I came, saw, and overcame,'"

and Falstaff makes a similar allusion at his capture of Coleville (*2 Henry IV*, IV.iii). Cloten speaks of "Caesar's ambition/Which swell'd so much that it did almost stretch/ The sides o' the world" (*Cymbeline*, III.i). We hear no more of Caesar's valor, glory, or wit, but a good deal of his fabulous military skill (*All's Well*, III.vi; *Othello*, II.iii; *Cymbeline*, III.i). The references to Caesar and Brutus in the earlier plays are also of value in indicating what must have been the attitude to the Caesar story of at least a considerable portion of the audience. If the majority of the spectators at the performance of *3 Henry VI* had in fact felt that the murderers of Caesar "did not offend, nor were not worthy blame," Queen Margaret's comparison would, to say the least, be ill chosen. In the same way Bedford's hyperbole would be a mere lapse into bathos unless a large part of the audience were in sympathy with the medieval apotheosis of Caesar. But there must have been other members of the audience, readers of Lucan and Plutarch, who, a few years later, could respond to Shakespeare's sympathetic presentation of Brutus in *Julius Caesar*, without the interference of preconceptions about Brutus' bastard hand that stabbed his friend and benefactor. And there were probably others, readers of Plutarch, Appian, and Suetonius, who were divided in their attitude, and who had not made up their minds. It is this variety and division of views among his audience which, as it seems to me, Shakespeare deliberately exploited.

I propose to begin with a discussion of Shakespeare's presentment of the character of Caesar. Its nature will be seen most clearly by being rapidly followed scene by scene, from the opening of the play until Antony's funeral oration.

In Flavius and Marullus we get our first glimpses of the republican opposition to Caesar's rule. Loyalty to Pompey's memory as well as fear of future oppression seem their chief motives. The metaphor which Flavius uses to justify their "disrobing" of Caesar's images strikes an ominous note:

> These growing feathers plucked from Caesar's wing
> Will make him fly an ordinary pitch,

Who else would soar above the view of men
And keep us all in servile fearfulness.

(I.i.75–78)

It points forward to the image of the serpent's egg applied
to Caesar in Brutus' soliloquy. There a more drastic opera-
tion is advocated, but in both cases the action is thought of
as preventive, directed not against what Caesar is but what
he may become if not checked in time. Both images are
probably indebted to a passage in Plutarch's "Life of
Caesar," where his favorite equestrian metaphor is used to
convey the same thought: "But in fine, when they had thus
given him the bridle to grow to this greatness, and that they
could not then pull him back, though indeed in sight it
would turn one day to the destruction of the whole state
and commonwealth of Rome: too late they found, that
there is not so little a beginning of anything, but continuance
of time will soon make it strong, when through contempt
there is no impediment to hinder the greatness."[9] Immediately upon Flavius' words Caesar makes his first appearance, and the imaginative impact of this short scene tends to
bear out rather than to discredit Flavius' fears. With the
utmost economy of words Shakespeare manages to create
the atmosphere of an oriental court with its cringing attendants and fawning favorites. "Peace, ho! Caesar speaks."
"When Caesar says 'do this' it is performed." And into this
atmosphere intrudes the first of the many warnings that
come ever thicker as the moment of the murder approaches,
and like all the others it is contemptuously brushed aside by
Caesar. "He is a dreamer, let us leave him: pass."

From this slow-moving and portentous scene we pass at
once to the rapid, feverish, and impassioned utterances of
Cassius in his great seduction scene. The contrast which
Cassius draws between Caesar's physical defects, which
make him succumb in a swimming match and shake when
suffering from a fever fit, and the greatness of his position,
is part of a general contrast, pervading the whole play,
between Caesar's frailties of body and character and the
strength of his spirit which has enabled him to become "the

[9] P. 5. All page references in the article are to *Shakespeare's Plutarch*,
ed. Tucker Brooke, 2 vols., in the *Shakespeare's Library* series.

foremost man of all the world." Cassius is genuinely per-
plexed by this contrast. He is like a schoolboy who is puzzled and angry that someone whom he has always beaten at
games should have become prefect and exact obedience
from his physical equals and superiors.

> Now, in the names of all the gods at once,
> Upon what meat doth this our Caesar feed,
> That he is grown so great?
>
> (I.ii.148–50)

Contrary to his intention, Cassius does not throw doubt on
Caesar's courage, but unwittingly testifies to it. It is the
fever fit that makes Caesar shake, not the prospect of
jumping into "the troubled Tiber chafing with her shores."
The story of the swimming match epitomizes the triumph
of Caesar's daring and resolution over his physical frailties.

It is significant that in this crucial scene, where Cassius
can be expected to make the most of the opposition's case
against Caesar, he makes no mention of any specific acts
of oppression or tyrannical behavior. There is only the
general assertion that Rome is "groaning underneath this
age's yoke." But the yoke to Cassius lies in one man's
usurpation of the honors and powers that previously be-
longed to many. To him the yoke is therefore very much
an existing reality, whereas to Brutus the threat lies not in
present but in impending conditions.

> Brutus had rather be a villager
> Than to repute himself a son of Rome
> Under these hard conditions as this time
> Is like to lay upon us
>
> (I.ii.172–75)

he tells Cassius in this scene. And in his soliloquy it is again
not what Caesar *is* but what he may *become* that causes his
fears.

What, then, is the effect of this scene upon our mental
picture of Caesar? It heightens, rather than alters, our
previous impression of him as an oriental monarch, a
Colossus, and begins the process, continuing through much

of the play, of disjoining and contrasting the human and
the superhuman Caesar, the man with his physical and
moral frailties and the God who is beyond human frailties.
Caesar, by constantly putting himself outside the pale of
humanity, collaborating, as Mr. John Palmer so well puts
it,[10] in his own deification, yet reminding us of his frailties
on each of his appearances, underlines this dissociation. In
the very next episode we find him angry at the mob's opposition to his acceptance of the crown, afraid of Cassius, yet
assuring Antony

> I rather tell thee what is to be feared
> Than what I fear; for always I am Caesar.

And at once follows the body-spirit contrast:

> Come on my right hand, for this ear is deaf
> And tell me truly what thou think'st of him.
> (I.ii.213–14)

As Dover Wilson points out (p. 113), the atmosphere is
again that of the oriental court. When Caesar is angry "all
the rest look like a chidden train." In his remarks about
Cassius we get our chief glimpse of the Caesar we know
from Plutarch, the shrewd politician, the keen observer of
men, the Caesar of the Commentaries.

In Casca's narration of the day's events a new Caesar is
revealed to us, again with Plutarchian traits, Caesar the
play actor, skillfully exploiting the passions of the mob.
While his fall in the market place is a sort of preview of his
later fall in the Capitol, his adroit play upon the feelings of
the mob adumbrates Antony's manipulation of them in his
funeral oration. Casca's report ends on an ominous note,
which, for the moment, makes the worst fears of the enemies of Caesar seem justified: "Marullus and Flavius, for
pulling scarfs off Caesar's images, are put to silence." Not
deprived of their tribuneship, as in Plutarch, but simply,
cryptically, "put to silence."

Up to this point Shakespeare has tipped the balance in
favor of the conspirators' view of Caesar and has made us

---

[10] John Palmer, *Shakespeare's Political Characters*, p. 37.

share Brutus' apprehensions. Now, by making Cassius, in
his soliloquy, so frankly impugn the integrity of his own
motives and show us so clearly the personal nature of his
opposition, we are brought to question the truth of our
impression of Caesar, so much of which we have received
through Cassius. And our doubts are strengthened by the
play's next image of Caesar, again drawn by Cassius, this
time for the terror-stricken Casca. For Cassius' picture of
Caesar and his explanation of the portents is clearly part
of an *argumentum ad hominem*. Cassius' himself is an
Epicurean and does not, at least not yet, "credit things that
do presage." But to convince Casca, who does credit them,
of the monstrosity of Caesar's rule, he is quite ready to put
them to use to prop up his arguments. Against Cassius'
explanation of the omens we have been indirectly warned
just before by Cicero:

> But men may construe things, after their fashion,
> Clean from the purpose of the things themselves.
>
> (I.iii.34–35)

The groundwork of Cassius' indictment of Caesar here is
much the same as in his scene with Brutus. There is again
the contrast between what Caesar really is and what he has
become, but what he has become is something slightly different, fitting the altered circumstances. It is no longer a
God or a Colossus who dwarfs his fellowmen, and thus
prevents them from achieving personal glory. This repre-
sentation of Caesar seemed to Cassius suited to Brutus in
whom he is trying to awake a sense of thwarted ambition.
But upon the terrified Casca it is a sense of the fearfulness
of Caesar that he tries to impress.

> Now could I, Casca, name to thee a man
> Most like this dreadful night,
> That thunders, lightens, opens graves, and roars
> As doth the lion in the Capitol;
> A man no mightier than thyself or me
> In personal action, yet prodigious grown
> And fearful, as these strange eruptions are.
>
> (I.iii.72–78)

But while the picture of Caesar as a God and a Colossus bore some semblance to the reality of which we have been allowed a few glimpses, the Caesar that "thunders, lightens, opens graves, and roars" is too obviously a fabrication of the moment for argumentative purposes to affect our mental image of the man. The ironic fact that Caesar later seems to bear out Cassius' description by referring to himself as a lion and Danger's elder twin brother does not alter this impression. For it is Caesar's most ludicrous utterance, and no more affrights us than Snug the joiner's impersonation of that "fearful wildfowl." Our image of Caesar receives its next modification in Brutus' soliloquy. Brutus' Caesar bears no resemblance either to Cassius' God and Colossus or to his roaring lion. He appears to Brutus in the image of a serpent's egg, someone yet harmless but potentially mischievous because of his desire for the crown. At the very moment when it is most in Brutus' interest to incriminate Caesar his intellectual honesty forces him to declare:

> And to speak truth of Caesar
> I have not known when his affections swayed
> More than his reason.
>
> (II.i.19–21)

It is an echo of Plutarch's "And now for himself, after he had ended his Civil Wars, he did so honorably behave himself, that there was no fault to be found in him" ("Caesar," p. 86). But are we to take this as a valid estimate of Caesar's character? Or is it as mistaken as Brutus' view of Antony and Cassius? His reference to Caesar's "lowliness" suggests this, for it is ludicrously inapposite to what we see of Caesar in this play. Thus Shakespeare calls in doubt the validity of Brutus' image of Caesar, just as he calls in doubt Cassius' image, and later Antony's, so that the nature of the real Caesar remains an enigma.

Nor is this enigma dispelled by what we see of Caesar in the following scenes. Even in the privacy of his home he is strenuously engaged in the creation of the legendary Caesar. There is never any real intimacy in his scene with Calpurnia, no momentary lifting of the mask in a soliloquy or

an aside. Here and in the Capitol Shakespeare gives us
above all the thrasonical Caesar, who sees himself as outside and above humanity.

> Caesar shall forth: the things that threaten'd me
> Ne'er looked but on my back; when they shall see
> The face of Caesar, they are vanished. . . .
> Of all the wonders that I yet have heard,
> It seems to me most strange that men should fear.
> . . . . Danger knows full well
> That Caesar is more dangerous than he:
> We are two lions littered in one day,
> And I the elder and more terrible.
>
> (II.ii.10–12, 34–35, 44–47)

Only upon the arrival of the conspirators does he unbend a
little, for the first and last time in the play. For his bearing
here Shakespeare is probably indebted to Plutarch's description of the youthful Caesar: "And the people loved
him marvelously also because of the courteous manner he
had to speak to every man, and to use them gently, being
more ceremonious therein than was looked for in one of his
years. Furthermore, he ever kept a good board, and fared
well at his table, and was very liberal besides" ("Caesar,"
p. 5). Plutarch's coupling of Caesar's hospitality with his
courtesy probably suggested to Shakespeare his

> Good friends, go in and taste some wine with me;
> And we, like friends, will straightway go together.
>
> (II.ii.126–27)

But these lines also call up memories of the ceremonial
sharing of wine before another betrayal, memories which
are strengthened by the kiss which Brutus gives to Caesar
in the Capitol ("I kiss thy hand, but not in flattery, Caesar"),
and later by Antony's reproach of Brutus at Philippi:

> In your bad strokes, Brutus, you give good words,
> Witness the hole you made in Caesar's heart
> Crying "Long live! hail Caesar!"
>
> (V.i.30–32)

("And forthwith he came to Jesus, and said, Hail master;
and kissed him," Matthew 26:49).

We are next given another estimation of Caesar and the
conspiracy in Artemidorus'

> My heart laments that virtue cannot live
> Out of the teeth of emulation.
> If thou read this, O Caesar, thou mayst live;
> If not, the Fates with traitors do contrive.
>
> (II.iii.12–15)

Having engaged our sympathies for Caesar more fully than
at any previous point in the play, Shakespeare loses little
time to alienate them again, so that by the moment of the
assassination our antipathies are more strongly aroused
than ever before. In his two short speeches in the Capitol
Shakespeare gives us a compendium of Caesar's most un-
amiable qualities: the cold, glittering hardness, the supreme
arrogance, and again the dissociation of himself from the
rest of mankind. A note of irony intrudes in his reference to
his constancy:

> But I am constant as the northern star,
> Of whose true-fixed and resting quality
> There is no fellow in the firmament.
>
> (II.i.60–62)

The whole speech is ironic both in view of the mental
vacillation which we have just witnessed, and his impending
fall. It anticipates Othello's similarly ironic comparison of
himself to the Pontic sea, which is equally belied by succeeding events. Shakespeare adds a final somewhat ludicrous
touch in Caesar's "Hence! Wilt thou lift up Olympus?",
which, juxtaposed with the immediately succeeding spectacle of his lifeless body lying at the foot of Pompey's statue,
crystallizes the contrast between the corporeal and spiritual
Caesar, which is summed up a little later by Antony's

> O mighty Caesar! dost thou lie so low?
> Are all thy conquests, glories, triumphs, spoils
> Shrunk to this little measure?
>
> (III.i.148–50)

From Antony we now receive our last image of Caesar. His is the Caesar of popular medieval tradition, the great warrior, the Mirror of Knighthood, the noble Emperor. There is Caesar's nobility,

> Thou art the ruins of the noblest man
> That ever lived in the tide of times;
>
> (III.i.256–57)

his fidelity,

> He was my friend, faithful and just to me;

his largesse,

> To every Roman citizen he gives,
> To every several man, seventy-five drachmas;

his military prowess,

> He hath brought many captives home to Rome;

his compassionate nature,

> When that the poor have cried, Caesar hath wept.
> (III.ii.87, 243–44, 90, 93)

Yet though we are not made to doubt the sincerity of Antony's tribute to Caesar in his soliloquy, the image of him created by Antony in his funeral oration is called into question by its forming a part of Antony's consummate and carefully contrived play upon the emotions of the crowd. As with Cassius' and Brutus' image of Caesar, we cannot accept it as a simple presentment of facts.

Throughout the first half of the play, then, we are given a series of images of Caesar none of which bear much mutual resemblance, though some of them are not irreconcilable with each other. There are the two Caesar's of Cassius, there is Casca's Caesar, Brutus' Caesar, Artemidorus' Caesar, and finally Antony's Caesar. But doubt is thrown in one way or another on the validity of most of these images. And to these Shakespeare adds his own presentation of Caesar, a presentation so enigmatic and ambiguous that none of the other images are really dispelled by it. It is a

Pirandellian presentation of the Caesar figure. "Which of all these is the real Caesar?" Shakespeare seems to ask. And he takes care not to provide an answer. But does not Shakespeare further anticipate Pirandello by making us feel that perhaps there *is* no real Caesar, that he merely exists as a set of images in other men's minds and his own? For Shakespeare's Caesar is continuously engaged in what Pirandello calls *costruirsi*, "building himself up," creating his own image of Caesar, until we are left to wonder whether a lifting of the mask would reveal to us any face at all.

What reasons lie behind Shakespeare's peculiar presentation of the figure of Caesar? The usual answer given by critics, that Shakespeare draws Caesar unsympathetically in order to preserve our regard for the conspirators, or, as Bernard Shaw more bluntly put it, that he writes "Caesar down for the mere technical purpose of writing Brutus up,"[11] will not do. For, as we have seen, what is involved in Shakespeare's presentation is something quite different from a mere writing down of the character. Another explanation is provided by Mr. H. M. Ayres who, as long ago as 1910, argued that, ever since Muret modeled his Caesar on the braggart Hercules of Seneca, the typical stage Caesar in the Renaissance was the vainglorious, hubristic figure of the French Senecans, and that Shakespeare had to endow his Caesar with these characteristics to fulfill the expectations of his audience.[12] However, there is no indication that any of the Elizabethan Caesar plays that were performed in the public theaters were influenced by the French Senecans. Muret, Grevin, and Garnier wrote only for academic audiences, and even a more popular play, like the anonymous *Caesar's Revenge,* may never have reached the public stage, for on its title page appears the note, "Privately acted by the Studentes of Trinity Colledge in Oxford." If Shakespeare endowed his Caesar with traits ultimately derived from the French Senecan Caesar plays he must have done so for other reasons than those suggested by Mr. Ayres.

Partly Shakespeare's presentment of Caesar was probably done in the interest of dramatic suspense. Shakespeare

---

[11] G. B. Shaw, *Three Plays for Puritans* (Constable, 1925), p. xxx.
[12] *PMLA,* XXV, 183ff.

appears to be playing on the audience's divided attitude to the Caesar story, giving encouragement in turn to each man's preconceived ideas. And since on our estimate of Caesar depends to a large extent our view of the justification of the entire conspiracy, the whole drama is thus kept within the area of the problem play. For though, as it seems to me, Shakespeare makes abundantly clear the catastrophic consequences of the murder, he does not, I think, make wholly clear its moral indefensibility. His ambiguous presentment of the Caesar figure allows responses like that of Professor Dover Wilson to be formulated, and I see no reason to doubt that there were also Dover Wilsons in Shakespeare's audience. In fact, the polarity of critical estimates of the character of the main *dramatis personae* and of the poet's attitude to the conspiracy bears witness to Shakespeare's success in making *Julius Caesar* a problem play. It is a problem play in much the same way as the *Wild Duck*, which has a very similar theme: the tragic mischief created by the actions of a young idealist in fulfillment of the highest principles, partly through his utter blindness to what people are really like. In both cases the question is put to the audience: "Was he or was he not morally justified in doing what he did?", and in both cases the dramatist's answer seems to me an insistent but not a compelling "No."

The main purpose of Shakespeare's dissociation of the corporeal and the spiritual Caesar throughout the play is, no doubt, to show up the futility and foolishness of the assassination. The whole second part of the play is an ironic comment on Brutus'

> We all stand up against the spirit of Caesar,
> And in the spirit of men there is no blood;
> O, that we then could come by Caesar's spirit,
> And not dismember Caesar!
>
> (II.i.167–70)

What is involved in the second half of the play is more than a grim pun, which makes the conspirators find that, while they have dismembered Caesar's body, his spirit, i.e. his ghost, still walks abroad, and exacts his revenge. For the spirit of Caesar is also that legendary figure, that God and Colossus, whom Cassius deplores, and whom Caesar seeks to impose upon the imagination of his countrymen and, it would seem, upon his own. In this he is handicapped by physical and moral frailties from which the murder frees him, and allows the legendary Caesar to come into his own, assisted by Antony's rhetoric, just as Antony later assists that other "spirit" of Caesar, his ghost, in executing his revenge.

That the spirit of Caesar in the sense of "Caesarism," the absolute rule of a single man, informs the second part of the play, as MacCallum, Dover Wilson, and others maintain, seems to me unsupported by anything in the text. Dover Wilson writes: "When Brutus exclaims 'We all stand up against the spirit of Caesar' he sums up the play in one line. For the spirit of Caesar, which was the destiny of Rome, is the fate against which Brutus struggles in vain" (p. xxii). And MacCallum, in a rather different spirit, tells us that "Shakespeare makes it abundantly clear that the rule of the single master-mind is the only admissible solution for the problem of the time."[13] Both these critics, and the many others who have expressed similar opinions, seem to me to be reading Plutarch's view into Shakespeare's play. Nothing in the play suggests to me that Caesar is to be thought of as the Man of Destiny or that the establishment of one man's rule is the inevitable outcome of the Civil War. As in Plutarch, the people are shown to be strongly opposed to Caesar's assumption of the crown, as the Lupercal scene makes clear. Over against this can only be set the plebeians' shouts after Brutus' speech, "Let him be Caesar," "Caesar's better parts shall be crowned in Brutus," but to take these as evidence of strong monarchic feelings among the Roman people is surely to miss their function in the scene's context. At Philippi it is not Caesarism or the providential scheme of Plutarch and Dante which defeats Brutus and Cassius, but their flaws of soldiership and character, which make Brutus give the word for attack too early, and Cassius slay himself rashly, in premature despair. As far as the super-

[13] Sir Mungo MacCallum, *Shakespeare's Roman Plays*, p. 214.

natural interferes in the affairs of men, it is Caesar's ghost rather than the hand of God that contributes to the defeat of the conspirators. Nor are we anywhere made to feel, as we are in Plutarch and Appian, that the Roman Republic has sunk into a state of corruption which only the establishment of one man's rule can cure.

Kittredge was undoubtedly right when, first among critics, he pointed to the element of "hubris" and ἄτη that pervades Shakespeare's portrayal of Caesar.[14] His infatuation, which makes him disregard all warnings, is repeatedly emphasized, from his first contemptuous dismissal of the soothsayer until his refusal to read Artemidorus' petition, and is pointed out by Calpurnia: "Alas, my lord, Your wisdom is consumed in confidence." His "hubris" is heightened with each appearance until it reaches its climax in his last speech in the Capitol. It is not difficult to trace the pedigree of this tragedy of "hubris," which is one of the several tragedies imbedded in the play. It is in a direct line of descent from Greek tragedy by way of Seneca, the adaptation of Senecan tragedy to the Caesar story by Muret and his imitators, and its adoption in the *Caesar's Revenge* play. But while the theme of "hubris" is dominant in all the plays in the Muret tradition, that of blind infatuation is only developed by Shakespeare.

We have seen, then, that in *Julius Caesar* Shakespeare puts a twofold problem before his audience: There is the psychological problem of the nature of the real Caesar; and hinging upon it there is the ethical prob'·m of the moral defensibility of the murder. Looked at in this way *Julius Caesar* reveals an unobtrusive kinship with Shakespeare's other chief problem play, *Measure for Measure*. Central to both is a moral choice imposed upon the protagonists, Brutus and Isabel. And in both cases Shakespeare, while, as it seems to me, strongly suggesting by the orientation of his dramatic material the wrongfulness of their choice, makes it remain sufficiently problematic to allow his audience to form varying views about it.

[14] *Julius Caesar*, ed. Kittredge, *Introduction*.

ROY WALKER

from *Unto Caesar: A Review of Recent Productions*

No major play of Shakespeare's has suffered more from democratic distortion than *Julius Caesar*. It seems improbable that the sympathies of the Elizabethan poet and his audience would be hostile to the aging, sick and childless personal ruler, brutally and treacherously assassinated by professed friends who then plunge their country into the dread cycle of civil wars that ends only with the disruption and downfall of the Republic. Although Hazlitt supposed that Shakespeare painted an entirely antipathetic portrait of Caesar, it was still possible, before two world wars darkened the scene, to recognize, as MacCallum did in 1910, that "Shakespeare makes it abundantly clear that the rule of the single master-mind is the only admissible solution for the problem of the time."[1] The Hazlitt tradition reached its patriotic peak in Dover Wilson's 1949 edition of the play. Meanwhile it had spread to the stage. After Orson Welles' 1937 modern-dress production (in which, of course, this powerful actor elected to play Brutus), other modern-dress *Caesars* in this country, and most costume productions too, presented the drama as the democratic doing-in-of a diabolical dictator. They could therefore make nothing of the celestial portents and still less of the fifth act in which the spirit of the dead dictator inconveniently triumphs.

From *Shakespeare Survey*, XI (1958), pp. 132–35. Reprinted by permission of The Cambridge University Press.
[1] M. W. MacCallum, *Shakespeare's Roman Plays* (1910), p. 214.

216

Now that the dogs of war are on the leash again there are signs of scholarly reaction on both sides of the Atlantic. In 1953 Virgil Whitaker argued that Shakespeare meant Caesar to seem "a great and good ruler"[2] and in the new Arden edition two years later T. S. Dorsch agreed that "Shakespeare wishes us to admire his Caesar."[3] A similar rehabilitation on the stage was overdue. It was peculiarly appropriate that this should be achieved in the year of the 2000th anniversary of the assassination, and in the Shakespeare Memorial Theatre at Stratford-upon-Avon, where Glen Byam Shaw produced the play. The main interest of this production lay in its bold centralization of Caesar, who became the real as well as the nominal protagonist, and in the means employed to keep this presence dramatically alive on the stage after the actual murder, with a consequent gain in coherency and in the significance of the last act.

Glen Byam Shaw's interpretation began at the beginning of the play. The curtain rose on a stage dominated by a larger-than-life statue of Caesar, raised on a tall plinth in the center of the stage. After the disrobing of this image by the envious tribunes, this statue pivoted backwards out of sight, the two walls of gray stone parted and against the blue sky at the back the living Caesar was acclaimed. The statue might easily have dwarfed the human figure, but the magnificence of the gold-embroidered crimson toga and the majesty of Cyril Luckham's bearing made him the incarnation of an immutable and pivotal principle of order. This ordered Rome was visible in the massive fluted monoliths of light gray stone, ranged outwards from Caesar as their personal center in two symmetrical lines, continued in the tall stone portals flanking the forestage. Here was the wide perspective of Caesar's Rome with Caesar himself the keystone.

When the procession had passed, that center was unfilled while Cassius, effectively played as a "little Caesar," a Corsican upstart, by Geoffrey Keen, maneuvered for the advantage of height with a Brutus (Alec Clunes) who was every inch Caesar's angel in presence and noble innocence.

[2] Virgil K. Whitaker, *Shakespeare's Use of Learning* (1953), p. 234.
[3] T. S. Dorsch (ed.), *Julius Caesar* (1955), p. xxxviii.

At the end of this scene of lurking disorder, the sky darkened with supernatural speed and an ominous patch of crimson appeared above the place where Caesar had stood. Cassius' defiance of the lightning was posed at stage center and met with a crackling blaze of white light from heaven, a warning which went unheeded by the arch-plotter.

The foremost monoliths converged again to close the main stage and leave the forestage for Brutus' orchard, but the central niche where Caesar's image had been was now eloquently empty while Brutus struggled to put away loyalty and friendship. When this orchard wall parted to reveal the interior of Caesar's house, the central entrance was hung with a divided crimson curtain, behind which was visible a head of Caesar, now isolated on a pedestal of his own height. The front walls converged again and Artemidorus paused before the empty niche to read over his warning to Caesar. They reopened on the Senate, with a raised central throne, its back a solid sheet of gleaming gold, on which Caesar took his place with his head high against the blue sky beyond. As he fell to the assassins' swords there was a fierce crackle of lightning from the clear sky, which was then rapidly overcast.

When the scene changed to the Forum, the two lines of monoliths had fallen back in disorder, leaving a wider gap in the center. Caesar's central throne had now given place to the popular pulpit from which successive demagogues harangued the changeable many who lined the front of the stage in dark silhouette, as though under a sinister shadow that had fallen on all Rome. Caesar's catafalque, the body shrouded with the crimson, gold-ornamented robe, was laid on the center of the forestage, below the pulpit. As Antony (Richard Johnson) passionately roused the mob to blood, the sky reddened, and at the climactic cry "Here was Caesar! when comes such another?" he was standing a little off-center in front of the now empty pulpit, his right arm thrust straight up to heaven; and suddenly in the true center of the sky the northern star shone out alone. After the tumultuous exit the stage was empty and silent for a moment with the star shining distantly down. The poet Cinna half turned his head toward it as he entered, saying "I dreamt tonight that I did feast with Caesar." Back surged the mob, now bearing lighted torches, bobbing and blazing symbols of disorder, the wandering fires of an earth from which the unmoved mover had been withdrawn. The interval arrived with an unforgettable stage picture of the murdered poet, flopped brokenly over the front of the pulpit like a discarded glove-puppet, and the star, blazing brighter in a sky that turned from blue to black, shining down in silent comment on the grim scene of chaos come again.

The second half opened with the triumvirate standing apart with their backs to a huge suspended map of the Mediterranean. Antony was in front of Italy, Octavius before the Balkans, Lepidus over against Asia Minor; the stretches of sea between the actors subtly suggested the space that always separated them, and the pattern of civil wars to come. Rome was now gone without a trace, and it was in a blood-red tent near Sardis that Brutus contended with Cassius and saw Caesar's ghost, which materialized in the open mouth of the tent, against the sky. When this tent was struck the bare stage was broken only by a low ridge of fissured rock which rose to a slight eminence a little off-center. It was from here that Octavius and Antony, with their troops and standards, saw Brutus and Cassius coming down to battle in the plains where dusty death awaits them. Cassius fell, then Brutus, their own swords turned against them by friendly hands, in the same central area and general posture as Caesar was, but further downstage, on a lower level. When Brutus came upon Cassius' body and exclaimed "O Julius Caesar, thou art mighty yet!", the northern star suddenly appeared again. There it remained, so that the final curtain recalled and resolved the first-half curtain. The dead body of the tragically deluded liberator lay in the center of the stage, not in Rome but in the wilderness he had helped to make of Rome, and high above him shone out the star of whose true-fixed and resting quality there is no fellow in the firmament.[4]

----

[4] It is necessary for the reviewer to disclose an interest. The present writer suggested to Mr. Byam Shaw the parallel between "that bright Occidental star," as the Jacobean translators of the Bible called the Queen, and the Caesar whose soul was taken up and made a star in the

climax of Ovid's *Metamorphoses*, an episode to which Shakespeare refers in the opening scene of *1 Henry VI*. He also suggested that the northern star speech in *Julius Caesar* draws poetically on that Ovidian climax, and that the promise that the ghost will appear again at Philippi may have been kept by displaying an emblematic star in "the heavens." (For a more elaborate staging of the transfiguration of a soul into a star on the stage, see the stage direction for the death of Hercules in Thomas Heywood's *The Brazen Age*.) Ways in which a comparable effect might be provided for modern audiences with present-day lighting equipment were also discussed. But a suggested interpretation is one thing; imaginative transformation is another. Mr. Byam Shaw transmuted the argument into his own art. If I am open to suspicion of being prejudiced in favor of the result, I may at least point out that the general opinion of responsible critics was that the production was conspicuously successful in its rendering of the true values of the play.

RICHARD DAVID

A Review of "Julius Caesar" (Royal Shakespeare, 1972)

At the opening of *Julius Caesar* the trumpets blared out, and a gigantic red carpet spinningly unrolled from the back of the stage to the very front. This was the cue for a production in which parade and panoply bulked large. These are features of our own received ideas of the Grandeur that was Rome, and I have already suggested that it would be particularly difficult to insulate *Julius Caesar*, of all subjects, from these habitual associations. There are other associations that may tend to color the play at least for the over-forties in a modern audience. The commentators never stop telling us that its real subject is dictatorship, and and that is a phenomenon of which some of us have had experience. For us Caesar can fall readily into the posture of Hitler or Mussolini, and this production with its heel-clicking and leather garments and fascist salutes strongly encouraged the connection.

Now this, while it adds resonance to the play, may be dangerous. Hitler and Mussolini, parodied as they have been by themselves as well as by others, are in one light too clownish for comparison even with that Caesar to whose failings Shakespeare gave some comic enlargement (he is pompous, hard of hearing, liable to fits, and the stories that Cassius tells against him are Shakespeare's deliberate distortions of incidents that Plutarch relates to his credit). In

From *Shakespeare in the Theatre* by Richard David. Cambridge: Cambridge University Press, 1978.

another light our modern dictators are too palpably and too seriously evil. Caesar must not be seen either as a comic monster or as a black tyrant. Only the lesser conspirators regard him as an unmitigated evil. Brutus sees in him a potential not an actual danger, and the other witnesses testify only to the good that his greatness has brought to Rome. He is another equipoise of right and wrong, and Shakespeare summed up his paradox in the line so mocked by Ben Jonson, which appears to have been edited out of the Folio in deference to that mockery, and which in this production I was glad to hear restored: "Caesar did never wrong but with just cause."

Fortunately Dignam's performance deftly preserved that balance and counteracted any undue pressure from the Hitlerian allusions. For his Caesar appeared a ruler of vision; a just judge if self-consciously so; and essentially a companionable man though too minded of his public position. He perfectly matched Cicero's account, in a private letter, of how the historical Caesar struck a contemporary. The masterly vignette of his call at Cicero's villa was engagingly translated in the theater program: "Nerve-racking —but it passed off tolerably. He was in a very good humor. The talk at table was all of literature, and serious subjects were avoided. Just a quiet man-to-man talk. Still, he wasn't the sort of guest to whom you'd say 'Look me up when you're passing this way again.' Once is enough." There you have the man whose public image has so engulfed the private person that personal relationships are no longer comfortable. The same dichotomy was in this production well conveyed by the introduction of Caesar's colossal statue into the one scene of his domestic life. Standing uneasily in the shadow of his public image Caesar cannot act naturally to his friends or even to his wife. I was not so happy about the continuous presence of this statue in the latter scenes of the play. The intention was good. The most significant irony of the play is that Brutus, regretting that in order to destroy the public Caesar he must kill the private one, ends by recognizing that although the private friend has been duly killed, the public Caesar persists indestructibly. This is the lesson repeatedly voiced by the characters and embodied in the visitation of Caesar's spirit to Brutus' tent on the night before the conspirators are finally liquidated at Philippi. For this visitation the statue, terrifyingly heralded by the nightmare cries of the sleepers, served well; but its later presence was incongruous. It is difficult enough to give reality to the battles without having them take place in a museum of sculpture.

The presentation of Caesar as a positive rather than a negative figure was enhanced by the treatment here given to his opponents. In passing let me call attention to the economy of brushwork with which Shakespeare fixes the conspirators for us. Brutus has a full-length portrait, Cassius a three-quarter-length. Casca gets a vivid head-and-shoulders; and I found Gerald James' hard-bitten black comedian refreshing and convincing in place of the usual bluff hearty. Ligarius is picked out by his illness, Decius is the smooth one who is set to appease Caesar's doubts while Trebonius heads off Antony, Cimber the banished brother and Cinna the poet namesake. More to my present purpose, however, is the emphasis placed by Shakespeare, and fully but fairly brought out in this production, on the incompetence and fatuity of the conspirators as a group. It is not only Brutus who is at fault here, though his blunders are the most obvious and are pinpointed by Cassius' comments. Brutus spares Antony's life, allows him to speak, and to have the last word at Caesar's funeral, marches out of his secure defensive position above Philippi, and gives the order to attack too soon. Cassius has no sooner killed Caesar ostensibly for dictatorially fixing government appointments by influence and bribes than he sees himself, with Antony, fixing future appointments and his taking of bribes is the cause of his quarrel with Brutus. The muffled conspiracy that visits Brutus' house is the height of amateurishness and the near-hysteria of the assassins shows them intoxicated by what they have done but utterly unprepared for what is next to do. The Citizens are eager to nullify the conspirators' action by making Brutus Caesar, and the triumvirate pledged to avenge Caesar at once demonstrate that they will resume all his political techniques and use them even more ruthlessly. Incidentally I was sorry that the director tacked this scene on to the funeral, before the interval. One need not pay too much attention to the purely editorial dispositions of the Folio, but it is, I think, pertinent that the Folio makes Octavius, Antony, and Lepidus open Act IV rather than end Act III. The first movement of the play concludes with Brutus and Cassius riding like madmen out of Rome. Their enterprise has failed, but it should not yet be clear what is to happen next. The emergence of the opposition is the start of the second movement. But the implication of the scene, wherever it is placed, is clear enough and was confirmed at the end of the play when, just before the curtain calls, the great red carpet again unrolled itself to signify that dictatorship had been reestablished as if the conspirators had never existed.

With this general structure of the play in mind, we may consider its central problem, Brutus. I will say at once that I found John Wood's continuously inventive and persuasive character study quite enthralling. I must add that I could not make it blend with the rest of the production. To put it in an epigram, he was more a Dane than an antique Roman. To this one might reply, why not? Brutus has often been seen as a preliminary study for Hamlet, and clearly at that moment in his career Shakespeare was mesmerized by something that the two have in common. The answer is that Brutus the Dane would be well enough if the whole play could be translated into, say, the Renaissance, but that the ties, actual and imagined, with classical Rome are too strong for this, and the introduction of Hamlet into classical Rome produces an effect on the audience like that of double vision. This is naturally less intrusive in those scenes in which the contrasting characters are few or none, and in such scenes the richness of the interpretation could be relished without qualms. In the soliloquy "It must be by his death," in which, before ever the conspirators arrive to persuade him, Brutus works out for himself the necessity of assassinating his best friend, the elucidation of the thought was so clear and the expression so limpid that one wondered how anyone could have found the speech difficult. When, at the end of the same night scene, Portia comes to upbraid Brutus for not sharing with her the secrets that so torture him, both the understanding between husband and wife and the irritability of one wracked by intolerable anxieties were movingly genuine. So, too, were Brutus' gentle courtesy to the officers bidden to share his tent on the night before Philippi, and to his sleepy servant.

Chief among these intimate scenes is the quarrel between Brutus and Cassius, and this quarrel was a fizzer. . . . Because Brutus had usurped the lean and hungry look and the thinking too much, Cassius had to fall back on other characteristics that certainly exist in the part, such as impetuosity and a quick temper. The violence of his anger was electrifying and he literally whipped the scene to its climax as, seizing Brutus' truncheon, he laid about him in his fury and beat the papers from the council table. With an equally characteristic gesture, Brutus, toward the end of the scene, signaled the extinction of the fires by going quietly about to pick up the scattered papers and restore them to their place. It seemed in keeping, too, that Brutus' fury should break out at the suspected mockery of the "poet" (here a masquerading soldier) while Cassius, now calm, could laugh at the joker. The end of the scene brought a beautiful touch. There is a famous crux here. Brutus, having revealed Portia's death to Cassius, pretends to Messala that he has heard nothing of it. The commentators on the whole have found it impossible to believe that Shakespeare can have meant to show the noble Brutus as so disingenuous, and before Cassius too, who knows that he is play-acting to Messala. The passage with Messala has therefore been written off as an alternative version that has accidentally remained uncanceled in the printed text, and it is usually cut in performance. Here it was retained and turned to advantage. As Messala speaks of Portia. Brutus signals to Cassius to keep silence. His dialogue with Messala is a public shield against the privacy of his grief being further invaded, and Cassius is the one sharer of the secret of Brutus' prior knowledge and real feelings. This second, personal conspiracy seals the bond of brotherhood that has just been renewed between them.

It was in the big public scenes that the difference in kind between Brutus and the others became disconcerting. That

Brutus does differ in kind is of course part of the point of the play. The director must not be blamed for bringing this point out, and that he was deliberately seeking to do so was plain. For example, there was no need to dress Brutus in a severe personal uniform that made of him a Roundhead rather than a Roman general. But the gap can be too wide, so that even credibility suffers: impossible to accept that a Caesar as hard-bitten as this one could have so close an attachment to a dreaming don, or that even such incompetent conspirators as these could think that they needed this Brutus to impress even so gullible a crowd as these citizens. It was not easy to believe that this Brutus would follow the example of his Roman associates and decide "not to be." A pity that the scene was cut in which Lucilius prepares us for the suicide, warning Antony in the fine words (taken over from North): "When you do find him, or alive or dead, He will be found like Brutus, like himself."

The Brutus is not to be blamed for the comparative failure of the biggest public scene of all, Caesar's funeral. The grouping was awkward. The rostrum was, perhaps inevitably, stage-center, and the people were crowded around it, backs to the audience. Between those backs and the audience was Caesar's bier. This was clumsy and created a double focus to the scene until Antony turned the people to look at Caesar's corpse. In addition all were in dingy colors. Perhaps this was to signify mourning, but it looked rather as if the artisans (who still apparently made up the whole populace of Rome) had not changed their clothes since Coriolanus' time. (Yet the tipsy revelers of the first scene had been quite gay.) As a result the whole scene had a clogged and muddy effect that gave Richard Johnson little chance to show his paces.

RALPH BERRY

On Directing Shakespeare: An Interview with Trevor Nunn, Director of the Royal Shakespeare Company

RB: I found your *Julius Caesar* startlingly original in at least two major ways, in terms of character presentation. Your Caesar was the first I've ever seen who's really struck me as being dangerous, an enemy to the state. Every other Caesar has appeared to me as a sort of company chairman, who's a little bit over the top, and the Board are getting rather restive about him. He doesn't really seem that much of a problem. He does in your production. And the other is Brutus. Every other production I've seen takes at face value the adjective that is applied to him constantly throughout the play, "the noble Brutus." Your production questions this. And taken together, this sheds a flood of light on the play for me.

TN: Yes. Brutus himself questions his nobility. He questions himself and his own actions constantly. When at the height of the tent scene Brutus turns on Cassius and says, "I shall be glad to learn of *noble* men," it's a vicious taunt at Cassius, but I also think it's an indication of the self-revulsion that is in him. We were able to find a complete continuity for the character by questioning that endlessly repeated adjective. Viewed through Cassius' (myopic) eyes, Caesar is fundamentally *ignoble* in wishing to retain and consolidate power. The aristocratic tradition is otherwise, a

From *On Directing Shakespeare: Interviews with Contemporary Directors* by Ralph Berry. (New York: Harper and Row, 1977), pp. 64–68.

commitment to preserve the idea of equality and freedom—
as John Wood (who played Brutus) once pointed out, freedom for Cassius to dislike Caesar publicly without fear of
arrest. Both Brutus and Cassius die amidst uncertainty, but
they know that a whole era has come to an end. "It is *impossible* that Rome shall ever breed thy fellow"—because
Rome has changed. "Our day is gone," says Titinius. The
opportunists and Empire builders have taken over. So far
as Caesar is concerned—I was reading recently a review by
Bernard Crick who, writing about the plays, lamented that
we had chosen a simple and naïve Mussolini-like solution
for the character, and pointed out that the problem Shakespeare is dealing with is less obvious than that. It seems to
me he has put his finger on the difficulty with the play in
performance. If one *doesn't* suggest that Caesar is fast becoming a military dictator—I mean, that after the civil war
he has total control of the army, and therefore cannot be
removed—he can't be *voted* out, and he's not going to
move over, to let somebody else enjoy that power he has
fought for—if one doesn't suggest that military power supports him, and if he doesn't in some way embody that military power, then obviously we get to the moment of his
assassination and we just think that it's dreadfully unfair
and dreadfully unnecessary that so many people should set
upon a harmless defenseless senator.

There's a great deal of evidence in the play that Caesar
has reached a point of dangerous insanity. Not only the
number of times that he refers to himself in the third
person, and as an institution, not only in the terrifying
"Northern Star" speech just before the assassination, but in
little references like from Casca, "there was more foolery
yet . . ." What happens to the two tribunes? This is something that I haven't picked up in any previous production—
maybe that's because I wasn't concentrating—but Casca
says that Marullus and Flavius, the tribunes of the people,
"for pulling scarfs off Caesar's images, are put to silence."
Surely he means they've been executed. It's been very sudden. Two men in high office have been executed and all
they did was to pull down a decoration off an image which
until last year no one was allowed to put up in the first

place. Now that's deeply sinister and deeply disturbing, the cult of the individual leader has arrived, Fascist control has happened. It can be argued that it's a tiny reference to it, but I believe that what Shakespeare is trying to do at the moment is to suggest that these things cannot be *openly* discussed; and why Brutus has to pluck Casca by the sleeve, is because it is no longer possible to go openly up to Casca and say, "Hey, what just happened?" It has to be secret, cloak and dagger. A police state is either in existence or is imminent, everybody is going to report on everybody else. Can Cassius trust Brutus, who after all when the play begins is a chief adviser to the supremo? Can Casca be trusted? Where does Artemidorus get his information from? So I think one *has* to be that graphic in a stage production. On the other hand, we did try very hard to show Caesar's humanity—wherever it exists in the text. Again, it seems to me it's not Shakespeare's primary concern—at the beginning of the play we tried to present a relationship with Antony from the little suggestions of "you and I like plays and Cassius doesn't" or "you and I laugh a lot and Cassius doesn't," but actually there are no opportunities in the play for Caesar to laugh a lot. He's constantly disturbed by soothsayers, by prophecies and by premonitions of one sort or another, he is decidedly unrelaxed, fainting, angry, disputatious.

RB: You worked in too that nice line that Jonson reports, "Caesar did never wrong, but with just cause."

TN: I'm sure that's the original. If one does take that to be the line, it's the ultimate statement of the power-obsessed dictator. Papal infallibility, etc.

RB: I'm glad you replaced that line. It was too good to be taken out just because Jonson laughed at it.

TN: I get the feeling that something like that must have happened.

RB: And *Coriolanus*?

TN: *Coriolanus* really is my favorite play, and I am annoyed that I can't get it as clear and as good in performance as I want it. Here is the example of the mature Shakespeare adopting every possible point of view through his charac-

ters, approving of nobody, but rejecting nobody—and so
allowing a complex debate to occur.

RB: How did your actors experience the problems of the
Roman plays? How did they react to the text and its difficulties? What did you find to be the major difficulties at the
rehearsal stage?

TN: We began in ideal circumstances. We had a four-
week period in London with a totally available company,
which is rare, a large bare rehearsal room, and no restric-
tions on the scheduling of rehearsals or undue pressures of
time. So we talked and we improvised a great deal. We improvised every single situation in *Coriolanus*, we improvised a lot of *Julius Caesar*, nothing more memorably than
the assassination. I only wish I could have recaptured what
happened in the rehearsal room when some of the actors
were using texts and some of the actors, overwhelmed, were
using the only words that occurred to them at the moment.

RB: If I can speak as a member of the audience here,
something special unquestionably did come through. What
was particularly powerful about the assassination as you
staged it was that the emotional effect came after the killing,
rather than the event itself. The reactions of the assassins to
the deed that they had done was the most powerful stroke
of theater.

TN: That's exactly what happened at the improvision.
The incident was quick, many people had no time to move,
and some people genuinely thought that some joke was being played. We discovered why it could be possible for the
Senate area to be surrounded by guards, yet for none of
them to prevent the killing. The four guards were posi-
tioned quite close to Caesar. They had been told that their
job on which their lives depended was to prevent any harm
happening to Caesar at any time, but they still didn't move.
We conducted a series of interviews after the event to try
to find out from people, as it would be TV reporters trying
to find out; what did they feel? What happened? Give us
your version. And the guards were agreed that it wasn't
their place to go into the middle of the Senate floor. That's
where the politicians went, that's where the great speeches
were given. Whatever happened there, it was not for them

to interfere. But then we also discovered that once the assassination had happened, there was a long, stunned time,
when nobody said or felt anything. Then there was pande-
monium, which of course is exactly noted in the text. Shakespeare's naturalistic writing amazes me. He is so accurate.
In improvisation John Wood desperately required to be
able to say to everybody, "stand still," he needed to impose
some order or pattern. And then contradictorily, he had the
feeling that everybody else must go away, for the double
reason that the responsible people must now deal with the
immediate aftermath, and if people were going to get hurt it
should be himself and his colleagues and not innocent people. In the improvisation it became absolutely clear how
different the assassins' attitudes were. Cassius just couldn't
stop stabbing at Caesar. That's a much more emotive part
of the improvisation process, but since there is more of a
personal vendetta between Cassius and Caesar—this was
the moment when it really got expressed. Cassius was
crazed, frenzied, and Brutus stopped him. In the tent scene
Cassius threatens Brutus, with "I may do that I shall be
sorry for" and Brutus replies, "You have done that you
should be sorry for." That always seemed to us to be a
paralyzing moment. Brutus is talking about the assassination, and what Cassius has revealed of his motives. I am not
saying that is unarguably the meaning of the line, but in
performance it could only mean that one thing to the actors.

RB: These improvisations that you practice are obviously superbly effective at bringing out the inner truth of the
lines, the energies of the drama if you like. How did you
deal with the more obviously technical problems of the
text—I think of matters like verse/prose distinctions, and
the like?

TN: In the Royal Shakespeare Company, we're very
fortunate in having John Barton, who is a Shakespeare
scholar, and who is specially talented in teaching actors and
helping actors with difficult texts. Consequently, at the beginning of rehearsals for the Roman plays, we had verse
classes and a great deal of Barton-led text work. Our attitude to the text has to vary from play to play, as Shakespeare's language varies from play to play—sometimes our

attitude has to vary from scene to scene, because Shakespeare's language varies from scene to scene. We mustn't *generalize*. The modern actor confronted with a complex Shakespearean text generalizes. He tries to suck out its emotional meaning; he re-presents the text with a generalized coloring of the words which he believes will somehow communicate that emotional meaning. And he won't be specific, he won't coin language at the very moment when it is emotionally necessary.

SYLVAN BARNET

"Julius Caesar" on Stage and Screen

> How many ages hence
> Shall this our lofty scene be acted over
> In states unborn and accents yet unknown!
> (III.i 111–13)

Thus speaks Shakespeare's Cassius a moment after he and others assassinate Julius Caesar; and indeed Shakespeare's lofty scene has for four hundred years been acted, often in tongues unknown to him, with only a few noticeable intervals. In the United States, the play was long a safe choice for all new theater groups, probably because at least until recently every schoolchild knew something about Julius Caesar. A version of *Julius Caesar* was among the first televised Shakespeare plays, and when the American Shakespeare Festival opened its new theater at Stratford, Connecticut, in 1955, *Julius Caesar* was its choice. But of course the play has not meant the same thing to every age. For instance, looking at Shakespeare's *Julius Caesar* the late seventeenth century saw a play about a heroic Brutus, the first half of the eighteenth century saw a play celebrating republican liberty, but (to skip to our recent past) the mid-twentieth century saw a play about fascism. For a painstaking discussion of most of the famous productions up to recent times, the reader is advised to consult John Ripley's *"Julius Caesar" on Stage in England and America, 1599–1973*. The following brief essay is deeply indebted to information in Ripley's book.

If the first thing to say is that throughout its history the play has been almost continuously popular on the stage (this can be said of only a minority of Shakespeare's plays), the second thing to say is that it has been ignored by some of England's most notable actors; Olivier, for example, has not played in it. Doubtless, part of the problem is that Caesar gets killed in the third act, and though generations of teachers have patiently urged their students to believe that Caesar's spirit dominates the entire play, actors have felt otherwise. The parts of Brutus and Cassius are substantial, of course, but the play is named after Caesar. Nevertheless . . . what leading actor wishes to die before the middle of the play? Moreover, some actors have seen unusual difficulties in the play. In *Early Stages,* one of his autobiographies, John Gielgud (who has played Antony, Cassius, and Caesar—but never Brutus) offers an actor's comment on *Julius Caesar.*

The verse pitched, almost throughout, in a lofty, rhetorical style, is very tiring and difficult for the actors to sustain without monotony in a large theater. There is little prose to vary it, and it is difficult for the leading characters to keep continuously alive against the mass of restless citizens, senators, and soldiers who must continually revolve and shout around them. There is little feminine interest to give the play domestic warmth and relaxation. The classical costumes, though becoming and graceful to players of fine physique, can be ridiculous and hampering to men who are too short, too tall, too thin or too fat. There is always a danger of the effect of a lot of gentlemen sitting on marble benches in a Turkish bath. There may be something to be said for experimenting with a production in Elizabethan dress, and yet it might only be confusing to see a Brutus looking like Guy Fawkes, or a Caesar crowned with laurel, wearing a beard and dressed in doublet and hose, thus adding further anachronisms to those which Shakespeare has already provided in his text. Unlocalized scenery—balconies, rostrums, and bare boards—may serve well enough for Roman streets, the Forum and the senate-house, but they will hardly serve to conjure up Brutus's orchard, his tent, and Philippi fields, even though Shakespeare's audiences may have found no difficulty in so imagining them on the open stage of the Globe three hundred years ago. The play bristles with hazards of all kinds both for actors and directors, even on the stage.

Hazards or not, the play has, we have noted, an almost continuous stage history. The first reference to a performance was by a Swiss visitor to London (see above, page xxi) in 1599; references to specific performances in the next few decades are scarce, but general allusions to the play make it clear that *Julius Caesar* was popular. In the late seventeenth century, when (after the restoration of Charles II in 1660) several of Shakespeare's plays were drastically adapted to appeal to the new taste, *Julius Caesar* survived virtually unchanged. The evidence for this assertion is a barely modified text of the play (for instance, a few speech prefixes are altered), printed at least six times between 1684 and 1691, which proclaims that it gives the play "as it is now acted at the Theatre Royal." Presumably acting in this virtually uncut text, Thomas Betterton performed the role of Brutus from at least 1684 until 1707. Twentieth-century viewers of the play, used to seeing Brutus portrayed as a stuffed shirt or a muddled idealist, may be surprised to learn that Betterton portrayed him as a philosophic man, in contrast to the passionate Cassius. An eye witness—though one who gave his report years after the fact—spoke of

the unruffled temper of his Brutus. . . . When the Betterton Brutus was provoked in his dispute with Cassius, his spirit flew only to his eye; his steady look alone supplied that terror which he disdained an intemperance in his voice should rise to. Thus, with a settled dignity of contempt, like an unheeding rock he repelled upon himself the foam of Cassius.

The almost unaltered text of 1684 gave way to a somewhat more altered text of the play published in 1719. This text bore the claim that it was *The Tragedy of Julius*

Caesar: With the Death of Brutus and Cassius; Written Originally by Shakespeare, And since alter'd by Sir William Davenant and John Dryden late Poets Laureate. As it is now Acted by His Majesty's Company of Comedians at the Theatre Royal. The attribution to Devenant and Dryden (both of whom were safely dead) is almost certainly false, but the text probably does give us a good idea of how the play was done in the eighteenth century after the first decade or so. The departures from the original (if we contrast them with the massive departures made in *King Lear*) are minor. In keeping with the period's idea of decorum, a few words that seemed absurd for one reason or another were cut, for instance Caesar's boast (II.ii. 44–48) that he and "Danger" are "two lions littered in one day." Brutus's remark (III.i. 171) that his pity for Rome prevented him from feeling pity for the Caesar whom he helped to murder—"As fire drives out fire, so pity pity"—was also deleted, perhaps because it seemed detrimental to Brutus's character. The most substantial cut was that of the horrifying scene (III.iii) showing the murder of Cinna the Poet. One other sort of change should be noted: a few lines were added, for instance four lines in which Brutus reflects on his first interview with the Ghost, a bit of dialogue between Brutus and the Ghost at Philippi (added because Shakespeare's Ghost promises to appear again at Philippi but doesn't), and in Brutus's dying speech some lines emphasizing Brutus's patriotism.

This version, or something very close to it, was staged in London almost every year in the second quarter of the eighteenth century; in the second half of the century performances of *Julius Caesar* were fewer, partly because David Garrick, the greatest actor of the period, never chose to do the play. It is probably fair to say, however, that throughout the eighteenth century *Julius Caesar* was regarded as a patriotic play showing the heroic Brutus nobly opposing the tyrannical Caesar. In the early nineteenth century John Philip Kemble continued along the same line. Because of this emphasis, Kemble omitted these world-weary lines that Brutus utters near the end of the play:

> So fare you well at once, for Brutus' tongue
> Hath almost ended his life's history.
> Night hangs upon mine eyes; my bones would rest,
> That have but labored to attain this hour.
>
> (V.v. 39–42)

Instead, Kemble adopted the passage that had been added in the 1719 version attributed to Davenant and Dryden, and he made some further alterations. The effect was to heighten the patriotic note:

> This was the justest cause that ever men
> Did draw with swords for; and the gods renounce it.
> Disdaining life, to live a slave in Rome,
> Thus Brutus strikes his last—for liberty!
> Farewell,
> Beloved country!—Caesar, now be still;
> I killed not thee with half so good a will.

Abundant evidence indicates that Kemble depicted Brutus not as a self-deceived figure but as a noble stoic. Only in IV.iii., when Brutus tells Cassius of the death of Portia, did he seem to have the weaknesses of other mortals. A stoic hero suited Kemble's style of acting which was what today we would call highly formal. "Statuesque" is a word often used to describe Kemble's style. The Roman grandeur of the style was supplemented by classical costume and an attention to grand pictorial effects, gained, for instance, by the use of masses of supernumeraries who set off the major figures. Ludwig Tieck, however, who attended a performance in 1817, saw in the formality not high seriousness but a "pretentious solemnity" that disguised the butchery of the assassination. Kemble's style, which of course also implies his interpretation of the role, dominated the interpretation both in England and in the United States until William Macready, playing Brutus in 1838, introduced a more intimate or (to use the word of a contemporary commentator) "amiable" note. The underlying idea now was that Shakespeare's Romans were not simply classical heroes but were also endowed with the strengths and weaknesses of all mortals. The assassination scene now was not the solemn ritual that Brutus intends, but the scene of shocking violence that it in fact becomes. Macready kept experimenting with the role from 1838 to 1851, but always in the direction of emphasizing Brutus's humanity.

Other actors, of course, also performed the role in the nineteenth century, notably Edwin Booth in the United States, and Samuel Phelps and (at the very end of the century) Herbert Beerbohm Tree in England. Edwin Booth inherited the role from his father, Junius Booth, who had performed it in the 1830s. In 1864, a year before Lincoln was assassinated, three Booths—Junius, Edwin, and Edwin's brother John Wilkes—performed in *Julius Caesar,* taking the roles, respectively, of Brutus, Cassius, and Antony. Edwin Booth's productions were known for their historical accuracy and also for the splendor of the scenery and costumes, but since the period of Julius Caesar—the age of the Roman Republic—seemed a bit drab, Booth followed Kemble in setting it later, in the more opulent Augustan period of Imperial Rome. Thus, instead of white buildings, he showed buildings of tawny marble, with crimson columns and colored friezes. For a text, he relied chiefly on Kemble's version, which cut some two hundred lines from the play, but he did not use the lines Kemble had added to the play. And in his interpretation of the role he apparently conveyed not only Kemble's heroism but a sense of psychological complexity (even a deep love for Portia) associated less with Kemble than with Macready.

Although *Julius Caesar* had been popular during the first two-thirds of the nineteenth century, when Herbert Beerbohm Tree staged it in London in 1898 it had not been done there (except occasionally by a touring company) for more than thirty years. Tree's highly successful production, often repeated during the next eighteen years, was influenced by a visit that the Saxe-Meiningen company had made to London in 1881. The Meiningen Players, a German company formed by the Duke of Saxe-Meiningen, were renowned for their emphasis on the relationship between the setting and the actors. For instance, they performed not on a uniformly flat platform but divided the surface of the stage floor into different levels and deployed the actors meaningfully on these levels. The company was also known for its handling of crowd scenes, so that the crowd in effect became another personage in the drama. (In fact, Macready had earlier achieved fame for his handling—orchestration, we might say—of the crowd in the forum scene.) Antony, the patrician who is attuned to the crowd, was the star in the Meiningen production, and Beerbohm Tree played this role in his production. A letter to his wife is revealing: "I like Brutus best—and he is so much deeper—but I still feel Antony has the color—the glamor of the play." Tree made the role more sympathetic by cutting the proscription scene (IV.i) in which Antony, Lepidus, and Octavius lightly consent to executing various enemies, and in which, after Lepidus departs, Antony speaks scornfully of Lepidus. Although *Julius Caesar* is short enough to be staged uncut, because Antony's role is not especially prominent after the forum scene, Tree made heavy cuts in lines spoken by others in the second half of the play. He cut, for instance, the whole of Cassius's birthday speech in V.i. 70–88. Tree performed the play in three acts, which John Ripley says might well have been called "Antony Introduced, Antony Contriving, and Antony Triumphant." The sets (Republican Rome, with some picturesque touches of Imperial Rome) and costumes were designed by Sir Lawrence Alma-Tadema, who gave Antony a splendid scarlet toga, steel helmet, and plume for the final act. The romantic portrayal of Antony established by Tree—more precisely, established by the Meiningen players—was continued by F. R. Benson, who, like Tree, played a dashing Antony and cut the discreditable proscription scene. Benson had, in fact, played Antony as early as 1890, that is, even before Tree did, and he continued to play the role until 1933 when he was seventy-five.

Tree and Benson worked well into the twentieth century, but their productions, with their splendid pictorial sets, are unmistakably of the nineteenth. What of productions born in the twentieth century? We can glance at some relatively recent productions in modern dress in England and in the United States, then will go back to Orson Welles's immensely influential New York production of 1937, and at last will end with a look at a Hollywood film made in 1953.

In 1963 John Blatchley produced the play with the Royal Shakespeare Company, at Stratford-upon-Avon. Stratford in the sixties, reacting against "museum theater," was much taken with the ideas of Artaud, Beckett, and Brecht, which means that the directors strongly imposed rather dark ideas on the production. Earlier interpretations had seen nobility and heroism and sometimes even warm humanity in Brutus; Blatchley's Brutus, played by Tom Fleming, was physically unprepossessing, and although this Brutus meant well he had little idea of what was happening. Antony's sensuality was evident, but reviewers found him unappealing. The set, regarded by many as equally unappealing, consisted of a ramp, some staircases, and a cloth for Brutus's tent. The costumes combined World War I uniforms with motorcycle togs and togas, chiefly grays, browns, and blacks.

The play is a tragedy, of course, but it has long been seen as a political play. At least as early as the late eighteenth century it was regarded as a display of Brutus's libertarian patriotism. That is, the tragedy was given a political interpretation that was seen as relevant to the audience. In 1770, for example, a group called the American Company performed the play in Philadelphia, saying that it showed "the noble struggles for Liberty by that renowned patriot Marcus Brutus." The political elements in the play lend themselves to those who wish to make statements about democracy and about political assassination. Two essays reprinted in this volume bring up the question of political implications in the play—the essays by Ralph Berry and by Richard David, on Trevor Nunn's Royal Shakespeare Company production of 1972, but here we can add that not all spectators of that production agreed on what they saw. Richard David found Caesar moderately sympathetic, but Peter Thomson (in a review in *Shakespeare Survey* [26]) reported that Caesar's appearance was "cold and cruel," and that "there was nothing attractive about this Caesar, except perhaps to the National Front." Thomson also observed that this "Caesar's Rome was a police state, with black-armored soldiers to enforce the law" (page 145). A production at Stratford, Connecticut, in 1979 somewhat similarly used modern dress in order to emphasize the political (and supposedly contemporary) aspects of the tragedy: Caesar was a Latin American dictator in the uniform of a general; Flavius and Marullus wore trench coats; soldiers wore fatigues and fought with guns (which made one wonder why in this play people committed suicide with swords). In a 1982 production at Ashland, Oregon, a roll of barbed wire was suspended across the rear of the stage; Arab and military gear suggested the contemporary Near East. The director, Jerry Turner, said he was influenced by the assassination of Egyptian President Sadat. Brutus was depicted as a serious but muddleheaded professor, Casca was a female revolutionary, and the Soothsayer—always a problem in productions set in modern times—was a bag lady. For at least one reviewer, this effort to make the play familiar served also to make it small, something routine rather than awesome.

The father of modern political interpretations of the play was the production by John Houseman and Orson Welles in New York in 1937, with Welles (then twenty-

two years old) as Brutus. (Strictly speaking, Houseman
and Welles had been anticipated by a modern-dress production at the Delaware Federal Theater in 1937, but the
Delaware production did not attract the attention that
Houseman and Welles received.) The set showed neither
Republican Rome nor Augustan Rome; rather, the brick
back wall of the Mercury Theatre, fire extinguishers and
steam pipes and all, was the backdrop. The main playing
area, the apron fourteen feet deep, rose gently to meet a
set of shallow steps that ran the full width of the stage.
The steps led to an eight-foot plateau, and the stage then
rose again with another set of steps. Thus, this bare stage
was not at all as simple as it looked, for it offered a variety
of playing areas. (Houseman describes the stage in detail
in *Run-through: A Memoir*.) Without scenery to change,
the play moved rapidly; columns of light illuminated a
playing space, then faded out and were replaced by others.
The players wore modern dress (Caesar wore a military
tunic and breeches, Brutus a double-breasted pin-stripe
suit), and there was a good deal of striding about and of
saluting with uplifted right arms. The play ran for an
hour and forty-nine minutes, without an intermission. It
was fairly heavily cut—no ghost of Caesar, no proscription
scene, almost no Octavius, and almost no battle, for instance—but one scene (III.iii) that for two centuries had
been absent from most productions was restored: the
murder of the luckless Cinna the Poet, which *Time* said
(November 22, 1937) became "a minor tragedy." Cinna,
pathetic in his innocent protestations, caught in a ring of
light, finds himself surrounded by hoods; the crowd closes
in, the ring of light diminishes, and suddenly there is
blackness. (For a photograph, see John Ripley's *"Julius
Caesar" on Stage,* page 229. For Houseman's discussion of
the scene, which in the early rehearsals seemed so unsuc-
cessful that it was almost dropped, see *Run-through,*
pages 310–12.) *Time* also found other aspects of the production impressive:

Lighting sets the mood and changes the scene. Notable effects: the giant backwall shadow of Antony, speaking over Caesar's body; a cross-hatching of light and shadow high up in the loft, unintentionally giving the impression of crossed fasces; the climax, patterned after *Life's* pictures of last summer's Nazi Congress at Nürnberg, vertical shafts of light stabbing up through the darkness as background for the eulogy of the noblest Roman of them all.

Subtitled *Death of a Dictator,* this production was widely regarded as antifascist—witness the reference in *Time* to the Nürnberg rallies. But Welles said the play was not antifascist; it was, he said, about Brutus. Brutus, he informed the theatergoer (in a statement reprinted in Ripley, page 223), is

the classical picture of the eternal, impotent, ineffectual, fumbling liberal; the reformer who wants to do something about things but doesn't know how and gets it in the neck in the end. He's dead right all the time, and dead at the final curtain. He's Shakespeare's favorite hero—the fellow who thinks the times are out of joint but who is really out of joint with his time. He's the bourgeois intellectual, who, under a modern dictatorship, would be the first to be put up against a wall and shot.

In a newspaper interview Welles referred to the mob as "the hoodlum element you find in any big city after a war." It is this hoodlum element, not any fascistic ideal, that tears apart Cinna the Poet, and so, though Welles and Houseman related the play to current events in Europe, the production scarcely made a coherent political statement about fascism.

This production, the most revolutionary and the most discussed version of our century, came close to being not so much a staging of Shakespeare's play as an independent work. Perhaps we should end, then, with a brief comment on a more traditional version, the 1953 M.G.M. film produced by John Houseman and directed by Joseph

Mankiewicz, with Louis Calhern (Caesar), James Mason (Brutus), John Gielgud (Cassius), and Marlon Brando (Marc Antony). Houseman, we have noticed, had already had some experience with Shakespeare; in addition to having been codirector of *Julius Caesar* in New York with Welles, he had directed *King Lear* on Broadway. Houseman in *Films in Review*, April 1953, and again in an autobiography entitled *Front and Center*, mentions that his conception of the play owes something to news-reels showing political figures signing pacts and making speeches, especially Hitler at Nürnberg—again, a *Julius Caesar* for our day—but the idea is not pressed, and the film is fairly true to the text. If not precisely exciting, it nevertheless is a highly competent film. (In *Front and Center*, Houseman discusses some of the problems of turn-ing Shakespeare's play into a film.) Movie buffs appreciate the fact that this is no mere filmed production of the play; it is a highly cinematic work, one that shows affinities with such films as *Double Indemnity* and *The Asphalt Jungle*, that is, with the *film noir* of the 1940s and fifties, films em-phasizing urban corruption. Furthermore, the film was shot (like *film noir*) in black and white—not, however, to save money but because Mankiewicz and Houseman saw the story as something intense, even gritty, to be told without the allure of color. The litter in the streets, the graffiti on the walls, and the menacing nighttime imagery or *film noir* appear here too, for instance in the scene in which Casca—played by Edmond O'Brien, who usually played detectives or crooked lawyers—encounters Cassius (I.iii) in the public square as a storm gathers. With its shots of dark alleys and rickety tenements, this was a Rome never before thought of as part of *Julius Caesar*. Possibly Calhern's performance as Caesar was overly in-debted to *film noir*, in which he had played cultivated crooks, for instance a dishonest lawyer in *The Asphalt Jungle*. In any case, some viewers found his Caesar suave rather than dangerous—but most viewers found his per-formance impressive, and there is general agreement that

Mason (Brutus) and Gielgud (Cassius) were excellent. Gielgud had already played (under Anthony Quayle's direction) a bitter, vehement Cassius at Stratford-upon-Avon in 1950, and he now repeated his performance. Brando's Marc Antony is more controversial; his appearance was appropriately athletic and voluptuous, but his delivery of the lines (despite abundant coaching from Gielgud) left something to be desired. The text for this film is fairly complete, but some cuts were made, notably the scene with Cinna the Poet, and the final speech of Octavius. (The scene with Cinna was filmed, but it appeared anticlimactic after the powerful forum scene, and so it was dropped.) The battle scenes near the end were reduced to a paltry ambush in a ravine. Houseman explains, in *Front and Center*, that although in the stage production Welles had omitted the battles and no one had noticed, the film audience would expect a good battle, possibly in the tradition of Oliver's *Henry V*. The budget, however, prohibited anything more than a perfunctory battle. The result was a battle that, although infinitely beyond what an Elizabethan audience could hope for, was vastly disappointing to a movie audience. In other respects, however, the film is impressive.

It is good to have so strong a version captured on film, but of course the film version does not make subsequent performances superfluous. The "lofty scene"—the assassination of Caesar—that Cassius speaks of continues to be acted around the world; that Caesar so often bleeds is a sign that the play is healthy.

Suggested References

The number of possible references is vast and grows alarmingly. (The *Shakespeare Quarterly* devotes one issue each year to a list of the previous year's work, and *Shakespeare Survey* —an annual publication—includes a substantial review of recent scholarship, as well as an occasional essay surveying a few decades of scholarship on a chosen topic.) Though no works are indispensable, those listed below have been found especially helpful.

1. Shakespeare's Times

Byrne, M. St. Clare. *Elizabethan Life in Town and Country.* Rev. ed. New York: Barnes & Noble, 1961. Chapters on manners, beliefs, education, etc., with illustrations.

Joseph, B. L. *Shakespeare's Eden: The Commonwealth of England, 1558–1629.* New York: Barnes & Noble, 1971. An account of the social, political, economic, and cultural life of England.

Schoenbaum, S. *Shakespeare: The Globe and the World.* New York: Oxford University Press, 1979. A readable, handsomely illustrated book on the world of the Elizabethans.

Shakespeare's England. 2 vols. London: Oxford University Press, 1916. A large collection of scholarly essays on a wide variety of topics (e.g. astrology, costume, gardening, horsemanship), with special attention to Shakespeare's references to these topics.

Stone, Lawrence. *The Crisis of the Aristocracy, 1558–1641,* abridged edition. London: Oxford University Press, 1967.

2. Shakespeare

Barnet, Sylvan. *A Short Guide to Shakespeare.* New York: Harcourt Brace Jovanovich, 1974. An introduction to all of the works and to the dramatic traditions behind them.

Bentley, Gerald E. *Shakespeare: A Biographical Handbook.* New Haven, Conn.: Yale University Press, 1961. The facts about Shakespeare, with virtually no conjecture inter-mingled.

Bush, Geoffrey. *Shakespeare and the Natural Condition.* Cambridge, Mass.: Harvard University Press, 1956. A short, sensitive account of Shakespeare's view of "Nature," touching most of the works.

Chambers, E. K. *William Shakespeare: A Study of Facts and Problems.* 2 vols. London: Oxford University Press, 1930. An invaluable, detailed reference work; not for the casual reader.

Chute, Marchette. *Shakespeare of London.* New York: Dutton, 1949. A readable biography fused with portraits of Stratford and London life.

Clemen, Wolfgang H. *The Development of Shakespeare's Imagery.* Cambridge, Mass.: Harvard University Press, 1951. (Originally published in German, 1936.) A temperate account of a subject often abused.

Granville-Barker, Harley. *Prefaces to Shakespeare.* 2 vols. Princeton, N.J.: Princeton University Press, 1946–47. Essays on ten plays by a scholarly man of the theater.

Harbage, Alfred. *As They Liked It.* New York: Macmillan, 1947. A long, sensitive essay on Shakespeare, morality, and the audience's expectations.

Kernan, Alvin B., ed. *Modern Shakespearean Criticism: Essays on Style, Dramaturgy, and the Major Plays.* New York: Harcourt Brace Jovanovich, 1970. A collection of major formalist criticism.

———. "The Plays and the Playwrights." In *The Revels History of Drama in English,* general editors Clifford Leech and T. W. Craik. Vol. III. London: Methuen, 1975. A book-length essay surveying Elizabethan drama with substantial discussions of Shakespeare's plays.

Schoenbaum, S. *Shakespeare's Lives.* Oxford: Clarendon Press, 1970. A review of the evidence, and an examination of many biographies, including those by Baconians and other heretics.

———. *William Shakespeare: A Compact Documentary Life.* New York: Oxford University Press, 1977. A readable presentation of all that the documents tell us about Shakespeare.

Traversi, D. A. *An Approach to Shakespeare*. 3rd rev. ed. 2 vols. New York: Doubleday, 1968–69. An analysis of the plays beginning with words, images, and themes, rather than with characters.

Van Doren, Mark. *Shakespeare*. New York: Holt, 1939. Brief, perceptive readings of all of the plays.

3. Shakespeare's Theater

Beckerman, Bernard. *Shakespeare at the Globe, 1599–1609*. New York: Macmillan, 1962. On the playhouse and on Elizabethan dramaturgy, acting, and staging.

Chambers, E. K. *The Elizabethan Stage*. 4 vols. New York: Oxford University Press, 1945. A major reference work on theaters, theatrical companies, and staging at court.

Cook, Ann Jennalie. *The Privileged Playgoers of Shakespeare's London, 1576–1642*. Princeton, N.J.: Princeton University Press, 1981. Sees Shakespeare's audience as more middle-class and more intellectual than Harbage (below) does.

Gurr, Andrew. *The Shakespearean Stage: 1579–1642*. 2nd edition. Cambridge: Cambridge University Press, 1980. On the acting companies, the actors, the playhouses, the stages, and the audiences.

Harbage, Alfred. *Shakespeare's Audience*. New York: Columbia University Press, 1941. A study of the size and nature of the theatrical public, emphasizing its representativeness.

Hodges, C. Walter. *The Globe Restored*. London: Ernest Benn, 1953. A well-illustrated and readable attempt to reconstruct the Globe Theatre.

Hosley, Richard. "The Playhouses." In *The Revels History of Drama in English*, general editors Clifford Leech and T. W. Craik. Vol. III. London: Methuen, 1975. An essay of one hundred pages on the physical aspects of the playhouses.

Kernodle, George R. *From Art to Theatre: Form and Convention in the Renaissance*. Chicago: University of Chicago Press, 1944. Pioneering and stimulating work on the symbolic and cultural meanings of theater construction.

Nagler, A. M. *Shakespeare's Stage*. Trans. Ralph Manheim. New Haven, Conn.: Yale University Press, 1958. A very brief introduction to the physical aspects of the playhouse.

Slater, Ann Pasternak. *Shakespeare the Director.* Totowa, N.J.: Barnes & Noble, 1982. An analysis of theatrical effects (e.g., kissing, kneeling) in stage directions and dialogue.

Thomson, Peter. *Shakespeare's Theatre.* London: Routledge & Kegan Paul, 1983. A discussion of how plays were staged in Shakespeare's time.

4. Miscellaneous Reference Works

Abbott, E. A. *A Shakespearean Grammar.* New Edition. New York: Macmillan, 1877. An examination of differences between Elizabethan and modern grammar.

Bevington, David. *Shakespeare.* Arlington Heights, Ill.: A. H. M. Publishing, 1978. A short guide to hundreds of important writings on the works.

Bullough, Geoffrey. *Narrative and Dramatic Sources of Shakespeare.* 8 vols. New York: Columbia University Press, 1957–75. A collection of many of the books Shakespeare drew upon, with judicious comments.

Campbell, Oscar James, and Edward G. Quinn. *The Reader's Encyclopedia of Shakespeare.* New York: Crowell, 1966. More than 2,600 entries, from a few sentences to a few pages, on everything related to Shakespeare.

Greg, W. W. *The Shakespeare First Folio.* New York: Oxford University Press, 1955. A detailed yet readable history of the first collection (1623) of Shakespeare's plays.

Kökeritz, Helge. *Shakespeare's Names.* New Haven, Conn.: Yale University Press, 1959. A guide to the pronunciation of some 1,800 names appearing in Shakespeare.

———. *Shakespeare's Pronunciation.* New Haven, Conn.: Yale University Press, 1953. Contains much information about puns and rhymes.

Muir, Kenneth. *The Sources of Shakespeare's Plays.* New Haven, Conn.: Yale University Press, 1978. An account of Shakespeare's use of his reading.

The Norton Facsimile: The First Folio of Shakespeare. Prepared by Charlton Hinman. New York: Norton, 1968. A handsome and accurate facsimile of the first collection (1623) of Shakespeare's plays.

Onions, C. T. *A Shakespeare Glossary.* 2d ed., rev., with enlarged addenda. London: Oxford University Press, 1953. Definitions of words (or senses of words) now obsolete.

Partridge, Eric. *Shakespeare's Bawdy*. Rev. ed. New York: Dutton; London: Routledge & Kegan Paul, 1955. A glossary of bawdy words and phrases.

Shakespeare Quarterly. See headnote to Suggested References.

Shakespeare Survey. See headnote to Suggested References.

Shakespeare's Plays in Quarto. A Facsimile Edition. Ed. Michael J. B. Allen and Kenneth Muir. Berkeley, Calif.: University of California Press, 1981. A book of nine hundred pages, containing facsimiles of twenty-two of the quarto editions of Shakespeare's plays. An invaluable complement to *The Norton Facsimile: The First Folio of Shakespeare* (see above).

Smith, Gordon Ross. *A Classified Shakespeare Bibliography 1936–1958*. University Park, Pa.: Pennsylvania State University Press, 1963. A list of some twenty thousand items on Shakespeare.

Spevack, Marvin. *The Harvard Concordance to Shakespeare*. Cambridge, Mass.: Harvard University Press, 1973. An index to Shakespeare's words.

Wells, Stanley, ed. *Shakespeare: Select Bibliographies*. London: Oxford University Press, 1973. Seventeen essays surveying scholarship and criticism of Shakespeare's life, work, and theater.

5. *Julius Caesar*

Ayres, H. M. "Shakespeare's *Julius Caesar* in the Light of Some Other Versions," *Publications of the Modern Language Association*, (1910), 183–227.

Barton, Anne. *"Julius Caesar* and *Coriolanus*: Shakespeare's Roman World of Words," *Shakespeare's Craft: Eight Lectures*, ed. Philip H. Highfill, Jr. Carbondale, Ill.: Southern Illinois University Press for George Washington University, 1982.

Bonjour, Adrien. *The Structure of "Julius Caesar."* Liverpool, England: University Press of Liverpool, 1958.

Charney, Maurice. *Shakespeare's Roman Plays*. Cambridge, Mass.: Harvard University Press, 1961.

Dean, Leonard (ed.). *Twentieth Century Interpretations of*

"Julius Caesar." Englewood Cliffs, N.J.: Prentice-Hall, 1968.

Dorsch, T. S. (ed.). *Julius Caesar.* Cambridge, Mass.: Harvard University Press, 1955.

Granville-Barker, Harley. *Prefaces to Shakespeare.* Vol. II. Princeton, N.J.: Princeton University Press, 1947.

Heilman, Robert. "To Know Himself: An Aspect of Tragic Structure," *Review of English Literature,* 5 (1964), 36–57.

Honigmann, E. A. J. *Shakespeare: Seven Tragedies.* London: Macmillan, 1976.

Knight, G. Wilson. *The Imperial Theme.* New York: British Book Centre, Inc.; London: Methuen, 1951.

Levitsky, Ruth M. " 'The Elements Were So Mix'd. . . .' " *PMLA,* 88 (1973), 240–45.

MacCallum, M. W. *Shakespeare's Roman Plays and Their Background.* New York and London: Macmillan, 1910.

Miola, Robert S. *Shakespeare's Rome.* Cambridge: Cambridge University Press, 1983.

Muir, Kenneth. *Shakespeare's Sources.* Vol. I. London: Methuen, 1957.

Palmer, John. *Political Characters of Shakespeare.* London and New York: Macmillan, 1945, 1946.

Richmond, Hugh M. *Shakespeare's Political Plays.* New York: Random House, 1967.

Ripley, John. *Julius Caesar on Stage in England and America, 1599–1973.* Cambridge: Cambridge University Press, 1980.

Schanzer, Ernest. *The Problem Plays of Shakespeare.* New York: Schocken; London: Routledge & Kegan Paul, 1963.

Smith, Gordon Ross. "Brutus, Virtue, and Will," *Shakespeare Quarterly,* 10 (1959), 367–79.

Smith, Warren D. "The Duplicate Revelation of Portia's Death," *Shakespeare Quarterly,* 4 (1953), 153–61.

Stewart, J. I. M. *Character and Motive in Shakespeare.* New York: Longmans, Green, 1949.

Stirling, Brents. *Unity in Shakespearian Tragedy.* New York: Columbia University Press; London: Oxford University Press, 1956.

Velz, John W. *The Tragedy of Julius Caesar: A Bibliography to Supplement the New Variorum Edition of 1913.* New York: The Modern Language Association, 1977.

Whitaker, Virgil K. *Shakespeare's Use of Learning.* San Marino, Calif.: Huntington Library, 1953.

SIGNET CLASSICS for Your Library